PRAISE FOR

PETER F. HAMILTON

"A Hole in the Sky *by SF master Peter F. Hamilton is a coming-of-age adventure that rapidly turns into the Poseidon Adventure aboard a failing generation ship. It's engaging, refreshing, and optimistic.*"
Kevin J. Anderson, New York Times bestselling coauthor of *Dune: House Atreides*

"A Hole in the Sky *is an excellent story, with a central mystery that builds tension throughout: the more you learn, the more you want to find out"*
Adrian Tchaikovsky, author of *Children of Time*

"The phrase 'modern master of science fiction' is not to be lightly bestowed. Peter F. Hamilton has earned it"
John Scalzi, author of *Old Man's War*

"We've said it before but let's say it again: nobody does BIG SF quite like Hamilton"
SFX

"Hamilton puts British SF back into interstellar overdrive"
The Times

"So long as there are writers like Hamilton who can blend the core and eternal human bits with the ultrahuman visionary stuff, science fiction will flourish"
Locus

"Science fiction authors don't get much more legendary than Peter F. Hamilton
New Scientist

"Hamilton handles massive ideas with enviable ease"
Guardian

"The master of his genre"
SFFWorld

"SF's go-to guy for adventure on a truly interstellar scale... Hamilton's storytelling is both staggering and poetic"
SFReviews

"Peter Hamilton doesn't just write Space Opera, he defines it"
SFBook.com

"One of the genre's leading exponents"
Daily Mail

"One of our greatest living SF writers"
Gareth Powell

"No one offers action-packed, meticulous, suspenseful, and consistent high-tech futures better than Peter Hamilton"
David Brin, author of *Startide Rising*

"Hamilton knows how to build a world, and he's one of the best in the field at imagining complex societies. Just as important, though, he knows how to populate his future environments with real-seeming people whose lives extend beyond the page"
Alastair Reynolds, author of *Revelation Space*

"An expert chronicler of humanity's far future"
Una McCormack

"The owner of the most powerful imagination in science fiction"
Ken Follett, author of *The Pillars of the Earth*

"A master of science fiction"
William C. Dietz

By the same author

THE GREG MANDEL BOOKS:
Mindstar Rising
A Quantum Murder
The Nano Flower

THE NIGHT'S DAWN TRILOGY:
The Reality Dysfunction
The Neutronium Alchemist
The Naked God

A Second Chance at Eden (shorts in the Night's Dawn universe)

THE COMMONWEALTH SAGA:
Pandora's Star
Judas Unchained

COMMONWEALTH UNIVERSE, THE VOID TRILOGY:
The Dreaming Void
The Temporal Void
The Evolutionary Void

Misspent Youth

COMMONWEALTH UNIVERSE,
CHRONICLE OF THE FALLERS:
The Abyss Beyond Dreams
Night Without Stars

THE SALVATION SEQUENCE:
Salvation
Salvation Lost
The Saints Of Salvation

THE QUEEN OF DREAMS TRILOGY:
The Secret Throne
The Hunting of the Princes
A Voyage Through Air

EXODUS:
The Archimedes Engine
The Helium Sea (published 2026)

STANDALONE NOVELS
Fallen Dragon
Great North Road

SHORT STORY COLLECTIONS
Manhattan In Reverse

Peter F. Hamilton

A HOLE IN THE SKY
BOOK ONE OF
THE ARKSHIP TRILOGY

ANGRY ROBOT
An imprint of Watkins Media Ltd

Unit 11, Shepperton House
89-93 Shepperton Road
London N1 3DF
UK

angryrobotbooks.com
Take the Blessing and give yourself to the future.

An Angry Robot paperback original, 2026

Copyright © Rutland Horizon 2026

Edited by Simon Spanton Walker
Cover by Sneha Alexander
Set in Meridien

All rights reserved. Rutland Horizon asserts the moral right to be identified as the author of this work. A catalogue record for this book is available from the British Library.

This novel is entirely a work of fiction. Names, characters, places, and incidents are the products of the author's imagination or are used fictitiously. Any resemblance to actual events, locales, organizations or persons, living or dead, is entirely coincidental.

Sales of this book without a front cover may be unauthorized. If this book is coverless, it may have been reported to the publisher as "unsold and destroyed" and neither the author nor the publisher may have received payment for it.

Angry Robot and the Angry Robot icon are registered trademarks of Watkins Media Ltd.

ISBN 978 1 83673 009 5
Ebook ISBN 978 1 83673 010 1

Printed and bound in the United Kingdom by CPI Group (UK) Ltd, Croydon CR0 4YY

The manufacturer's authorised representative in the EU for product safety is eucomply OÜ - Pärnu mnt 139b-14, 11317 Tallinn, Estonia, hello@eucompliancepartner.com; www.eucompliancepartner.com

9 8 7 6 5 4 3 2

To James Ohlen, who really knows how to fly an arkship.

(1)

It was a Cycling Day – my Cycling Day, actually. Not that it made any difference; as always, I was woken up by Frazer moving round our room. He's my little brother. Although he's actually fourteen now, and nearly as tall as me, that's how I still think of him. I suppose I always will.

"Sorry, Hazel," he whispered, completely unapologetically, when he saw me peering blearily at him. He was like a solid shadow in the gloom, except for his hair, a shaggy white-blond mass, shining in the silvery moonlight leaking round the shutters. His round face is cute and energetic, with wide blue-grey eyes. I've noticed several village girls his age start to give him attentive looks at meals, nudging each other and whispering, but mainly giggling. He never sees them, of course – too busy. Frazer is always busy, either with his hands, helping Dad in the village carpentry shop, or with his brain. If he looks at anything for more than a few seconds, you just know his thoughts are taking it apart to figure out how it works. Maybe someday he'll be the one that gets all the ship's machines working again.

He put on his shirt and trousers and waved to me before slipping out. It was strange; nobody had been sleeping well for a while. I'd spent another restless night shuffling about on the thin mattress, waking intermittently. It'd left me as tired as when I went to bed.

I snuggled back under the blanket, all comfy and warm like a baby bird in its nest. On the other side of the room, hanging on the dresser, was my new dress. Dad's partner, Tanari, had made it for me, and didn't charge me a single food kilo – which was so kind of her. I just kept staring at it in the low light. That dress was the loveliest thing I'd ever owned, emerald-green to complement my red hair, with a long elegant skirt and wide shoulder straps. And right in the middle of the front was a Cycling symbol, a circle divided by an S-line down the middle, one half black, one half white, each with a dot of the opposite colour top and bottom.

The whole village was going to be watching me at the Cycling, especially now I'd got the dress. I was the ceremony's flower girl, presenting the posies to those who were to be Cycled.

It's a real honour to be chosen as the flower girl. After so many years of being overlooked, I was kind of surprised when the mayor asked me. Nobody over seventeen is selected, so I'd only got a few months left.

Cycling Day is the best time. For a start, nobody works. Well, the cows have to be milked, pigs and chickens fed, and the cooks have a lot to prepare, but that's all during the morning, when the families are saying goodbye to members who are going to be Cycled, which is kind of a sad–happy time. Then, once the morning's over, we have the ceremony at midday, followed by a big remembrance celebration and feast in the afternoon. The kids play games; there's singing. Then, when the daylight goes off, the flower girl lights a big bonfire in the village square and there's dancing until late.

So it was my day, and it was going to be wonderful. The only possible downer would be Zawn. He's twenty, and a couple of months back he got appointed a probationary Regulator, so he thinks he's important because of that. There's a real swagger to him now as he walks about. Truth is, he only got the Regulator job because Elijah, his older brother, is deputy Regulator. And Zawn likes me – a lot. My fault; he was a mistake, a rebound from Scott. By the time I realized that, he'd gone and got all serious about us and decided I was The One for him. I broke it off, of course, but I handled that badly.

Out of the twenty-three precious books we had at the school, my favourite was *Pride and Prejudice*. I always see myself like Elizabeth Bennet, who keeps having all those mixed-up conversations with Mr Darcy. Except *under no circumstances* can Zawn ever be compared to Mr Darcy. So, basically, my love life is an ongoing disaster.

I clambered up out of bed a few minutes before the daylight switched on. I really, *really* wanted to put the dress on, but I had chores to do first and I wasn't going to mess it up. No way.

I pulled on my usual trousers, a shirt that wasn't too scratchy, and slipped a jerkin on over that. My boots were soft leather and fitted perfectly, but the soles were worn. I'd have to visit the cobbler again before long, which will cost plenty of food kilos.

It took a couple of minutes sitting on the edge of the bed to comb out my hair, which falls nearly down to my waist. I inherited my red hair from Mum. It's thick and tangles easily, which is a real pain, but red hair is rare in the *Daedalus*, and to be honest it is my best feature. Everyone says that. I let it grow long because I wanted my best friend, Alice, to have it for a wig, but in the end she said no, so now I just let Mum trim it when the ends get all split. I'm well practised at braiding it so that it only takes a minute.

I picked up my basket and the nightsoil bucket, then tiptoed carefully across the cabin's living room so's not to wake Mum. I needn't have bothered. I could hear her coughing away in her room. It's quite an epidemic in the village right now, which is maybe why we're all finding it harder to sleep. Outside, the morning air was fresh from last night's three-hour rain. I took a deep breath, smelling the lavender in the garden, and looked round.

Our village is called Ixia, and its layout is typical of a *Daedalus* habitat village. Right at the centre – in every sense – is the hall, one of the arkship's old buildings that date back before the Mutiny, a broad circle with a white roof that has radial curves, like a melted flower. Its glass walls have big, open archways leading inside. Above the largest, there's a sign carved into whatever the roof is made of:

IXIA STATION
BLUE LINE

Nobody knows what blue line means. Maybe there was a blue path on the ground before the Mutiny, but if so it's long gone now.

There aren't many rooms inside the hall. There's the main hall itself, which has the Electric Captain's screen at one end – that's where we all eat and have village meetings. It has the kitchen along one side, with the ovens and cold cupboards that work from electricity, just like people had before. Behind the kitchen is the hospital, which has a medicine machine that got smashed up by the Mutineers but still works a bit.

The Regulators have their rooms near the centre, too, along with the mayor's office. But best of all is the school. I'm too old to go anymore. Besides, I know all of Ixia's twenty-three books. Maybe not as good as Frazer does – he can recite them all by heart – but I enjoyed them plenty. I liked just sitting and learning. I know all my numbers and letters; I can write and do arithmetic, and draw. I also learned how to play the guitar, which is what I like the most.

Outside the village hall, laid out in neat concentric circles, are the cabins where everyone lives. Ours has bamboo walls and a reed roof, though some are constructed entirely from wood. We have a bigger garden than most, with long beds full of Mum's herbs. There's also some fig trees, and grape vines on a frame that Dad built before he left.

It was early so there weren't many people about. I quickly dumped the nightsoil into the drain and left the bucket by the cabin door. Frazer and I are supposed to share that chore, but he never does it.

I made good time walking out of the village. All the barns and stables and pens form a border around Ixia's cabins. The smell from the animals is ripe, but I don't mind it. Farming is all part of the life Cycle. Without it, the arkship would be dead.

I'd been assigned a chicken coop next to one of the plough-horse stables. Teenagers always get an interim job once they finish school, so the mayor can see how reliable we are before we settle down into a profession. There are twenty-five chickens in my coop. It isn't particularly hard work, but it's important. Everyone eats eggs.

The birds were just starting to stir when I arrived. I tipped some grain and kitchen scraps into the feeder trough outside. Yesterday I'd spent a couple of hours giving the hutch a good clean so I wouldn't have to do much today. As the silly creatures came strutting down the ramp into the silver light, I went inside and checked for eggs. I got seventeen, which I put carefully into the basket.

As I left the hutch, the light strips running the length of the habitat roof a kilometre and a half above me turned from a gentle silver radiance to a dazzling white, like an incandescent rib cage holding up the solid sky. It's never an abrupt transition, taking maybe ten seconds, but it always makes my eyes water.

I blinked the tears away and looked down the length of the habitat. Ixia is midward, almost equally spaced between the two endwalls. I knew the forward wall was twenty-eight kilometres away but couldn't see it clearly. The landscape of farmland and forests sort of shimmered into a distance haze where the light strips overhead seemed to merge with the ground. They don't, of course; tower mountains rise out of the land every five kilometres like titanic black pillars, helping to hold up the habitat roof.

To spinward and antispinward, the ground appeared to curve up, again until it reached the solid sky. Another optical illusion. Wherever you stand in the habitat, it always looks like you're at the bottom of a curve.

Daedalus is basically a colossal cylinder flying through interstellar space on its way to our new world. It spins along its axis as it travels, giving us gravity on the habitat floor – apparently it's the same strength gravity as Earth had. To start with, the ship was an asteroid, just a huge lump of stone floating round Earth's sun. The Builders hollowed out the habitat section in the centre, making a cylindrical chamber fifty-five kilometres long and eleven in diameter, which gives it a circumference of thirty four point five kilometres. In the middle of that, the axis is another solid cylinder of rock – our sky. I always wish they hadn't designed it that way, that instead they'd left us with an open cylinder so we could look up and see the land above us. But they chose this layout. Too late to change now – by nine hundred years.

I walked back to the village hall. Even twenty metres outside the glass wall, the marvellous smell of fresh-baked bread was thick in the air. Inside, the kitchen the cooks were working hard, shouting at each other and their helpers. No way was I going to interrupt that, so I left my eggs in the rack along with all the others. Hauer was on duty that morning, one of the village Regulators. Some of them try to make out they're aloof, implying they're better than the rest of us, but Hauer's not like that. He smiled at me and put an entry in the food-kilo ledger that I'd completed my task. At the end of every week, Mayor Fininen and Chief Atov tally up everyone's work hours and issue food-kilo coins for them. I had my eye on some blue cloth that I wanted Tanari to turn into a skirt for me, but I was still about eight food kilos short.

I thanked Hauer and looked round, trying to see Alice. We grew up together, played together, got into trouble together, sang together in the choir. She is my sister, more than any family could make her. Not that anyone can mistake us for family. First off, her skin is a lovely rich black. Second, she's the pretty one. I'm just tall and skinny, while she's almost as tall and has a figure which makes boys stare silently then talk like they have brain damage. And her smile... Even I feel happy when she smiles. I can't smile like that. Don't bother trying.

She's also bald. According to Marana, it's some kind of very rare disease, which is otherwise completely harmless. Poor Alice didn't think so a few years back when she started to lose her hair. That's when I volunteered my hair for her. I couldn't bear how much she cried – it used to set me off as well. But in the end she decided a wig of red hair with black skin would be even more weird. As it turns out, she made the right choice. Having no hair just makes her look even more striking.

At the party after the Cycling ceremony, it'll be Alice who'll have all the boys in Ixia lining up pleading for a dance while I'll be left fending off Zawn.

The mayor had assigned her as a cook's helper. I caught sight of her taking a batch of loaves out of an oven on a long wooden peel. There are seven ovens in our kitchen, all of them the same: hemispheres a couple of metres across the base with an open arched doorway in the side. The floor inside is some kind of tough stone that the electricity heats up. They're always hot, about two hundred degrees Celsius, so everything gets cooked in them.

Alice slapped the loaf tins down on a table, then slid a couple more fresh ones into the oven. That was when she saw me and came over, snagging a couple of rolls on the way.

"You're not in the dress yet, then?" she teased and handed me one of the rolls. It was still warm in my hands.

"I'm getting ready after breakfast," I told her.

"I want to help braid your hair."

"How long till you finish?"

"Going to take a while," she said resentfully. "There's five didn't come in this morning. Five! Can you imagine that? On Cycling Day! So the rest of us have to cover, and it's not like we'll get extra food kilos for it. Itzy got taken to hospital in the middle of the night – she won't stop coughing. They say Marana's worried something is in her lungs, an infection maybe."

"That's terrible."

"Yeah." She coughed, then looked annoyed with herself. "Hope we haven't all got it."

"We'll be fine," I assured her. I knew Itzy. She's three years younger than me. Yes, it's wrong to judge people, but Itzy always looked frail; she was shorter than everyone else in her year and had really thin limbs. At school she'd hang back at playtime, never joining in the games. We'd whisper behind her back that she'd likely be going for an early Cycling. That's horrible, I know, but Dad always said school is really for toughening you up ready for adult life.

"I'll be as quick as I can," Alice said. Her expression soured as she caught sight of something behind me. "Uh-oh. He's been asking when you'd be in."

I turned to see Atov, Ixia's chief Regulator, walking towards me, a powerfully built man in his early fifties with brown hair just starting to show strands of grey. He got the job three years ago, when Shamus, the last chief, Cycled. Actually, he's not a bad Regulator – a pragmatist, Dad says. Whatever. I always feel guilty when I see him. Having him come towards me so purposefully was troubling. I've never done anything wrong – well, technically. I'm too young to drink alcohol... but surely he doesn't care about that? If he did, he'd have to fine every teenager in Ixia.

"Hazel. I'm glad you're here."

"Chief Atov." I bobbed about pathetically as he looked me up and down.

"Is that your flower-girl dress?"

I frowned crossly. "No, sir!" Then I realized he might be making a joke. His thin face was regarding me quizzically. I'm not used to Regulators trying to be funny. I suppose he wanted to put me at my ease. Why would he want to do that? What–

"Can I have a word with you, please?" he said. "Nothing to worry about."

"Yes, sir," I mumbled.

He led me towards his office in the centre of the hall building. Behind me, Alice pulled a wicked face. I gave her a shrug in return, grinning.

"Are you looking forward to the ceremony?" he asked me.

"Uh, yes, sir. I thought I might never be asked. I'm nearly too old."

"Nonsense. A girl like you, with your head screwed on right, you were always going to be asked. You're a credit to your family and your village."

"Thank you."

His office was a simple circular room with a big desk in the middle. Sheets of whiteleaf were piled up on its broad wooden top. The Regulators keep notes on everybody – when you were born, parents, school marks, infractions, good citizenry citations, illnesses. Your Cycling Day.

On the wall behind the desk was a long cabinet. I noticed it because it's made out of metal, which is unusual – most of the furniture in the village is made of wood. So the cabinet was obviously pre-Mutiny. Its lid was glass, which allowed me to see Ixia's five Regulator pistols inside, sitting neatly in their cradles.

Our Regulators don't carry them often, thankfully. They're nasty dull-black things with a fat barrel. I remember old Shamus coming into school to explain them to us. The pistols suck up electricity when they're not being used, he said, and that powers the mechanism that fires the dart.

Darts are dangerous. If you're too close when a Regulator shoots his pistol, they can punch a big hole in you. Really close, and the damage can be fatal. They're intended to inject a fleeing infractor with a simple anaesthetic, knocking them out. The darts themselves are reloaded with anaesthetic from the hospital medicine machine.

I never thought about it before, but looking at the pistols made me wonder... That's quite a coincidence, that among the very limited number of medicines the machine in the hospital can produce – biotics for infections, painkiller pills, contraception pills, creams for sick skin – the bit that makes the anaesthetic drug still works. You'd think the Mutineers would've smashed that part first. And it's not just Ixia's medicine machine – all the *Daedalus* villages have the same kind of machine and each one can make the dart drug for their Regulators.

Atov got me a chair and sat behind his desk, looking at me in what, presumably, he thought was a kindly fashion. "It's like this, Hazel," he said. "Your job today is nice and simple. You award everybody who's being Cycled with a pretty bunch of flowers."

"A posy," I corrected. I didn't like that he was disparaging the flower girl's role. "It's a posy of flowers, not a bunch."

"Quite. It's the symbolism, you see. Flowers are bright and colourful when they're open, full of life, but they also contain seeds, which are the future."

"The life Cycle." I knew all this, we did it at school the whole time. I didn't understand why he needed to bring me in here to tell me again.

"Normally, we Cycle when we're sixty-five." He gestured at the stack of whiteleafs on his desk.

With a start, I realized a sheet with my name on it would be there, sitting among all the others – Savin (Dad), Mum, Alice, even Frazer. All those sheets with our Cycle Day written on them. Everything decided, because that's how it has to be. They explained it all at school: despite how big the *Daedalus* is, it's not a wide-open world like Earth from before. Even though the Builders did their very best to make it planet-like, it's a closed system which only works because of the Cycle.

"It is a great time," he continued. "An honourable time. We Cycle to make room for the new generations. We return to the soil, which grows crops, which we eat. Thus we live."

"Yes."

"Everyone knows this. Everyone accepts this. So everyone whose Day it is takes their posy from you before they're Cycled; and when they do, they smile and say thank you. There's never normally any fuss."

Now I knew why he'd brought me in here. "The Cheaters," I said.

"Exactly."

It had been the talk of the village for the last four days, ever since the Regulator squad had brought back three Cheaters they'd found stealing our sheep. I'd caught a glimpse of them sitting in the cart as they were taken to the village hall and locked in the cells, two men and one woman, so terribly old. They had run away before their Cycle Day, run off and hidden somewhere inside the arkship's habitat – actually, in the tower mountains. Everyone knows that's where Cheaters go.

Now they'd been caught. Our diligent Regulators had brought them to justice. They were going to be Cycled this afternoon.

"They can't physically run," Atov told me. "They're too old now, anyway. And my people will be escorting them to the Cycle platform. But they may resist when it comes down to it. We don't often have to Cycle a Cheater; I'm old enough to have seen it a couple of times. There could be shouting, a lot of anger. It might be unpleasant."

"I understand," I told him, and I really did. And that was accompanied by a nasty thought: had I been chosen because I was old? That a five-year-old flower girl wouldn't be able to cope with Cheaters at the ceremony?

"Good. You need to be prepared, that's all. If it looks like they're going to be trouble, if they start kicking off, we'll use a dart to put them under." He gestured at the pistol cabinet behind him. "Nobody wants the ceremony ruined, especially not by a Cheater. Today is a celebration. It's *your* celebration, Hazel."

"Right."

"So if they can't receive the posy gracefully like they're supposed to, like a decent citizen would, just lay it beside them and move on. Got it?"

"Yes."

"Good girl. I knew we'd chosen well. You just keep your head and tonight we can all have a great party." He winked. "I might just be not looking your way when you and your friends have a drop or two of something you shouldn't."

"But…" My forehead must have crinkled up, I was puzzling away at this so hard. "If you disable them with a dart, how will they take the Blessing?" The Blessing is the little glass of liquid that everyone being Cycled drinks as they go to lie down on the platform. In school, they told us it has the best taste imaginable. It sends you peacefully to sleep and slows your heart until it eventually stops. Then *Daedalus* Cycles you.

"The Blessing can be injected if necessary," Atov said flatly. "That's something the Regulators will take care of. It's our job. Don't you worry about it."

"Yes, sir," I nodded hurriedly.

But I couldn't stop thinking about it all the way back to our cabin. Life in *Daedalus* is the Cycle. You know when your Day will come. It's written down there on the whiteleaf in the Regulator's office on the very day you're born. And when it comes around, you take the Blessing and give yourself to the future. That's the only way the *Daedalus* will eventually reach our new world.

I never questioned it my whole life. Cycling is so simple, so obvious. Everyone is brought up understanding the necessity of it.

Cheaters don't. They believe in something different altogether. They're not like us; they're arrogant, greedy and horrible. But they're still people. And if Chief Atov is right, they might not take the Blessing drink willingly. It will be forced on them.

I suppose that means – if you take away all the smooth, soothing words – we're going to execute them.

(2)

Alice and I got ready in my room. She brought her dress over, a grand ruffled skirt and a scoop-neck top in purple and white. Standing beside her, I knew I looked great in my green dress but once again she'd outshone me without even trying. She spent a long time doing my hair, weaving in white flowers – bouvardias and peonies. Mum had given me a basket of them – she must have spent a day selecting them from other gardens and the fields outside Ixia.

"Wow," Alice said, as she put her arm round my shoulder. We both stared into the mirror. "You look amazing. Like mother nature Herself."

I had to admit I did like the effect. My hair was thick with blossom. She'd arranged it perfectly. The only downside was a headache growing behind my eyes. I'd been getting them a lot recently.

"Thank you," I said.

"You'll knock 'em dead tonight," she said. "Who are you going to dance with?"

"I don't want to go anywhere near the dance. I thought I'd bring my guitar and help the band."

Her nose wrinkled in disapproval. "They won't let you play. And it's *your* Cycling Day. You need to make the most of it. Be the queen of the dance."

I groaned in frustration. I did love to dance. But… "Zawn is going to be there. I don't want to be stuck with him all night. I don't want to be stuck with him for one dance, actually."

"Then don't. He needs to get it into his thick skull he's been dumped, and with good reason. Come on, you're the flower girl. You get to dance with who you want. I know Garril said he wanted to dance with you."

"Garril?" Oh dear. Garril is shorter than me and has crooked teeth. He's already working in the pig pens like his father. I know, don't judge. But...

"No? Well, how about Makkus?"

"Definitely not. He's already twice my weight. His mother must give him all her food."

"It's not fat." Her eyes had *that* gleam. "I've seen him with his shirt off."

"Makkus?" I asked, mock-scandalized.

"And *this* is why you have the likes of Zawn thinking he's still in with a chance. Stop being so dismissive of everyone else. We need to get boys to realize how fantastic you are. Scott did." She pouted at herself in the mirror. Wiggled her hips and shimmied. "Go get 'em, girl."

I sighed and my shoulders drooped, remembering Scott. "I wish I was like you."

"No, you don't. You're you and you're fabulous just as you are. We need to make people realize that. And this dress will go a long way to making that happen. Trust me."

"I just–"

The door banged open and Frazer charged in.

"Hey!" I yelled. "Girls changing in here!"

He gave both of us a jeering laugh and pulled his shirt off. "Yeah, yeah. Boy changing now. Oh my dayz, what is that *smell?* Hazel, why've you got a garden on your head?"

"She's the flower girl, idiot," Alice told him.

Anyone else, *anyone*, calling him an idiot would've got a barrage of abuse back. If it'd been me, he'd have thrown something. Mind, I may have lobbed things in his direction on occasion. Brothers are a complete pain. I always wish I had a sister instead.

But because it was Alice, Frazer just grinned and said, "You two! Mad, the pair of you."

"Come on," I told her. "It's about time anyway."

We left just as Frazer tugged his trousers down. He is so embarrassing at times.

"You need your own room," Alice said as we went out into the living room.

"Tell me about it," I replied in my best martyred tone. There were even times when I wondered if I should just go and move in with Dad. Except that would devastate Mum. It always amazes me that, in a small village where everything flows along smoothly, life can be so complicated.

Georgi was waiting with Mum in the main living room. He's the council clerk, sorting out all the administration. They'd been seeing each other off and on for a few months, though he's a lot older, only six years off Cycling. He's nice, quiet and patient, which is good for her. I guess I may have been a bit resentful about how he made Mum start to feel good about herself again. Finally. It was a long painful climb out of the sullen anger that had claimed her after Dad left. Mum had withdrawn to some inner place that not even me and Frazer could pull her out of.

I kept a grip on my disappointment as I looked at Mum. She was in the same dress that she'd worn to every Cycling Day for the last ten years. There's nothing wrong with it; I just wish she'd try something new, something that might jolt that weary expression off her face. Georgi, by contrast, was wearing an immaculate black jacket and matching trousers.

Mum came over and started fussing, adjusting the dress when it didn't need it. "You look so fine," she said. Her voice was all choked up. "I'm so proud." She hugged me tight. "You know that, don't you?"

I squeezed her back. "Thanks, Mum."

"You're going to be fighting off the boys at the dance tonight," Georgi said, giving me a thumbs up. All I could do was return a slightly forced smile. Why does everyone focus on me and my chances at the dance? If they're not setting me up with someone, they're speculating who I'll wind up with. Why can't they leave me to find my own friends? It's tough enough without all eyes being on me. Besides, I've grown up with all the Ixia boys. I know them too well – the choice isn't exactly inspiring. That's what makes the invitation dances to other villages so popular. I get to meet boys like Scott.

"The flowers were lovely, Jolene," Alice said brightly.

"Thank you, sweetie," Mum said. She handed Alice a single scarlet rose. Alice smiled happily and took it.

"Are you all right?" Mum asked me.

"Headache, that's all."

"Oh, we can't have that." She went over to the dresser that held all her jars of herbs and fruits. "Here," she said, handing me a handful of almonds. "Chew these. They should help."

"Thanks, Mum."

Frazer charged out of our room, greasy hair tufted up and full of sawdust, shirt hanging out of his trousers. All four of us groaned at him.

"Oh my dayz, what now?" he demanded.

"Come here," Mum said fondly. She and Alice smartened him up, and we were finally ready to go.

Walking down to the village hall together, we joined in the procession of other families who were emerging from their cabins, all wearing their finest clothes. I love it when everyone dresses up; we spend so much time working it's hard to remember there are times when we can just ease off and be happy.

"You nervous?" Alice asked me.

"No."

"Lucky you. I was in a complete panic."

"Were you? Nobody could tell."

"So what did Atov want?"

"Just to tell me to be calm when I greet the Cheaters."

"Oh, that's a relief. I couldn't think you'd be in trouble over anything."

Which I slightly resented. I can be bad if I want. "What do you think about the Cheaters?" I asked her.

"I think I'm glad they're caught. Breathing our air, taking up our rightful space. *Daedalus* isn't infinite."

"But they didn't actually harm anyone."

"What's wrong with you, Hazel? Those were our sheep they were stealing. We would have had to go without. And they know more than anyone *Daedalus* has to Cycle. Everyone's life depends on it. They Cheated that."

"I know, I know. It's just... if they don't take the Blessing, we're going to kill them."

Alice looked mildly shocked. "We kill sheep and cows and deer so Ixia can eat. People Cycle so life can carry on until we reach the new world."

"Yeah. I just wish they'd been caught for a different Cycle Day."

"Oh, Hazel." She put her arm round my shoulder. "They will not spoil your day, okay? It's going to be magnificent."

I managed to produce a smile of sorts. "Thanks."

The Cycling platform is right behind the village hall, a metal square three metres to a side with a guard rail around it. An old metal sign above it says: MAX LOADING 1,500KG.

Mayor Fininen was already standing there, along with Chief Atov. As I joined them, I noticed the chief was wearing his pistol holster. I took my place next to Marana, who was looking very unhappy. Her fingers kept stroking the leather medicine satchel she always carried with her.

I tried to quell my nerves as I faced the assembled villagers. Yes, I wanted to be flower girl, but I wasn't used to so much attention. Alice did an exaggerated mime and I stopped hunching my shoulders.

As the stragglers arrived, I found myself looking at the front row: those to be Cycled. There were nineteen of them. It was odd, but to my eyes it seemed like they were the ones about to lose family members rather than the other way round. Quite a few had red eyes from crying. A couple of them appeared sullen. I quickly moved my gaze away.

Cycling is deliberately intended as a celebration, rejoicing the departure of the old people so it doesn't upset the young children who are likely watching a grandparent disappear. It's open and honest, so everyone knows it will happen to them, that it's perfectly natural, the way the habitat is sustained. We thank those being Cycled and reaffirm our commitment to the voyage of the *Daedalus* so one day our children will reach the new world.

The chatter faded away as Regulators escorted the Cheaters out of the village hall, where they'd been held. Two men and one woman, their faces all wrinkled, hair thinning so much it reminded me of the awful six months Alice had suffered. Their appearance made me wonder exactly how old they were, how long they'd Cheated the Cycle.

Zawn was escorting the woman Cheater, looking insufferably proud at the duty. I saw his hand gripping her arm so tightly it must have been painful for her. Typical.

Mayor Fininen began his address. I could practically recite it myself, I've heard it so many times. How *Daedalus* travelled from Earth to the first world, taking four centuries to reach it. The discovery that although the first world was mostly ocean, it had evolved a species that was almost sentient. Then came our finest hour: we renounced the first world as it did not belong to us; the aliens who were born there deserved their chance to reach their full potential on their own.

With great sadness, Captain Kruger ordered *Daedalus* to fly to another new world – the one we were still heading to. It was even further away, a flight of at least five hundred years.

Thirty years after the ship left the first world came the Mutiny. The Mutineers wanted to turn back; in their arrogance they claimed the aliens were never going to amount to anything and we should have our chance. They wanted to establish their shiny new cities on the islands of the first world and claim it for their own. It was the ultimate betrayal of our ancestors, whose society had risen above Earth's ancient conflicts and imperialism to a noble era where everyone played a part in building the *Daedalus*. Fortunately, many on board were appalled by the Mutineers; they remained loyal to Captain Kruger and resolved to uphold the decency of the Builders and continue onwards.

The conflict raged for over a year, with the Mutineers smashing all the food machines in an attempt to force Captain Kruger to turn round. Then they began on other machines. It was a terrible time; so many adults died in the fighting – on both sides. Finally the Mutineers laid siege to the bridge, where Captain Kruger and her remaining loyalists had retreated. So the captain made her glorious sacrifice: she cast herself into the remaining thinking machines to become the Electric Captain. If the Mutineers smashed the thinking machines, the arkship would die. So in the end, she won. *Daedalus* remained under her lawful control and never turned round.

But the machines they'd already broken no longer produced food and medicine and clothes. Thankfully, our magnificent Builders were smarter than the Mutineers ever realized. With the guidance and knowledge of the Electric Captain, it was possible to farm the habitat parkland. It would be a simpler life, she warned the young survivors, a harder life involving many sacrifices, but people would live to continue the great star voyage. As she explained, the parkland is finite; its resources must be carefully nurtured. It cannot support expansion. To keep it stable and alive, everything must be Cycled.

"And so we are gathered today to acknowledge the wisdom of the Electric Captain," Mayor Fininen said. "Today we Cycle. Those who are to be Cycled, we salute you. *Daedalus* will reach the new world because of you. One day, our children will live under open skies."

"Open skies," everyone repeated dutifully. Then they started cheering and clapping. The first Cycler stepped forward. I was nearly crying myself when I handed him his posy of purple iris and yellow roses. "May you blossom again," I said formally.

"By the grace of the Electric Captain, I will," he replied.

I always find Cycling a very emotional time, ever since I watched my grandparents Cycle.

After they collected their posy from me, those to be Cycled were given their glass of Blessing from the mayor. They drank it, often knocking it back in one, then went over to the platform.

They lay down side by side on the cushions placed on the cold, hard metal. The mayor pressed one of the two buttons on the box fixed to the guard rail and the platform sank down. Once it was below ground, a pair of safety doors flipped out so no one fell in, but they also shielded the platform from view as it descended.

A couple of minutes later, the safety doors moved aside and the platform slid back up, empty.

Only three people could lie on the platform at a time, so it took half an hour before the last one went down. Then the Regulators brought the Cheaters forward. Nobody applauded them. The whole village watched in silence.

The first one, a man with the whitest hair I'd ever seen, had to be lifted up and carried. There was a Regulator on either side; Elijah was one of them, stiff with the effort of holding him up – but the Cheater wasn't struggling. I realized he was unconscious, his head was lolling forward. They stopped in front of me. I picked up a posy from the tray. I couldn't put it on the ground next to him, like I'd been told – that just felt wrong – so I spent a few seconds tucking it into the top of his shirt. "Blossom again," I whispered. Then Atov stepped up and made a gesture like he was gripping the Cheater's shoulder in friendship. I saw the injector pod in his hand.

For one wild moment I wanted to yell out, *No, stop it!* but somehow I managed to stay silent. In my heart, I knew this was wrong.

Then the old man was being lowered onto the platform and the second one was escorted up to me. I held out the posy. His expression was contemptuous, but he took it from me. Next thing, he was chewing the flowers. I was so surprised all I could do was stare at him.

"May you bloss–" I began.

He spat out the wad of pulp and laughed mockingly at me.

The Regulator holding his arm twisted it and grunted: "Behave."

Mayor Fininen held up the glass of Blessing. The Cheater practically snatched it from his hand and tipped it back, swallowing the drink fast. Then he screamed as if he was in agony and clawed at his throat, his knees buckling. Everyone jumped. I cried out, covering my mouth with my hand. The Blessing drink was supposed to be painless.

"Doctor!" Fininen yelped. She rushed forwards, then stopped.

The Cheater had abruptly fallen silent. He stood up perfectly straight and sneered at poor Marana. "What exactly were you going to do?" he asked. "Save me?"

"Get him on the platform," Atov hissed.

The Cheater started a manic laugh as the Regulators lifted him off his feet and carried him away.

Out of the corner of my eye, I could see Marana standing perfectly still, except for her hands, which were trembling.

The last Cheater came forwards. Zawn had let go of her arm, allowing her to walk with dignity. Her face was heavily wrinkled. I wanted to ask how old she was but didn't dare.

"Hello, my dear," she said. "What lovely hair you have."

"Er, thank you."

"So like our dear Electric Captain."

I just stood there all gormless. Plenty of people say the same thing.

"Oh, is that for me?" she asked. "It's very pretty."

"Huh?" I'd been so thrown by the last Cheater's mischief, I hadn't picked up the final posy. "Uh, right."

"You have headaches these days, don't you, my dear?"

I froze as I was about to hand her the posy. "How did you know that?"

"We all get them. It's because the habitat air is running out."

"What?"

"The pressure's falling; it has been for years, and now it's become critical. If you don't believe me, ask Alisha. She knows all about these things."

"Give her the flowers," Atov told me curtly. "And you, be quiet."

The old woman took the posy from me.

"May you blossom again," I said automatically.

She smiled, such a warm, sympathetic smile it made me feel so guilty at what we were doing. Before Zawn and Atov could stop her, she put her arms round me. "Alisha is in Tressaco," she whispered in my ear.

"Come on," Atov tugged her away from me.

The mayor offered her the Blessing glass. She drank it down in one, all the while staring unnervingly at me. "Think for yourself, my dear. Save yourself."

I watched numbly as Zawn led her over to the platform. She was almost there when she stumbled. Zawn had to carry her the last few steps. The last thing she did was put her arm round the man who'd chewed the posy. I thought I saw her smile, then she flopped down.

Were they married? They'd been caught together.

I was fighting back tears as the platform sank away. Marana's arm went round my shoulders. "It's okay," she said soothingly.

Then Zawn walked over. He was smiling as if everything had gone smoothly. "Well, that's over," he said cheerfully. "You look lovely, Hazel. Really. The finest girl in the village."

"Thanks."

"Time to celebrate now."

"Celebrate what?" I asked him numbly. I couldn't forget the image of the three dead Cheaters lying on the platform. The guilt was like an all-over ache.

He gave me this puzzled look, his broad forehead all crumpled up, brown eyes narrowed. "The feast, remember? Then tonight, after you light the bonfire, I thought... I hoped, you and I could dance."

"Zawn. No–"

"Hey, come on, you owe me an explanation, at least. I thought we were good together. Weren't we?"

His face – which, if I'm honest, was reasonably handsome – was very still, with his jaw muscles all tensed up. After the stress of dealing with the Cheaters, I really didn't need that needy self-pity directed at me full strength. "Affairs of the heart don't follow reason," I told him, which was pretty much what Elizabeth Bennet might have said.

"What did I do?"

Nothing. The idea of spending every day of my too-few years being with you, here in the same village, of having no choice in my life, of never seeing the new world – I want to cry and scream at the very idea. "It's not you. it's me."

"Everyone knows that means the opposite. Why? What did I do wrong? Most girls would jump at the chance to go out with a Regulator."

"Lucky you, then. Go and dance with them all tonight."

Marana's arm tightened round me. "Thank you, Probationary Regulator," she said levelly. "That will be all."

Zawn gave her a resentful look and marched off back to the village hall.

"Thanks," I mumbled.

"If he gives you any more trouble, you let me know." As the village doctor, Marana was really important. She sat on the village council and even the mayor had to listen to her. She also happened to be Dad's cousin, which makes her someone I could always turn to. I wound up visiting her cabin a lot after Dad moved out.

"I will."

"So what did she say to you?"

"Who?"

"The old woman. When she hugged you."

Interesting that Marana didn't call her a Cheater. I looked at Zawn's distant back, then at Atov, who was talking to the mayor. "She said the flowers were nice. That's all."

"Right." Marana gave me a very judgemental look.

Tressaco is a tower mountain seven klicks spinward from Ixia. So I guessed there was a bunch of Cheaters hiding out there. I didn't want the Regulators going there and hauling them in for Cycling. Not after today. "Marana, what do you think she meant about the air running out?"

She glanced over at the mayor and Atov, who were still talking heatedly. "Not much ambiguity there, Hazel. She believes the air is running out."

"Is it?"

"I don't know."

"Well, we have to find out!"

The mayor and Atov stopped talking. They both stared at me. I blushed hot red.

"Hazel," the mayor said amiably. "You did a wonderful job there. It can't have been easy at the end. Thank you."

"She said the air's running out," I blurted.

"She was lying," Chief Atov said.

"We don't know that. We have to find out."

"Hazel," he said, using a voice like a teacher patiently explaining something at school. "If we were in any danger, the Electric Captain would warn us. Wouldn't she? She'd tell us what to do."

"Oh. Yes."

"The Cheater was trying to cause trouble. It's what they do, you understand? They're rotten to the core."

I turned to Marana, who gave a small nod.

"Yes, Chief Atov," I said meekly.

"So don't go mentioning what she said to anyone. Lies like that only upset everybody – which is what the Cheaters wanted. Don't let them win."

"I understand."

"Good girl. Now come on, the cooks have prepared another amazing feast for us. I don't know about you but I'm starving."

I found Mum and Georgi sitting at one of the long tables in the hall. Frazer was with them and I slid onto the bench beside him. He barely looked up from his plate.

"You did a fantastic job," Mum told me. "And you looked gorgeous."

The cooks had prepared several pigs for us, along with a deer and half a dozen swans, with just about every vegetable we grow piled up steaming hot, and baked potatoes, and jugs full of thick gravy and apple sauce. I could see flans and cakes and meringues for pudding, all lined up on the counters along with tall pitchers of cream.

I reached for the nearest dish of roast pork. "Thanks, Mum."

"It was so funny," Frazer said.

"Funny?" I asked, annoyed.

"That old Cheater who made out he was in pain." Frazer's hands went to his own throat and he thrashed about, going cross-eyed as he made wailing sounds.

"Stop it," Mum said sharply. People were looking round.

"What?" he snorted. "Everyone was having a heart attack. *Daedalus* nearly got fifty extra bodies to Cycle. It was funny. I couldn't stop laughing."

"You are seriously warped," I told him.

He just chuckled and went back to stuffing his face.

The pork tasted great, and the roast parsnips, and the sweet potatoes, and the eggplant, and the tomatoes. I had two helpings, then sat back and chewed on a long strip of crackling before collecting a slice of pear flan.

"Can I go?" Frazer asked eagerly after he'd gulped down his pudding.

"Already?" Mum said. She sounded disappointed.

"Mum!" he waved wildly at the archway where a dozen boys were already hurrying out. One of them carried a football. "If I don't get out there now, I'll have to play in goal. I hate playing in goal. I'm the best striker there is."

She smiled indulgently. "Go on then."

"Thanks, Mum!"

He nearly fell backwards off the bench, he was in such a hurry.

Bottles of wine were appearing at most of the tables at this point. The afternoon was for relaxing, catching up with friends and gossip. Alice caught my gaze and winked as she raised a glass. I knew it would have wine in it. Her parents are a bit more liberal than mine.

"I'd better go and talk to Dad," I said.

"Yeah," Mum said. "You'd better."

Dad was sitting at a table down the other end of the hall, about as far away from Mum as physically possible. Naturally. Tanari was with him, a woman with a round, cheerful face, wearing a blue-and-red dress with a tassel hem. As I got closer, I saw she had turquoise streaks in her brown hair. That was new.

Dad stood up, trying not to grimace. Just like I tried not to look at his leg. He'd made it himself in the carpentry shop. It's very clever, with an ankle joint that bends just like a real one. His knee stump fits into a padded cup and leather straps hold the whole contraption in place, allowing him to walk almost normally. But he's always in pain. I feel that hurt just looking at him.

When he did it, that stupid accident in the waterwheel house, I was so scared he'd be Cycled. If you can't contribute to the village, that's what happens to you – it's the law. But Marana saved what was left of his leg and Dad designed and built the artificial limb for himself. Nobody had ever seen anything like it before. He could resume work, but living in constant pain changed him. Too much for Mum.

"Hi, Dad." I kissed him gently and waited until he'd eased himself back onto the bench.

"Sweetheart," he smiled happily. "You were the most perfect flower girl ever."

"Thanks." I studied his face. As always, he looked like he hadn't slept for a month, but at least today the usual worry lines had gone. I suspected wine had something to do with that. He and Tanari had already finished one bottle, and now she was refilling his glass for him.

"Thanks again for the dress," I told her.

She winked and held up her glass. "My pleasure. You wear it well."

"So who are you dancing with tonight?" Dad asked.

I groaned. "Don't you start."

"That idiot Zawn being a nuisance?"

"I can handle Zawn."

"That's my girl."

I leaned in a little closer. "Dad, did you ever hear of someone called Alisha?"

The surprised expression on his face told me he wasn't as tipsy as I'd thought. "Where did you hear that name?"

"So you do know her?"

"Yes," he nodded slowly. "I remember her, anyway. I never saw her much, though. She ran off when I was still a child."

"Who is she?"

"My grandmother."

Shock immobilized my throat muscles. It was a few heartbeats before I managed to breathe again. So this Alisha woman was my great-grandmother. And she was still alive.

(3)

A week after Cycling Day, there was an assembly in the village hall. Everybody came, without exception. Marana even helped Itzy walk through from the hospital. The poor girl was still coughing, but not as bad as before. I saw Elijah and Atov both study her before she sat on a bench at the back. That chilled me.

Mayor Fininen came and stood in front of the screen. It's a big rectangle of black glass stuck up on the wall at the head of the hall. Glowing red numbers in the top-left corner were counting down. Whenever the Electric Captain had something to say, those numbers appeared, usually a day in advance.

He eyed the red digits and held up his arms. "Okay people, quiet down. Please stand for our Electric Captain."

We all clambered to our feet. As always, Mayor Fininen had timed it perfectly.

The screen amazes me. For a start, it's a pre-Mutiny machine which works, which is always a rarity. Not only that, it's a solid link to the past. Everybody used to have screens, and dozens of other machines, before the Mutiny, when they all lived in the tower mountains. It's how the Electric Captain talks to us. She never says very much. If I'm truthful, the talks she gives us are sort of a let-down because all she does is basically read out lists. I guess that doesn't matter so much; it's reassuring seeing her, knowing she's still there somehow inside the thinking machines that guide *Daedalus* through space. And because of that, we will reach the new world one day. She gives us a reason to carry on.

The little red digits all reached zero and the blank rectangle lit up. The Electric Captain appeared to be staring out at us, her face filling the screen, allowing only a tiny glimpse of the background, which is always the same huge room with walls of rock. Tall columns of shiny metal stand behind her. She has a strange, plain face which is always devoid of emotion, though I suspect she might be sad – a mind imprisoned for centuries in the machines has to be the greatest burden anyone could endure. I am so grateful she does that for us and wish I could tell her so. Her face is quite thin with a small nose, and red hair much darker than mine pulled back and fastened somewhere behind her head. She is civility and authority.

"Good day to all of you," she said in her calm, measured voice. I could see the children smiling at the sound, while adults just looked relieved. "And my congratulations on yet another successful Cycling Day. With your commitment to maintaining the environment of the habitat, respecting the order we must live by, you have ensured our magnificent ship will continue its flight to the new world. As a result, I am happy to announce an invitation dance."

Several people clapped. I could see a lot of smiles around me – indulgent from the grown-ups, eager from all my fellow teenagers. I forced a smile. True, I was genuinely pleased about the invitation dance, but some part of me was hoping that today would be the day of *the* announcement. The one we've been waiting for five hundred years to hear. That the Electric Captain would finally tell us the voyage was coming to an end and we would soon arrive at the new world. I always pray it will happen in my lifetime, that Alice and I are the generation that would walk under that unimaginable *open sky*. It's what we were always told in school, that it would take five hundred years. Which is now! About now, anyway. There are many uncertainties in travelling so far, and the Mutineers did damage the ship.

I was always resentful about that, not understanding why the Electric Captain never tells us how much longer the voyage will last. Dad always said it was to avoid taking people's hope away. That we keep on hoping *Daedalus* will arrive, so we do what we have to and live our lives without fuss, all the time believing that our children will reach the new world. Dad can be quite cynical.

The Electric Captain started announcing the twenty villages taking part. A list. Always lists.

"Ixia's girls are invited to attend a dance thrown by Akebia."

Cheering and squeals broke out across the hall. I had to admit, that was exciting. Akebia was a village right up by the forward endwall, twenty-five kilometres away. That would mean I'd finally have travelled the whole length of the habitat. Two dances ago, we'd been invited to Viride, which was a fishing village on the edge of the ring lake. I'd met Scott there. At the time, it had been the best two days of my life.

Then the boys were cheering and clapping.

I turned to Mum. "What?"

"Ixia has invited the girls from Crinum to a dance here."

I pulled a face. "Those poor Crinum girls."

Mum shook her head at me, but she was chuckling.

We had three days to get ready for the dance. The first thing I did was take my green dress to Tanari.

"No problem," she said. "I can unpick the Cycling symbol in an hour."

"Oh, thank you!" Nothing wrong with the symbol, except everyone in Akebia would know it was a Cycling Day dress.

"You want me to do anything else?" she asked.

"What do you mean?"

Tanari gave me a knowing look. "Lower the neckline? Raise the skirt hem?"

My cheeks became quite warm. "No, it's okay, thank you."

"Quite right. You'll have your hands full fending them off as it is."

I couldn't meet her gaze. "That's Alice, not me."

"Forget about Alice for once. You are allowed to have fun, Hazel. That's the whole point of invitation dances – have fun, meet people, break hearts. And remember: what happens when you're away dancing stays away."

"I know." As always, Scott's smile drifted into my mind. Maybe I'd made a mistake. But it had been such a lovely mistake.

"Good. Just make sure you do enjoy yourself, then. These last few years haven't been easy for you. Now everything has settled down here, it's about time you started enjoying yourself."

"I will," I promised.

"Don't forget to visit Marana and get your contraception booster pill before you go."

"Tanari!"

She grinned at my reddening cheeks and opened her sewing box.

We left on Kirill's barge an hour after daylight came on. There were hundreds of the long, shallow craft sliding serenely along the canals of *Daedalus*. Water always flows in one direction through the habitat, from the waterfalls on the forward endwall to the ring lake around the aft endwall. The canals meander a lot on their way, merging and splitting to form a comprehensive network across the habitat. All of the hundred villages are sited next to a canal, not just for easy transport but so everyone can have a waterwheel to power the mills and looms and saws we need to keep our society running.

There was an odd ornament mounted on the bow of the barge, a pincer claw of black bone, sort of like a bird's talon but bigger than any bird in the Daedalus. The outside edge was razor sharp and the tips were like needles too. It'd been well polished over the years.

"A dragon's foot from before the Mutiny," Kirill said, all solemn-faced when Alice asked him what it was. "There were big flocks of them flying all over the habitat back then."

He walked away aft, but not before I saw him start to grin. Alice and I exchanged a glance. Why do adults think saying things like that is funny?

There were twenty-five of us in the barge, all the Ixia girls over fifteen and still not committed or married. Well, mostly – I know Jane and Chloe were going pretty steady, but there they were on the barge, looking eager at the prospect of the dance. We sat on long benches facing each other, along with four of the older women from the village who were there to make sure we didn't completely disgrace ourselves. Elijah was accompanying them too, sitting up at the prow, trying to look all confident – as if he was in charge. Nobody paid him any attention, which I guess helped cultivate his stern expression.

Alice and I sat together, trying to ignore the stink of previous cargoes whose dank juices stained the wood. There was a lot of giggling as we set off. The ducks and swans that paddled up and down the calm waters of the canal parted to let the barge glide past. We sang, too, as the black shire horse on the towpath pulled us along. Kirill, the barge master, told us her name was Shella, and that she was seventeen hands. I didn't know what that meant, except: big.

Kirill walked alongside her, guiding the huge beast over bridges and taking the correct fork at every junction pool without even slowing. He bragged that he knew all the canal routes in the *Daedalus*.

I learned that barges going forwards always travel on the left of the canal, while anyone heading aft goes to the right.

"I could do that," I told Alice sometime around mid-morning.

"Do what?"

"Be a barge master."

"You're kidding?"

"It'd be nice. Visit somewhere different every day. Handle different cargos. Meet new people all the time."

"Have a boy in every village. Walk away from Zawn!"

We both laughed.

"If you did, then most of the time you'd be all by yourself with a ton of guano," she said. "That would be seriously lonely. Not to mention sad."

"I know," I sighed. Guano time is something nobody can avoid, not even the mayor. We get regular deliveries of guano every month. Every village does. That's one set of machines that the Mutineers didn't wreck. All the human waste we produce, along with every piece of organic rubbish from the farms and kitchen, all gets flushed out of the village down a big sewer pipe to a composter machine (most likely many composter machines) somewhere beyond the rear endwall that's been sealed off since the Mutiny. That's where the Cycled bodies go, too. The machines take all the harmful toxins out of the waste and pump it back into the habitat as a thick sludge, guano, which is a great fertilizer. Trouble is, there isn't a machine to spread it back onto the vegetable gardens and fields. I doubt there ever was.

About a third of the tower mountains have a spill pipe where the guano comes out like a sluggish black waterfall that reeks. From there, the barges load up to take it back to the villages. Every time we get a delivery, the whole village turns up at the wharf, every one of us pushing a wheelbarrow, and out we take it to whatever piece of land is on the rota. Those are long, wearisome days. When you tip out your wheelbarrow, you can't just leave the stuff in a big squishy pile; you have to rake it into the soil. Then you go back for another barrow-load.

And the compost machines aren't perfect, either – not anymore. You often get small chunks of bone, or bits of animal carcass that haven't been broken down properly. Once, a couple of years ago, I was raking guano into Mum's herb beds when I pulled out this disgusting length of flesh like a piece of black-and-red rope. It was as thick as my arm but didn't have a bone in it like a limb should.

One of the village school books is called *Ocean Creatures* and has pictures of a whole load of interesting fish from Earth. The flesh rope stuck to my rake reminded me of an octopus tentacle, but this thing didn't have sucker rings.

I had no idea where it came from. I'm pretty sure we don't have an octopus family swimming round in the aft ring lake. Scott would have known about them. It must have been some bit of fetid animal guts I didn't recognize. So I just buried it, and let the horrid thing decompose in the soil.

No, guano time is not the most popular activity. Alice was right – that's what barge masters spend most of their time moving round. I needed to think of a different job.

The *Daedalus* endwalls are really something. I mean, the tower mountains are impressive, but the endwalls form a near-vertical cliff of smooth rock holding the ground and sky apart. The forward one has waterfall outlets high above the ground, spaced every kilometre or so the whole way around, sending out thick jets of water which splash into circular pools, where the canals start. I stared in fascination at the foaming tract of water as we approached Akebia. It curved sideways like a scythe blade as it fell. I'd heard about it but never seen the phenomenon. It's because of the spin, Frazer says. The water coming from the outlet isn't spinning quite as fast relative to the habitat floor so it arcs through the air as it comes down. That's how we know which way *Daedalus* is spinning.

We really do live in a strange place.

Akebia was just below a waterfall pool, spread like a semicircle along the start of the canal. The current outside the pool was strong, too – poor old Shella was straining hard for the last kilometre to pull us up to the wharf.

We were greeted by Damaso, the mayor, and half the village council, who were quite sweet and made us feel genuinely welcome. No eligible boys, though. That's tradition. We don't get to meet them until the dance starts.

They showed us to the cabins we'd be sleeping in. The one Alice and I shared had a window that looked out towards the pool. I pushed the shutters open and stared out at the thick waterfall. It made a constant low grumbling sound. I supposed I'd get used to it. After all, it was only for a couple of nights.

"I didn't realize the waterfalls were so big," I said to Alice as she joined me."

"Course they are," she said breezily. "*Daedalus* has to keep the canals full. There's more water in the canals than in the aft ring lake."

"Really?" It was hard to believe – the aft ring lake was huge, measuring an easy five kilometres from the shore across to the circular drain-weirs that made up the base of the aft endwall. I know because Scott took me out there on his boat.

"Yeah. Kallik told me."

I was surprised. "Kallik?" I confess the query might have sounded slightly sceptical.

"Yes. He's quite smart, actually."

Alice had this mental list of all Ixia's boys. She knew all their good features – and their bad ones. Zawn was at the bottom, she'd assured me, because he has no good features.

"They're so powerful," I said, gazing at the cascade. "How does *Daedalus* move so much water around?"

She shrugged. "Pump machines. Gotta be. Who cares?"

"Be nice to know."

"Promise me something."

"What?"

"Don't talk about canal-water circulation at the dance tonight."

* * *

We took hours getting ready. Our hosts had provided large bowls of warm water and soap in every cabin. For once I could give my hair a thorough wash. Back home we just go down to the bathing pond, which is cut into the canal bank downstream from the waterwheel and shielded from view by a big hedge of bougainvillaea. Men and women go at separate times to wash – and gossip. But the water is cold; you don't waste time there.

Alice helped me style my hair, then we got dressed. All the Ixia girls were led down to Akebia's village hall. Like ours, it had a sign carved into the edge of the roof:

AKEBIA STATION
GREEN LINE

There was a delightful courtyard area just outside (no green line on its flagstones), surrounded by tall cherry trees and roofed over by wooden beams that were invisible under a dense web of honeysuckle. A small raised stage at one end had five guitarists and a drummer playing as we arrived. Tables and benches had been set up around the edges, with candles flickering amid the food and drink. The boys were waiting beside them, looking as eager and anxious as I supposed we did.

"Just remember I'm here," Elijah said. He'd walked down from the cabins with us.

"So?" I said irritably.

"Have a nice time dancing, sure, but don't get too friendly with anyone. Zawn is still crazy over you."

"If you were a proper brother to him, you'd tell him to get over me."

"You need to think strategic. You're going to spend the rest of your life in Ixia, and he has prospects."

"No one in Ixia has prospects," I mocked. "There haven't been *prospects* in *Daedalus* for five hundred years."

"You think you're so much better than the rest of us, don't you?"

"No. I'm just a realist."

"You hurt my brother and that upset me. Don't do it again. I'd be really disappointed, and you wouldn't like that."

"Oh, really?" I looked round the Akebia boys. Yeah, there was nothing exceptional on show there, but they weren't from Ixia so, to me, every one of them was full of unknown potential. My gaze went back to one. My intuition can take over conscious thought sometimes – Mum calls it being impetuous. He was a couple of centimetres taller than me, and probably a couple of years older, too. Nice dark-olive skin and a baby beard which highlighted firm cheekbones. He wasn't compellingly handsome like a couple of them were (Alice was already sharing sly smiles with them). He wasn't trying to catch anyone's attention, which gave him an air of reserve. Which was kind of endearing.

I walked right across the courtyard to him. That's just not done. The invited girls are supposed to wait to be asked to dance by the host boys. Both groups stopped eying each other up to stare at me. I even heard a few dud notes coming from the guitars.

When I was about halfway over, he realized I was heading right at him. His eyes flashed with surprise but he soon recovered, straightening his back.

I stopped half a metre in front of him. "Hi," I said. "I'm Hazel."

"Uh, Rell. Pleased to meet you, Hazel."

"Would you like to dance?"

Rell must have been wanting to look round, to see everyone else's faces, maybe exchange wry grins with his friends. Me too. Specifically, I so wanted to see Elijah's face, but I wouldn't give him the satisfaction of knowing how significant that was to me.

"I would be delighted to dance with you, Hazel," Rell said formally. But he was smiling that way you do when you're sharing a secret.

So I was first out on the dance floor. Me and Rell, all by ourselves, with everyone gawping. We – all right, *I* – would be the talk of both villages for weeks.

Rell was twenty, and he'd been accepted as Akebia's apprentice doctor. That impressed me. I told him about Dad's wooden leg, which fascinated him. "I'd love to see that," he told me eagerly.

Other couples started to join us on the dance floor. That allowed me to relax a bit. I even sneaked a glance at Elijah as he slunk around the edge of the courtyard, sullen and glowering, refusing to talk to anyone.

After a couple more dances, Rell asked if I'd like a rest and a drink. We sat at the table he'd been standing beside. I thought he'd thank me kindly and move on, but no.

"Mind if I ask why that happened?" he said pleasantly.

"I'm really sorry. I didn't mean to embarrass you."

"Believe me, you didn't. My status among my friends has just reached the highest point it's ever going to get."

I took a sip from the glass he'd given me. The wine tasted as sweet as honey. Better than anything Ixia makes. In fact, everything about Akebia was better than home. "The Regulator who came with us, Elijah... His brother has a thing for me, so Elijah thinks he's some kind of chaperone. I was cross. Oh, that must make me sound horrible."

"No. I must remember to thank Elijah before he leaves."

"Thank *Elijah*?"

"Well, yes. He's the reason you stomped over to me. I was already scheming harder than I ever have, trying to work out how I could possibly get you to dance with me. And... pow, it just went and happened. I am incredibly grateful to him for being an arse."

I drank some more wine. "I think you mean you were scheming how to get my friend Alice to dance. She's the one over there, in the white-and-scarlet dress."

"No," he said intently. "Not her. You."

I could feel my cheeks heat up. But by then the moonlight was on, so he couldn't have seen that. I drank some more wine, hoping that would cool me down. "I didn't stomp," I muttered.

"Oh, that was definitely a stomp."

His teasing smile was rather charming. I realized how much wine I'd been drinking and switched to water. Then we were up and dancing again.

Half an hour later, I was standing in the queue at the buffet table, alone for a few seconds while Rell gallantly collected some plates. There was a swirl of white-and-scarlet cotton, a strong scent of morning flower perfume, and there was Alice, a huge smile on her face. "You *baaad* girl," she exclaimed in breathless delight. "Who is he?"

I tried not to grin. Failed. "Rell. I just... you know."

"No, I do not. Who are you and what have you done with my friend Hazel?"

"It's all Elijah's fault."

"Ah, who cares about that idiot? This is why I love you, Hazel. You're always full of surprises."

"So who's the boy you were dancing with?"

"Don't try and change the subject. But... which one? They're both deliciously hot, aren't they?"

Thankfully, Rell came back, and I introduced the pair of them. Alice fluttered her eyes and flirted outrageously with him as we served ourselves with slices of beef and egg salad and rolls. The two boys Alice had danced with, Shao and Tamran, joined us at the table to eat, both of them lovesick, hanging on every word she said, laughing obediently at the dumbest things. Tamran talked a lot while Shao said nothing – to be honest, I didn't actually hear him speak the whole evening. Rell and I shared quiet knowing glances while Alice got on with the job of being Alice. He seemed to be as amused by the whole performance as I was.

Shao and Tamran were dispatched to fetch us all dessert. I let my shoulder rest against Rell, and not long after his arm appeared round me. It was a really good fit. In fact, I hadn't felt this content for quite a while, not since Scott had carefully steered his fishing boat into the shelter of the mango trees which overhung the lake shore, and it wasn't just the wine producing that sensation.

Beyond the village, the endwall was a black expanse, kind of what I imagined space would be like. When I tipped my head back, I could see the light strips on the sky end just a few metres short of the sheer cliff. It made me acknowledge *Daedalus* is actually finite. In Ixia the habitat stretches away in every direction – I wasn't used to a limit. The silver moonlight radiating from the strips illuminated wisps of mist drifting above us. I frowned, narrowing my eyes to focus better.

"What's that?"

Rell grinned and squeezed a little tighter. "What?"

"Up there between the light strips, where the sky roof meets the endwall. Those little streamers of cloud... they're moving in a circle."

"That? We call it the Swirl. You can only see it at night, of course. The light strips are too bright in the day."

"I've never seen anything like it before." All I could think of when I looked at it was the way water drains through a hole.

"It appeared after the Jolt. Did you hear about that?"

I remembered the Jolt, though not everybody did. It was maybe three years ago. The habitat shuddered. Not much. It was night, so most people never even noticed it, but I was awake. My bed wobbled, just briefly, as if someone had shaken it. But that was it. Over the next few days, we found that most of the hundred villages had felt it. The Electric Captain never mentioned it, so everyone knew the ship was still okay. Just like always.

I stared up at the streamers of cloud as they slithered into a spiral and *vanished* where they merged. "We're losing air," I said numbly.

Rell's expression was puzzled. "What?"

"She told me. The Cheater – she said we're running out of air." I sat up abruptly. "Are people here getting headaches?"

"Oh, Hazel..." Alice groaned. "Don't. This is a dance."

I turned to Rell and gave him an intense stare. "Are people getting more headaches than usual? Maybe coughing as well?"

I could see he was getting alarmed by my behaviour, that he wanted to say something funny, to get the evening back on track. But to his credit, he answered honestly. "Yes. We have been getting more cases than usual, I suppose. What Cheater?"

Goosebumps were rising all along my arms, yet the evening air was mild. "I was a flower girl. A Cheater woman talked to me before she Cycled."

"And she said the air was running out?" he asked incredulously. "But it's not."

"We don't know that. The headaches! I've started coughing sometimes, too."

Alice sighed in dismay and rolled her eyes.

I ignored her. My gaze went back to the Swirl. It was small, yes, but if air had been leaking out into space for years...

"The Electric Captain would have warned us if there was a problem with the air," Rell said, his voice rich with concern for me. "We're fine."

I never got a chance to answer him. Someone rode a horse right up to the edge of the courtyard. The band stopped and everyone on the dance floor turned to look at the rider as he dismounted. With a shock, I recognized Hauer. And nobody rides at night unless it's extremely urgent. Alice and I automatically gripped hands, knowing it was going to be bad.

Hauer searched round at all the still figures who were staring anxiously at him. Then he was walking – towards me.

"Hazel," he said awkwardly.

"What is it? What's happened?"

"I'm really sorry. Frazer was playing in the date-palm grove. He fell out of a tree."

"Is he dead?" I gasped fearfully.

"No. But he can't move his limbs."

(4)

I don't remember much of the trip home. I rode with Hauer the whole way – he seemed to know the paths as well as Kirill knew the canals. We stopped once in a village called Polreith, to change horses, then we were off again.

The moonlight was still on when we arrived back in Ixia. Hauer dropped me off right outside the village hall.

I rushed through the glass archway. The cooks were just starting to arrive and get breakfast ready. They said nothing as I ran past them and into the hospital. Mum, Georgi and Tanari were dozing on a settee outside Marana's office. Mum sat up as I came in and put her arms out to me. We hugged for a long moment. I could see she'd been crying for hours – her face was all pale and blotchy the way it goes when she's suffering. I'd seen it all before with Dad, months and months of it.

"How is he?" I finally asked.

"He's asleep now," she said, wiping her eyes again. "Marana gave him something. He was in shock, and very distressed."

"How bad is the pain?" I asked fearfully.

Mum's tears welled up again. "There is no pain. He can't feel anything. Nothing! I can't stand it. Not Frazer, not this."

I gave Georgi an entreating look. He came up and gently took Mum from me.

"I want to see him," I said.

Mum nodded. I went through into the ward. Itzy was lying on one of the beds, fast asleep. At the other end of the ward, Dad was slumped in a chair. He glanced up and gave me a forlorn grin. I saw he'd been crying as well.

Marana was standing at the end of Frazer's bed, looking exhausted. I forced myself to walk forwards.

Frazer was lying there sound asleep. He looked absolutely fine, and so peaceful with his eyes closed. His blond hair was fanned out over the pillow, chest rising and falling softly. He wasn't sweating, wasn't flushed. Nothing wrong at all.

I leant over and gently kissed his forehead.

How he'd hate that.

A couple of weeks back, he'd been out after supper. It was only a few minutes until the daylight switched off and Mum was getting worried and cross that he wasn't home, so as always I got sent to find him.

It wasn't difficult; I just followed the noise of boys shouting. Frazer was in the canal with some of his friends, upstream of the mill – which was a big no. People aren't supposed to swim there, not even the adults, in case the current pulled you into the wheel. I yelled at him to get out and come home.

All his friends jeered at him as he waded out.

"Thanks a bunch," he sneered at me.

"You know swimming there is dangerous," I told him.

"What are you, a Regulator?"

"I'm just saying–"

He laughed in that dismissive way he has to tell me what a pain I am. Then he gathered up his clothes and started to run.

"Hey!" I yelled. "I haven't finished telling you–"

He made an obscene gesture and laughed at me again. Every time! He knows exactly how to wind me up. I didn't want to be his nursemaid. I didn't want to be sent out to find him like some eight-year-old child running an errand for her mother.

I set off after him. I'm taller than him, with longer legs. You'd think catching him would be easy. But Frazer isn't just fast; he's nimble with it. He dodged off the path into an orchard, zipping round the trunks as the daylight switched off and pale moonlight was left to bathe the habitat. Next thing I know, a ripe peach came flying out of the gloom and only just missed me.

"Right!" I yelled. *Two can play at that game.* I reached up and snatched some of the pulpy fruit from a bough above. The chase was on!

I managed to get in a couple of good strikes to his one by the time we piled in through the cabin's front door, both out of breath and giggling. Mum took one look at the pair of us and scowled. We were both sent straight to our room.

That's Frazer. Not...

Dad got up and put his arm around me as I stared down at my brother in the hospital bed.

"He'll be all right, won't he?" I asked. It was really hard fighting back the tears, but Frazer might wake up and see my crying, and that could not be allowed.

"He can't feel his legs," Dad said quietly. He looked down at his own wooden limb – guiltily, I thought.

"What does that mean?" I asked. I knew. I knew right from the second Hauer told me. I just didn't want to believe.

"He landed on his back," Marana said. "It's caused some damage to his spine. The good news is that his right arm is unaffected, and he has partial use of his left hand."

"That's good news?" I exclaimed.

"Yes. It indicates that the nerve damage may be due to swelling, in which case feeling may return as the swelling subsides naturally."

"So he'll be able to walk again?"

"I said *may*. It is far too early to tell."

"How long, then? A day? A week?"

"Come on," Dad said, and steered me away from the bed. "You've been riding all night. You need to rest."

"No I don't!"

"Yes you do. You're no use to anybody in this state, least of all Frazer. Now lie down here and get some sleep. He won't be awake for a few hours yet."

I sat on the edge of the next bed along from my brother. "You'll wake me when he wakes up, won't you?"

"Of course."

I don't know how long I was asleep. When I opened my eyes, Dad was in the same chair as before and Mum was sitting on the edge of Frazer's bed. Frazer had been propped up on a pile of cushions. There was a chess board on his lap. He and Mum were playing.

"Hey you," I said.

Frazer smiled. It wasn't his real smile. This was like someone had told him what a smile was and he was trying to achieve it. "You were snoring," he said.

"I don't snore," I said automatically. "You do."

"Do not."

I went over and hugged him. Or tried to. People normally lean forward to receive a hug. Frazer didn't; his torso stayed there, resting on the cushions, so I just squeezed his shoulder fondly. "How's it going?"

"I can use my arms," he said brightly.

"That's good. You'll be able to swim okay, then."

"Hazel!" Mum snapped.

"Oh my dayz, she's right," Frazer said. "I never thought of that. You know what, I could become a fisherman – in some kind of canoe. That doesn't need legs. I can get about just by paddles." He gave Dad an eager look. "Right?"

"Good idea," Dad said, pressing his lips together as if he was considering it.

That was so Frazer – take an idea and run with it at right angles to everyone else. My brain would never make a connection between swimming and canoeing, let alone using that to contribute to the habitat's Cycle by fishing.

"Let's just do what the doctor advised and see what happens when the swelling goes down," Mum said.

"Okay," Frazer said. He held up his left hand. His fingers were curled up, not quite tight into a fist but closed against his palm. He managed to open up his index and middle finger, showing them to me proudly. "I could barely do that last night," he said chirpily.

"Well done," I said, hoping that my misery wasn't bleeding into my voice.

"You should get some breakfast," he said. "It's great in here. You get first choice on everything."

"I'll do that," I said, and turned away before I started crying.

We spent the first week in the hospital by Frazer's bedside. It was hard, but we took it in shifts, overlapping so there was always two of us there at any one time. Georgi and Tanari helped. Mum didn't really approve of Tanari but Frazer liked her a lot, and her jolly personality cheered him up. All his friends visited. We had to work out a rota for them.

Alice turned up as soon as the barge docked a couple of days later. That produced the biggest smile on Frazer's face since the accident. She treated him as if nothing had happened, teasing, pouring derision on him being a canoe fisherman, giggling wildly at him having to use a bedpan. Frazer loved it.

I walked out of the ward with her when she said goodbye. "So what happened at the dance after I left?" I asked.

Her smile became coy. "It happened away. I can't possibly say," she chanted.

"Alice!"

"All right, but not a word to anyone."

"Of course not."

"Tamran insisted on escorting me back to our cabin after the dance."

I was silent for a moment, thinking there was going to be more. Then I must have blushed.

Alice caught it, and smiled like the proverbial cat who's found a canal's worth of cream. "And you remember how quiet Shao is?"

"Yes."

"I got him to make a lot of noise the second night."

"Alice! You are impossible."

"Speak for yourself. Rell couldn't stop asking questions about you the rest of the evening, and at breakfast as well. In fact…" She produced a neatly rolled-up whiteleaf. "For you."

"Really?"

She smirked. "Who are you trying to kid? You are all that village is talking about."

After she went home I sat in the main hall, which was practically empty. I should have gone back to Frazer, but I was desperate to unroll the whiteleaf.

Rell's letter was really sweet. He said how sorry he was about Frazer's accident and hoped he'd get better soon. He said he'd never forget seeing me for the first time. How he adored dancing with me. How much fun I was. How interesting. How smart. How pretty. How he couldn't wait to see me again, and was going to visit me as soon as possible.

My ears were bright red when I finished, but the really stupid grin on my face took an age to fade. If Frazer ever read it I would simply die of embarrassment, so I rolled it back up neatly and tucked it into my pocket.

* * *

After three more days, Marana allowed Frazer to come home. Everyone was encouraging, saying how he must be improving for the doctor to let that happen. It wasn't true and, in its heart, Ixia knew that. There was no change at all.

Mum and I spent a day getting our old room ready. My bed got moved out to the living room, where I'd sleep. Frazer's bed got raised on blocks so people didn't have to bend over so much to help him. He and Alice might have giggled about the bedpan, but in reality lifting him on and off it was hard work. Some despair-withered part of my mind was thinking about having to help him for another fifty years until it was my Cycling Day, how it would turn me into an old crone who couldn't stand up straight by the time I was thirty.

Dad and his friends in the carpentry shop made a tray on a tall leg that straddled the bed, so it was like a table for Frazer. Friends contributed big bowls and piles of extra towels so we could give him proper bed baths. They're not easy for him, either. Or us.

A team of men, led by Dad, carried him back to the cabin on a stretcher. Frazer was really quiet as they made their way through the village. I knew what he was thinking, of course – how he used to run along this path so easily. Maybe it was that trip back home which made him realize how serious this was. He was certainly a lot more subdued when we got him back into his own room than he had been in the hospital. Hospital is only ever temporary. That's what everyone tells themselves. Hospital is where you stay while you recover. When you're discharged, you're no longer ill.

The real trouble after settling him in was that there was nothing for him to do. What can anyone do if they're stuck in bed all day every day? There's only so many games of chess you can play. Frazer never learned how to play a guitar. I suppose he can learn, but it's not him, and his singing voice is truly rubbish – that's not just me taunting him. That didn't leave him with anything to do except lie there and think. Which wasn't good for anyone, let alone Frazer with his hyperactive brain.

His friends kept visiting, just not quite as often as they did while he was in hospital. Marana came to check him twice a day. She was encouraging, but there was absolutely no change.

If anything, it was getting harder for him to open his left hand. He'd never admit that but I could see the effort it cost him, the dark shadow lurking behind his eyes that threatened to swell out and consume him.

That was when I had to face the worry that I'd been in denial about from the very beginning. Just like I did with anything serious, I went to see Alice.

"Cycle Frazer?" she exclaimed, outraged. "That's ridiculous."

I was lying on the cushioned bench in her cabin. It had a curved neck support at one end, to hold your head up. Alice gives the most amazing scalp massages; she can soothe away any stress. She learned from her Mum, the best hairdresser in the village. There's a lot of gossip gets traded in their cabin.

"Is it?" I asked as her fingers worked their way along the sides of my temples. "Mayor Fininen and Chief Atov have never come to visit him; everybody else has."

"Of course not. They don't want to worry you into thinking they're making an assessment."

"But they will come eventually, won't they? It's their job. They have to assess him, to see if he can make a full contribution to village life. He has to be able to earn his food kilos." I started to shake. "They came and saw Dad. I remember that." When it happened, I was so scared Mum had to take me out of the hospital. I was crying and yelling.

"Hey," Alice moved her fingertips behind my ears and rotated them gently. "You've got to stop thinking like that. Frazer needs you."

For once the massage was having no calming effect on me. "That's it, though, isn't it? He *does* need me. He always will. He can't look after himself anymore. He can't contribute. And if you can't contribute…"

"He's fourteen. It's not even been a fortnight. If anyone can prove an invalid can earn food kilos, it'll be Frazer. Now breathe deep and try to relax."

I nodded, grateful for the reassurance as her hands began to rub the very top of my scalp. Finally, I could feel the pressure that'd been squeezing my whole body start to ease off. I wasn't convinced, though.

* * *

It was a day later when Dad asked me to accompany him down to the carpentry shop. He had this blank expression when he spoke to me, like he was trying to hold in his emotions. At first, I thought it was going to be bad news. Then we arrived at the big open-walled shed beside the canal.

I don't go in often. It's a funny old place, with long benches and tools of sharp metal. All the tools stay sharp – just like the knives and forks and things we use, which are all pre-Mutiny. Dad says the Builder machines did something to the material they shaped which makes it unnaturally strong. All the things we make are good but they don't last, at least not for centuries.

The day he told me that, I got so angry with the Mutineers. All the machines they destroyed for their own selfish ends would have made our lives so different, so much easier. When we do arrive at the new world, we'll have earned that better life the Builders wanted us to have.

At the far end of Ixia's carpentry shop there are three circular saws, each a different size, powered by the waterwheel outside. Thick leather belts and pulleys turn them, making a constant thrumming noise. And when someone shoves a tree trunk through to cut it into planks, the noise is like the screech of a beast in the slaughterhouse.

Nobody was sawing anything when we arrived. The carpenters were all clustered round the end of Dad's bench. They looked at me, nudging one another as I went over to them.

Dad had made a chair. But instead of legs, this one had wheels. They were smaller versions of the cartwheels which were made in the carpentry shop – a little pair at the front that you could turn from side to side with a curved steering handle, and a bigger pair at the back.

My mouth dropped open with surprise and delight. "Dad! Frazer can go anywhere in this."

"Yes," Dad said slowly. "I hope so."

"It's brilliant. No one can say he has to be Cycled now."

Dad's smile faltered slightly. "No, they can't."

There were two handles at the top of the backrest, like the ones on a wheelbarrow but shorter. I gripped them and pushed the chair out of the carpentry shop. The carpenters and apprentices clapped me out.

It was mid-morning, so there were lots of people about as I pushed the wheeled chair back through Ixia to our cabin. Everyone stopped to watch. It was obvious what the chair was for, so I saw a lot of approving smiles. Dad and I were given plenty of thumbs up. My face was red when we got home, half from embarrassment at all the attention, half from happiness.

I trundled it through into Frazer's room. The incredulous expression on his face when I came through the door was one of the best moments of my life.

Tears were running down his face as he said, "Thank you," to Dad. Mum was all choked up, unable to say anything.

"Want to go for a ride?" I asked blissfully.

"Oh my dayz, do I!"

My, but word had got around fast. People were gathered outside our cabin as I triumphantly pushed my brother out. He was greeted with a big cheer. Frazer grinned wildly and waved with his working arm as I pushed him along the path to the village hall.

At the back of my mind, I was concerned they were only applauding the chair, another marvel Dad had crafted. Did they also see the liberation it had brought Frazer? The hope? Maybe.

I parked him at the end of a hall table and Mum collected food from the counters for him. We had lunch as a family for the first time in a fortnight. It was the best meal I could remember.

Me pushing Frazer around the village became quite a regular sight. I took him out to my chicken coop every morning – Jane had been looking after them for me since the accident. He carried the basket full of eggs on his lap as I wheeled him back down to the village hall. Then we had breakfast. It was important to Frazer – joining in with everyone else made him feel like he was taking part again. To help with that, some days Mum or I would take him to the carpentry shop. Dad and the others had rigged up a special vice so he could use a tool to carve wood into shapes with his working hand.

But it was only some days. He got tired quite easily, which upset him, and he was really susceptible to headaches now. When he was low, I would wheel him round the barns and pens to look at the animals, or out to an orchard where I'd pick some fruit so we could deliver it to the kitchen.

It was four days since he'd got the wheeled chair. I was pushing him back to our cabin late in the afternoon. It had been a tough day for me. Jane had been really kind to take care of the chickens, but her heart wasn't really in it. I'd needed to give the coop a thorough clean-out, which was exhausting and dirty work. It hadn't been helped by three of the dumb birds escaping, so I'd spent twenty minutes running round trying to catch them. After that I'd had to do the pile of laundry which had accumulated. Then Mum brought Frazer home early – he'd messed up the cuts on a piece of wood at the carpentry shop. He was upset and moody, which is why I wheeled him out to the orchard. But the path I came back along at the edge of the village was rough, with stones sticking out of the soil and so many little ridges and folds that from the side it must look like the serrations on a bread knife. And we'd had a three-hour rain the night before, making the earth soft.

Every one of those snags had clearly been designed to catch the wheels on his chair. It was taking all my strength to manoeuvre him over the stones.

"Turn me round and pull the chair over the stones," Frazer said. "It'll be easier than pushing."

"Don't tell me how to push you about," I snapped back, trying to ignore my growing headache. "It's all I do now. Nobody else is ever going to do it." Yes, I know I shouldn't have said that, but I was short of breath, seriously tired and frustrated, and in truth it had been preying on my mind. The wheeled chair was wonderful for Frazer, but there weren't a whole lot of volunteers stepping up to push him round all day long. It was all down to me and the family. And if he didn't improve, I could see it stretching out to become my whole life. I already despaired at the idea of living a *Daedalus* village life – marry a *nice boy*, have the two kids which the Captain allows, work hard, get Cycled. And all for what? So those children could do the same? If we just knew how far away the new world was, it might be bearable, but having to endure that life and take care of Frazer as well – I knew I wouldn't be strong enough, and I hated myself for that.

"Need a hand there?"

I turned round. Zawn was walking towards us.

It just had to be him. I was reluctant but my aching arms and dizziness told me to forget pride and just let him. "Thanks," I said. Maybe it came out a bit more grudgingly than it should have.

"You know this doesn't make any difference to me," he said with a lopsided smile.

"What?"

"Frazer."

"What are you talking about, Zawn?"

"Family is important to me. If we marry, I'll be there for you all the time. We can help him together." He patted Frazer on the shoulder. "How does that sound? Would you like to move in with me and your sister?"

"That could work," Frazer said. He looked up at me for approval.

I was so shocked I couldn't say anything.

Zawn gripped the handles at the back of the wheeled chair and the first thing he did was turn Frazer round so he was pulling him over the rough stones, not pushing.

"See?" Frazer said smugly. "Everyone knows you pull over tough ground."

"Oh, just shut up," I snarled. Then I was running, ignoring the two of them calling out behind me. I was in tears when I got home.

"What's happened?" Mum demanded with panic in her voice as I burst through the door alone. "Where's Frazer?"

"He's with his friend," I yelled. "Apparently he's always going to be with him."

I couldn't even go to my room – it wasn't mine anymore, was it? I just curled up on my bed and shouted at Mum and Georgi to go away and leave me be.

Zawn turned up ten minutes later, easing Frazer into the cabin. Mum was so grateful that for one wretched moment I thought she was going to ask him to come in. But he simply accepted her thanks politely and said he'd see us around.

"Hazel," Frazer said in the meekest voice I'd ever heard coming from that reckless mouth. "I'm sorry."

"It's okay," I said, still curled up and not looking at him. "I should have pulled."

"It's not going to be like this always," he said. "Really it's not. I'm going to get well again. I promise."

That just made my tears flow even faster. But I forced my jaw shut so he couldn't hear me whimper.

(5)

The next day, Frazer brought back a model of a canoe he'd been working on in the carpentry shop. It was a marvel of detail, which he delighted in showing off to me. It was designed to hold his legs in place and keep his back upright while he paddled. He demonstrated the fishing mechanism, giving a breathless running commentary. If he turned a wheel, it would lower a net into the water then winch it back out again once it was full of fish.

"You've got a friend at Viride, haven't you?" he asked. "Could you ask him to take a look at it for me? I'd appreciate a real fisherman's opinion. I expect it'll take a few modifications before I get it working properly."

My cheeks became warm. "Scott's not really a friend. And he's married now." Three weeks after the dance, *actually*. I shouldn't dwell on it. Alice wouldn't. It's what happens at every dance – it's what dances are for: fun. I'd known that.

"But you could ask him?" Frazer persisted. There was so much hope piled up behind the question, so much desperation.

"Sure, I'll write to him." I bent over the model again, so he couldn't see my face. As always, I was impressed with his ingenuity, yet at the same time depressed at where his flight of fancy had taken him. The canoe with all its intricate parts would take months to build – which would cost plenty of food kilos. It assumed he'd have both arms to paddle with, and that wasn't looking good; he could only move his left hand's index finger now. It was also an admission that he'd never use his legs again. That was probably subconscious for Frazer, but it was what everyone else, including me, was thinking.

But I told him it was brilliant and I couldn't wait to see him in it.

That evening, I pushed him to the village hall for supper. Mum and Georgi had wheeled him about all day, giving me a break. All that did was make me feel guilty.

I parked him at the table in his usual place and went to collect our food. It was sweet potatoes and poached trout with egg salad. It was no use putting much salad on Frazer's plate – it would just go to waste – but I liked it. I was scooping up my third spoonful when Elijah came up beside me. I gritted my teeth and said nothing, hoping he'd get the message, but oh no. Not him.

"That's how you respond to an act of kindness, is it?" he asked. "Classy."

"What?"

"I heard what happened yesterday. Zawn was showing you a whole load of sympathy by pushing your cripple brother, and you just ran off in a huff."

I was too stunned by him calling Frazer a cripple to answer. I just stared at him in hot indignation.

"That was a nasty way to treat my brother," he said. "I get you're upset over Frazer, but you might want to start being a whole lot nicer to Zawn. Families support each other. You're going to need that."

"What are you talking about?" I spluttered.

"They're going to assess Frazer. Who do you think is going to speak in his favour at the review, huh? I can, if I'm minded to, and Chief Atov listens to me."

"Frazer doesn't need anyone to speak for him. He'll pass any assessment easily."

"Really? Because all that fancy chair of his does is take someone else away from contributing to the Cycle. How many food kilos do you earn pushing him about, huh? I've seen the ledger – you've got zero in your column. So as long as he's around, that's two people who'll be freeloaders. And you know the Electric Captain's rules: everyone has to contribute to the habitat Cycle. If you can't do that then you're Cycled."

"You're not Cycling Frazer," I snapped, maybe too loud. People were turning to look at us.

"I hope not," Elijah said. "Genuinely, I do. What's happened is awful. Which means you need to start making smart decisions about the future, yours and his. Just saying it as it is here. Don't blame the messenger."

I turned my back on him and walked back to the table.

"What was that all about?" Frazer asked.

"Nothing. He's an idiot, that's all."

"Funny how he's so different from his brother," he said. "I quite like Zawn."

"Good. You can go out with him, then," I growled back.

They came to the cabin the following afternoon, Mayor Fininen and Chief Atov. Marana was with them to formally explain Frazer's condition and offer an impartial prognosis.

We knew they were going to assess him – Georgi had told us the previous evening – so we were ready. Frazer was dressed in clean clothes. His bed linen was fresh. The canoe model was within his reach, as was his chess set.

Mum and Dad welcomed them into the cabin. I wasn't sure I could keep control if I said anything to them. I hated them, even Marana. It was so unfair. We'd done so much for Ixia. We don't cause any trouble. If we chose to look after Frazer, what business was it of theirs? They should never have this kind of power over other people. Nobody should.

The three of them trooped into his room and shut the door. I could hear what they were saying, of course; I didn't even have to eavesdrop for that. Mum and I sat on my bed while Frazer gave his typically animated description of the canoe and how he would use it. He told them how he'd made the parts himself, that he was as useful as ever to the carpentry shop. Then they started asking questions. They were kind about it: *Show us what you can do with your left hand. Can you feel anything in your legs? How do you use the bedpan?* Mayor Fininen made encouraging sounds – *That's good. Well done. Ah, clever* – but I knew what he was thinking: that none of us was earning enough food kilos anymore, that Frazer was a burden and he'd never stop being one.

They were polite when they left, but it was awkward. Mayor Fininen couldn't meet Dad's gaze.

I went in to Frazer. He was sitting up, supported by his pile of firm cushions. He looked at me, but wasn't seeing me. His mind was focused on something a long way outside *Daedalus*.

"I think our family's cursed," he said. Even the voice didn't belong to my brother Frazer. It was meek, broken.

"Don't be silly. There's no such thing."

"First Dad's leg, now this."

Zawn and Elijah, I added silently. "They were accidents, that's all. Chance."

"I've been working out the probability of injuries like ours happening in the same family. The odds are so massive, they don't happen. Not in real life."

"I don't think you can use maths to analyse accidents. That's the thing with accidents: they're completely random."

"Maybe."

"Want a game of chess?" I asked brightly.

"No thanks, Hazel."

I don't really recall how the rest of the day went. I know people were staring at us in the hall that evening when we went down for supper. Word of the assessment had gone round the village. I detested their sympathy. None of them wanted Frazer to be Cycled, yet no one was ever going to support us against the assessment verdict when it came. Disagreeing with authority was mutiny. Everybody knew another Mutiny could never be allowed on *Daedalus*. We had to live by the rules of the Electric Captain.

That night, as I got ready for bed, Rell's letter fell out of my pocket. I read it again, the nice words, his supposed affection for me. But it had been weeks now and he hadn't visited like he'd promised. *What happens away on a dance stays away*. Not like anything had happened, not like it did with Scott.

As I crawled into bed, trying not to weep, everything returned in an icy rush of darkness. I'd been so absorbed by caring for Frazer, I'd forgotten or supressed all of it. How slow I'd become. The recurring headaches. The physical effort it took to push Frazer. The Cheater woman's warning about the habitat air. The Swirl I'd seen *with my own eyes*. All of it deliberately pushed away because it was too big, too shocking, to think about.

Cycling Frazer was nothing. Everybody was going to die when the air ran out. Myself included.

Hauer called us down to the mayor's office the next day. I suppose they did it after breakfast so not too many people were about. It didn't matter. Those that did see me and Mum and Dad troop down to the village hall all studiously ignored us.

The mayor's office is one of the finest rooms we have in Ixia – as befits his status, I suppose. It's a lot bigger than Chief Atov's. A semi-circular shape with the outside wall that was all glass, allowing him to see across the canal and the grazing meadows beyond. Some of his furniture is salvage from the tower-mountain homes where everyone used to live.

"It's a difficult decision," Fininen said, as if the pain was all his. "It always is, and doubly so because of Frazer's age. But at the moment he obviously requires full-time help from one or more other persons. Chief Atov has checked your ledgers, and you're all down on food kilos. That cannot continue."

"You're not Cycling my son," Mum said in a fierce voice. "Now Frazer is settling in, I'll be able to work my usual hours."

Mayor Fininen glanced at me. "And what about you, Hazel? You've spent a lot of time helping your brother. How long do you think you can keep doing that?"

I cocked my head to one side and gave him a hard stare. "Until the air runs out. Which isn't going to be long, is it?"

Which clearly wasn't what he'd expected me to say. "That's nonsense," he blustered. "Hazel, you're upset. I understand that. I know this is difficult–"

"Difficult! You expect us to stand here meekly while you tell us you're going to execute Frazer?"

"Not execute!" Fininen said, red-faced and shaken. "That's not what we do. He'll be Cycled so the rest of us can live our lives and the great voyage can continue."

"No it won't! You heard the Cheater woman – the air is running out. We all get the coughing and the headaches now. You *know* it's true, but you're not doing anything about it. You're killing us, you're killing all of us! Because you're a useless, stupid coward!"

"Okay," Dad said firmly as his arms went round my shoulders. "That's enough."

I let out a wordless scream and shook him off, then ran out of the office.

* * *

It was Dad who found me later. I was sitting on the end of the wharf, staring at the ridiculous ducks paddling along the canal. It's a good place to be alone. And I'd finished crying by the time he sat down beside me.

"How are you doing, sweetheart?"

I shrugged.

"Mayor Fininen is postponing the decision."

"Typical," I said. "He's too scared to do anything. He knows people don't want Frazer Cycled."

"Our next Cycling Day isn't for another two months. He's prepared to wait and see if Frazer improves. They'll reassess him a fortnight before the ceremony."

"Fininen will Cycle him. You know that."

"It's not a certainty, sweetheart. Not even Marana knows what's going to happen."

I let out a long sigh and looked at him. He was in even more pain than usual – I could always tell. "Offering hope is a good way of making us all keep in line."

His arm went round me again. This time I didn't twist away.

"When did you grow up?" he asked quietly.

"Dunno."

"You know you actually scared Fininen. I've never seen him so flustered."

"I wasn't joking, Dad. The Cheater woman was right. We're going to die if someone doesn't do something about the air."

"If she was right – and I'm not convinced – the only person who can do anything about that is the Electric Captain."

"Then we have to ask her. Simple."

"She doesn't talk to us. Not anymore."

"But she used to, didn't she? That's what they said at school. She told everyone what to do after the Mutiny – how to farm the land and build the village houses, how to get the medicine machines going again. Everything we needed to carry on the voyage. The mayors used to ask questions when the screen came on, and she'd answer them directly. So why has she stopped doing that?"

"I don't know. Maybe the mayors just ran out of questions. There's not much uncertainty about life in *Daedalus* anymore. Everybody knows what to do."

"Fine. So what do we do about the air running out?"

He gave me a fond squeeze. "You can raise it at the next village meeting. If people vote for it, Fininen will have to ask next time the screen comes on."

I shook my head in despair. I couldn't ever imagine the villagers doing something so out of the ordinary; they just don't think in those terms. "Might as well ask for free bread every day, or to arrive at the new world."

"I know." He hesitated, giving me a strange look, almost as if he was uncertain. "Hazel, I might have to... leave."

"Leave?"

"Frazer and me. If the reassessment isn't favourable. Do you understand?" he asked anxiously.

I was so surprised, I couldn't say anything at first. Dad even thinking in those terms was having the universe turn upside down. He was ready to defy the mayor and the Regulators to defend Frazer, to risk his own life for his children. That was utterly wonderful.

I put my arms round him. It was like being five again, when there was nothing greater in the whole ship than hugging Daddy. "I'll come with you," I promised.

"No. That's too big a risk. You have your whole life ahead – I want you to live it well."

Which annoyed me. Hadn't he listened to what I'd just been saying? Didn't he believe me?

There is no future. The air is running out. We're all going to die.

"Whatever you say, Dad." I leaned into him a little further, welcoming the feel of him against me, the warmth, his love. It was probably going to be the last time.

Mum had told Frazer the mayor's verdict by the time I walked back to our cabin. Georgi was comforting her, the two of them sitting together, hunched up, not saying anything. Defeated.

I went into Frazer's room. He looked drained, as if he wasn't fully alive any more.

I loved Dad for being so bold, for putting himself on the line for Frazer, but he wasn't thinking straight. When Fininen delivered his reassessment verdict, Atov would be ready for us doing something stupid like Cheating. The Regulators would be watching. But today, poor, weak Fininen had *graciously* given us hope. We wouldn't be troublesome for months.

"Snap out of it," I said to Frazer.

He gave me a wounded look. "Didn't you hear? If I don't improve, they're going to Cycle me."

"I don't care what they say. I need your big brain working properly. Right now."

"My brain?"

"You and I have to plan something. It's got to be perfect, and we don't have much time…"

We were lucky – if you could call it that. There was a three-hour rain due that night. We have them every third night, starting at midnight. No one likes to be out in it.

I lay in bed waiting for it to start. The drops falling on the cabin's reed thatch make a soft but constant pattering sound. Mum was asleep, exhausted after such a terrible day; I could hear her snoring lightly.

Carefully, quietly, I eased the covers back. I was fully dressed, wearing a pair of dark trousers and a turquoise blouse, with a brown sweater on top. I picked up my boots and tiptoed into Frazer's room.

He was wide awake, eagerness animating his features – so much so, it was like having the old Frazer back.

"You ready?" I whispered.

"Yeah!"

I opened the shutters and peered out. Rain reduced the moonlight to a low glimmer. I could barely see the next cabin, let alone the rest of the village.

I'd been worried about lifting him, but a couple of weeks shifting him on and off the bedpan had clearly toughened me up. I managed to carry him over to the window.

"Legs first," he grunted.

"I know!"

Frazer had thought it through, just like I'd known he would. That afternoon we'd put a table in front of the window ready, so now all he did was sit on that. I lifted his ankles up, and he swivelled round so his legs were overhanging the window sill. He slipped through and I lowered him down.

Then I grabbed the bags we'd prepared and shoved them through. The blankets went next. I followed them out.

The wheeled chair was parked next to the window, waiting for us. I'd taken Frazer down to the carpentry shop earlier, and the chair had –oops – somehow got very muddy coming back. So I'd washed it, leaving it under the roof overhang so it could spend the night drying.

Frazer pulled a crossbow out from where we'd hidden it under the cushion, and I boosted him into the chair. While he was perching the bag and crossbow on his lap, I pushed my head through the hole I'd made earlier in the blanket and settled the heavy fabric over my shoulders. It fell almost to my knees. Another of Frazer's ideas, the heavy wool should help keep the rain off.

I put the second blanket over him. "You sure about this?" I asked.

"Let's go."

I pushed the chair out into our garden, then started tugging him along. "I'm pulling, see," I teased.

"You're the best, Hazel."

The wheels did sink in a bit, but the tracks through the village were so compressed the going wasn't that hard. We'd made a whole ten metres when I saw Zawn.

He was standing under the overhang of Torbin's cabin on the other side of the track. So – I wasn't as smart as I thought I was. Atov must have known we'd do something like this. Zawn was on lookout duty.

Frazer would be Cycled. I'm not sure what the punishment is for helping someone Cheat. Nothing good.

I stood perfectly still. The constant rain had already soaked my hair, turning it to straggly ropes that hung down over the blanket. Strands were sticking to my face. I blinked them out of my eyes, staring at Zawn. He stared right back at me.

The rain used to be our thing, me and Zawn. We'd both sneak off when it started, and meet up in an unused cabin. It had been romantic and exciting and fun, and I'd enjoyed it for a few weeks. Then he fell for me the way I'd fallen for Scott. So I hurt him – quite badly, I suppose, which he didn't deserve.

Life in *Daedalus* really sucks.

After the longest moment the universe had ever known, Zawn slowly turned away and walked round the corner of the cabin. I whimpered softly in relief – and confusion. Zawn hadn't just helped me; he'd saved me, showing unparalleled kindness. Again. I felt... I don't know what I felt. Guilt, mostly, I guess.

"What's up?" Frazer asked. "Are we stuck?"

"No." I started pulling him again. "We're not stuck. We'll never be stuck again."

It was a long, bad slog out to the stables. By the time we got there my arms were almost numb, they ached so much. I don't have much to do with the village horses – they're all working beasts, pulling ploughs and wagons across the fields. We went out with the farmers during school, learning the basics, but that's all.

I found Bronwyn's stall. She was a brown mare almost as big as Shella, who'd towed the barge to Akebia. I doubt she remembered me from the school trips, but she was pleased enough with the carrots I brought. While she was munching them, I buckled on her bridle and led her out to where Frazer was waiting.

Then the real fun began. I had to keep Bronwyn still while somehow shoving Frazer up over her back. I wound up jamming the wheeled chair against the stable wall and standing on it myself, grunting and straining until he was in position, lying across her, arms dangling down one flank, legs down the other, as if he was a long sack of flour.

We'd brought a leather belt with us to hold him in place. I fastened it round his ankles then looped it under poor Bronwyn, who was more patient than I'd expected. Frazer held the free end in his hand, wrapping it round his wrist.

"You okay like that?" I asked.

"No problem," he assured me, even though I could see how awful it was for him.

I slung the crossbow over my shoulder along with the small bag, and took hold of the bridle. Then we set off towards Tressaco and our great-grandmother, Alisha.

I didn't mind that it was raining. After all, it provided us with perfect cover and wiped out any tracks we left. But the sheer monotony of it was depressing. It was perfectly constant and never ever let up. It didn't seem to matter which way I turned my face; the rain just kept coming straight at me.

Tressaco was seven kilometres away in a direct line. I chose the straightest route we could walk, which I reckoned made it closer to nine kilometres. According to the map, which takes up half a wall in the village hall, there were seven canals I'd have to cross. At supper I'd sat facing it, memorizing the bridges for all of them.

I don't know if it was Frazer or myself who was most surprised when we actually found the first bridge. After crossing two more canals, we left the grazing meadows behind. It was all untended land ahead now, where there were no real tracks and the woods grew in long sprawling patches.

As well as wild ostriches, there are deer herds living in the woods. Villagers cull them regularly, which gives us extra meat for the kitchen. That was why we'd decided to bring the crossbow. I thought that I could learn to shoot deer or some of the swans and geese that fly around the habitat so we'd be able to contribute to whatever community the Cheaters had. They'd need food just like everyone else.

It took over two hours to reach the forest that sprawled around the base of Tressaco. It was a wild one. I was pushing through a huge variety of fruit trees – apples, olives, cherries, loquat, jackfruits, pears, breadfruit, and a whole lot I didn't recognize in the gloom. All of the habitat woods form a vast natural reserve of food if a village ever goes short. Not that we ever do in Ixia – we manage our orchards and groves so well these days.

Calling the route through the trees a "path" was just a joke. If the one on the village hall map ever had been there, it was long since overgrown. The trunks were close-packed and their boughs tightly interlocked. Then there were the grape vines, which swamped the whole place, making it completely impassable. After ten minutes, when we'd gone maybe thirty metres, I gave up and turned round.

After that I skirted round the edge of the forest until I reached the canal and used its towpath for the last kilometre. Tressaco, like all the mountain towers, is a giant pillar of rock, three hundred metres in diameter. Apparently they're solid in the centre, but the Builders cut a honeycomb of rooms and corridors into the outer surface – a hundred floors of them, they told us at school. Standing at the base, blinking up against the rain, I could see the neat rings of the metal-and-glass balconies stretching on up until I lost sight of them. My mind filled them with ghosts, the smiling families who had set out from Earth, whose descendants had spent four centuries gazing out across the marvellous vista of the habitat as they voyaged to their new world – only to find it occupied.

I wondered what they would think, those ghosts, as a soaked girl and her disabled brother came trudging out of the rain, desperate for sanctuary in the deserted ruins of their grand homes?

There was no sign of life on any of those imposingly high levels. No movement, no glimmer of light seeping out into the damp night. For one awful moment I wondered if the Cheater woman had lied to me, her final cruel payback on the village that had caught her.

"Let's find the way in," I said.

"Okay," Frazer agreed. He sounded utterly miserable. I would be too, slung over a horse like that for hours.

The canal merged into a broad, circular harbour pool close to the foot of the tower. There'd be no problem finding a way in – the whole of the ground floor was inset with great archways five times my height, opening into lightless caverns that reached some indefinable distance into the tower mountain – but I could sense it was a long way. The forest formed a tangled boundary just a few metres out from the base, with what must have been the oldest trees in *Daedalus*.

"What do we do?" I said piteously. There was no part of me that wasn't soaking wet and, with that, numbingly cold. I was tired, hungry, frightened, concerned for Frazer… I didn't know quite what I'd been expecting, but not this. The black emptiness of the entrance caverns was sucking the last sparks of hope from my body.

Frazer craned his neck, which must have been difficult for him given his position. "That one," he said.

I squinted at the archway he was indicating. A broad expanse of stone spread out from it until it reached the huge, ancient trees.

"All right." I didn't have the energy to argue with him.

"The stone on the ground means you can go in and out without leaving a trail in the vegetation," he explained. "So that's the one the Cheaters will use as their entrance."

I tugged on Bronwyn's bridle and led her onto the uneven, cracked stone. She snorted as we drew near the archway, with its lightless cavern beyond, but I coaxed her a few metres inside. I think even she was glad to be out of the rain.

Frazer had clearly quadrupled in weight during the trip. I could barely hold him as he half slithered, half fell off Bronwyn's back. We both collapsed groaning onto the floor. The cavern air seemed to drain sound away, leaving us isolated from the rest of the ship.

Right up until the moment a man's voice said, "He's a smart one, that boy."

(6)

I started. "Who's that?"

"Shield your eyes," the voice said.

"What?"

"I'm going to switch a torch on."

"What?" I repeated dumbly.

Suddenly a beam of light stabbed out, illuminating me and Frazer. It was amazing, as if a splinter of the daylight had been captured and brought down from the sky. Poor old Bronwyn whinnied in surprise, trotting a few metres away. I had to put my hand in front of my eyes to ward off the glare.

Another of the torches came on. Then a third. There was enough light now to reveal several silhouettes standing around us. When I looked round, two more people were coming in through the entrance. Old people.

"Who are you?" the voice asked.

"Please, I'm Hazel."

"And why are you here, Hazel?"

"My brother's injured. They're going to Cycle him, so we ran away to join you. That, and I'm looking for Alisha."

Which caused a few murmurs of surprise.

"What do you want with her?" a woman asked.

I tried to squint in the direction she'd spoken. "I think she's my great-grandmother."

A woman with thick white hair came forward. She knelt down beside us and reached out tentatively to touch Frazer's face. "Just like little Savin," she said in amazement, and promptly burst into tears.

* * *

I slept late into the next morning. Waking up was odd. Every muscle ached from our night-time hike through the rain, yet I was dry and warm and strangely content. The mattress must have helped. I didn't know anything could be so soft yet supportive at the same time. And the covers, too – they were thin and amazingly smooth. It was luxury even the mayor didn't have.

I sat up cautiously and the memories came rushing back – this was Alisha's home, and it was on the sixty-seventh floor of the tower mountain! I was wearing some kind of white bedshirt, something Alisha had given me last night. I'd barely got it on before I fell asleep. But now I could look round properly, I saw the room was almost as big as our whole cabin back in Ixia. One wall was hidden behind a thick curtain, with slivers of light probing round the edges.

The Cheaters – and I must find a more polite word to call them – had brought us up here on a moving platform they called a lift. It was a rectangular shaft that ran all the way up the inside of the tower mountain to the one hundredth floor. The platform had a big metal wheel at the back which Karval and Noran, two of the old men, started turning. When they did, the platform began to slide upwards.

I jumped at the motion and looked round anxiously as the walls glided past us. Frazer just said, "That is a very cool winch."

"This platform has a counterweight," Noran explained, pleased by Frazer's interest, "so it doesn't take too much effort to go up and down. Put it this way: it's a lot easier than walking up and down the stairs, but it still keeps you fit."

"We think the Builders installed the winch mechanism as some kind of emergency system for the platform," Karval said. "All the other lifts work off electricity. One day we'll get one working properly again."

"You can do that?" Frazer asked excitedly.

"Maybe."

I was more interested in their torches, which they said were also electrical – metallic purple cylinders ten centimetres long and two in diameter, with a glass end that shone a powerful beam of light which could be wide or narrow, depending how you twisted it. Alisha used one to light the way along the corridors to her home. Her friend Mortos – who claimed he was a hundred and seventeen – had carried Frazer. I didn't ask Alisha how old she was.

I stared at the purple torch she'd left on the bedside table for me. She'd shown me the little button that switched it on, but I was nervous about doing that. School always said electricity was dangerous, that it could kill you if you came into contact with it. That was why we should never touch any of the old machines.

There was just enough light sneaking round the curtains for me to see by, so I went over to the door and opened it. "Hello?"

"You're awake. Lovely," Alisha called. "Hang on, I'm coming."

She arrived carrying a bundle of clothes. "How are you feeling, my dear?"

"Okay, I guess."

She dropped the clothes on the bed and walked over to the curtain. "Brace yourself," she warned, and pulled the curtain back, revealing a glass wall. Light flooded in. I gasped in astonishment. We really were very high up the tower mountain. Kilometres of the habitat were spread out clearly below us. Being so high up meant I could see the aft ring lake, which sparkled in the distance. But everything looked so tiny; the trees in the forest below appeared only a few centimetres tall. It was such an unusual perspective, the backs of my legs started to tingle, which was the strangest sensation. I swayed back.

Alisha's arm went round my shoulders, holding me steady. "The height affects a lot of people that way," she said sympathetically. "It's called vertigo. Don't worry, it'll pass."

I looked at her face. And, yes, there was so much of her I recognized. Her grey-blue eyes were darker than mine and Dad's, the nose a little sharper.

"How old are you?" I blurted, and promptly blushed.

"I'm ninety-three," she said. "I left Ixia when I was fifty-six. Your father was only five. I haven't seen him in all that time. How is he?"

"He had an accident. His leg – the doctor had to amputate."

"Oh, sweet Captain!"

"He's okay!" I said hurriedly. "He made himself an artificial one. They didn't Cycle him."

"An artificial leg?" she said incredulously.

"Yes. He's the head of the carpentry shop. He's really smart. So's Frazer."

Her lips tweaked into a secretive smile. "I'm sure he is," she murmured.

"Oh, but Dad's going to be so mad with me. I didn't tell him what I was going to do." Saying it made me wonder what was going on in the village right now. The mayor and the Regulators would be furious. Would they punish Mum and Dad? Alice would be happy, I'm sure. For a start, she'd be the centre of attention, with everyone asking her what she knew. I grinned at the image that conjured up. Then I thought of Zawn, which kind of broke my mood.

Alisha stroked my face. "Your father won't be angry. Trust me. He'll be proud of you, just like I am. It takes a great deal of courage to do what you've just done. I remember. But it is so worthwhile."

"Is it?"

"They would have Cycled me twenty-eight years ago if I'd stayed. The Electric Captain's rules are barbaric."

That startled me. I wasn't used to anybody, let alone adults, challenging the Electric Captain. "But being part of the Cycle is how we all survive."

"Indeed. But why didn't the Electric Captain ever teach us how to rebuild the machines the Mutineers wrecked? She has the knowledge inside the big thinking machines that keep *Daedalus* flying. Why are we kept in complete ignorance?"

"I don't know," I said, suddenly intrigued. "I always wanted to know how much longer it's going to be till we get to the new world."

"Questioning what you see is a good start," she said. Her fingers started examining my hair. "We need to get you washed. I've got plenty of olive-oil soap. You know the secret to a good bar is to let it cure for at least six months?"

"Um, no, I didn't know that."

She laughed and gave me a hug. "You turning up is such a miracle. But let's start with breakfast, shall we?"

My mouth started to water at the mere mention of food. "I am hungry," I admitted.

* * *

I put on the clothes Alisha had brought – a pair of supple deerskin trousers and a dark purple shirt that was a little big for me. Then she led me through her home, which was a line of big rooms around the outside of the tower mountain, linked by a corridor running round the back, and all with a window wall looking out over the habitat.

The living room had a long table. Frazer was sitting at it, chatting to Mortos. Part of its glass wall was actually a door out to the balcony, which was open, allowing the air to gust in. It was cooler than I was used to.

"Hazel!" Frazer shouted. "Check this out." He pushed off from the table with his good arm.

His chair was pre-Mutiny, with a metal frame holding tough black cushioning. It had a single shiny central leg, which branched out into six horizontal spokes at the bottom. Each of them had a small spherical wheel at the end.

He went gliding over the floor, laughing happily. When he reached the back wall, he pushed again, sending himself back to the table. Mortos had to grab him as he reached it.

"Nice," I said approvingly.

"Karval and I can rig up some ropes," Mortos said. "That way Frazer can pull himself around the apartment."

"That sounds like a great idea," Alisha said, as we sat at the table. "But I do want Findell to take a look at Frazer today. Findell's our doctor," she explained to me.

"Ixia's doctor said I might improve," Frazer said enthusiastically. "I just need time."

I couldn't meet Alisha's gaze.

"That's lovely," she said.

Breakfast was poached eggs and fruit, with peach juice. As much as I wanted. I was curious how they cooked the eggs. I hadn't seen a fire, and I couldn't imagine how you could have one up here.

"An oven that Noran wired into a working electrical circuit for us," Alisha said when I asked. "It's called a microwave – and no, I don't know why. That's just what it says on the front."

"You're going to miss bread," Mortos said. "But we can't really steal wheat from the village fields."

"Most of our food comes from the forest," Alisha said. "There's just so much of it. And we keep chickens and goats up on the seventy-fifth floor for eggs and milk. It's a regular farmyard up there."

"Why do you live this high up?" I asked. "Are all the floors occupied?"

"Not at all. We're up here because the Regulators have an aversion to climbing up this many stairs – especially as they're unlit. They don't know about the lift platform with the winch mechanism. And if they do come, we'll have plenty of time to vanish into the interior. There are a thousand rooms and corridors further inside. It's quite a maze in there."

Alisha showed me round Tressaco, introducing me to people, explaining how they lived, how they were trying to find out how the old relics functioned. I loved it. Even though the tower mountain was ancient and most of it didn't work, it was all new to me. And the single greatest achievement of the tower-mountain homes had to be the flush toilets. After years of emptying out the nightsoil bucket, they were a revelation.

There were sixty-seven people living in the tower mountain, Alisha said, which intrigued me – the way the Regulators went on, you'd think the terrible Cheaters practically outnumbered us and were sucking the life out of the habitat.

Some of the other tower mountains also had elderly communities, as she called them. They favoured the ones that didn't have guano spill pipes, so they didn't have regular visits from the canal barges. It meant there were fewer opportunities for them to be discovered.

As we started looking round, I asked Alisha what I should call them instead of Cheaters. She gave me a hard look and said, "People." So now I know where Dad gets his attitude from.

Karval had left early that morning. He'd taken Bronwyn back along the canal towpath, then walked round the forest. He'd decided to leave her close to Hameri village's grazing meadows, four kilometres forward. The villagers would find her before long, and when she got taken back to Ixia, Chief Atov would have another mystery to ponder.

The Tressaco people keep a constant watch on the two towpaths, which, thanks to the forest, are the only way to reach the tower mountain. Even though Tressaco doesn't have a guano spill pipe, several barges travel along the canal each day.

Caylin was on duty that morning. She sat on the fifth-floor balcony, which gave her a decent view along both of the canals that stretched away from the harbour pool. "If anyone's outside, gathering food in the forest or hunting, we post another lookout directly below," she said. "Mind you, we mostly go out at night. The moonlight is bright enough to pick fruit by."

I peered over the balcony rail and experienced another vertigo tingle. Below me I could just see the lookout's head. "Do you shout down to them?"

"Oh, no," Caylin said. "Noise carries a long way. If anyone knew for certain we were here, the Regulators might make a bit more effort trying to find us." Her foot nudged a big jug of water on the floor by her chair. "I just tip this over the edge. Then the lookout knows to go out and warn everyone to either hide or scoot back into the tower mountain until the barge has passed."

"Did you see me coming?" I asked.

"Yes, dear. Just. The three-hour rain gave you good cover. That was clever."

"Frazer's idea," I admitted.

Alisha and I found Frazer in the sixty-eighth-floor workshop that belonged to Noran. He was so happy, pushing himself around on his six-wheeled chair, zipping from bench to bench. Noran was slowly delving into the mystery of electricity. "Been at it for thirty-two years now," he told me cheerfully. Then he glanced over at Frazer. "Never had a pupil this smart before," he told me in appreciation.

"Electricity makes everything go," Frazer said exuberantly as I went over to his work bench. "Everything! Oh my dayz, I had no idea. It flows through wire – which is a conductor. There's positive and negative. You can store it in batteries. Coils of wire make magnetics. You need insulators round conductors or it'll short out. Every room in Tressaco has an induction band. It powers the water pumps and the habitat light strips – but that's big electricity. And–"

"Whoa, slow down," I said. I might have just as well asked *Daedalus* to stop spinning.

"Look at this," Frazer said, and picked up a dark green cylinder with a handle coming out at right angles. There was a slim drill bit at the other end. He pressed a button on the top of the handle and the drill bit blurred with speed. I've seen Dad drilling wood in the carpentry shop. The drill bits in Ixia do not blur with speed. "Power tools," Frazer pronounced grandly.

"Very good," I told him.

"Don't you get it? I can use them all one-handed. They're perfect for me."

"That's great, Frazer," I told him, even though I was thinking how much Dad would love all this.

"Noran is showing me how to repair one," he said, gesturing at a larger version of the drill. Its casing was open, allowing him to spread intricate components across his bench. I peered closely, fascinated by the little pieces of wire and grey cubes.

"It's the best way to learn the fundamental principles," Noran said in a voice that was almost apologetic.

"There are so many tools," Frazer said, and hauled himself along the side of the bench, stopping to pick them up for me. "Saws – three different sizes. A screwdriver with a dozen heads you can swap round, see? Microdrill, flexible scope, clip lock, charge detector. Torch." He slapped one of the little purple cylinders into my hand. "This way." He shoved off again, zipping backwards across the workshop.

I put out a hand to grab him, but he was laughing at me. Somehow he managed to spin the chair round before he hit the wall. "This is how you charge things, look." Running round the room at waist height was a metal strip ten centimetres wide. I'd seen strips like it in most of Tressaco's rooms and assumed it was just part of the tower mountain's decoration, but no – this was the induction strip, Frazer explained. He produced a small grey disc the size of his palm and a couple of centimetres thick. It had a circular indentation on one surface and a length of cable sticking out like a skinny tail, ending in a small silver nub with a flat end that made me think of a metal grape cut in half.

"Stick this on here like this," Frazer said, and touched the nub to the induction strip. And it did stick – it just clicked on and stayed there, fastened to the vertical wall. I waited for it to fall but it never did. "How–" I began.

"Magnet," Frazer said smugly. "Now put the torch into its charge slot." He took the purple cylinder from me and pressed it into the indentation on the larger disc. "And it charges up the torch's battery. Simple, but so clever. The Builders were amazing."

I could see a pinpoint of red light blinking at the centre of the torch's button. After a couple of seconds, the red changed to green. "It's ready now," Frazer announced triumphantly.

"Just like the Regulator pistols," I murmured.

"Exactly the same principle," Noran said. "It'll last for about ten days continual use before it needs charging again. The induction strip has a low power rating, which is presumably why it's still working. The big stuff, the high-voltage circuits on every floor, are all off. I haven't found out where to turn them back on."

"But you can still do so much with what we've got," Frazer insisted. He shoved off again, heading for another bench. "Look, Hazel, these are charging pads for all the tools. And there's shapes for machines Noran hasn't even found yet." He was holding up charging discs of various sizes, all with their cables dangling, going through them like he was dealing cards. One was the size of a dinner plate, with a broad X-shaped indentation. My mind simply couldn't conceive what tool or machine that would fit.

"Frazer–"

"And there's electrical motors here, too," he said. "I want to try and fit some to the chair so they can power the wheels. Oh my dayz, do you get what that'll mean? I can drive around–"

"Frazer!"

He looked up at me with such a delighted face. There was simply no way I could bring him down from that much bliss. "I'm really glad you've got all this."

"You brought me here," he said, and there was a hint of moisture in his eyes, as if he was about to start crying. "I would never have known these things without you, Hazel. You made this happen." His good hand gripped mine. "Thank you."

"You don't have to thank me, you're my brother. But we need to take things slowly, okay? We've only been here half a day. And even you can't learn everything at once."

"Yes. Of course. I understand."

"Good. So what did Findell say about your spine?"

"Oh. About the same as Marana. That I may get some feeling back, but it'll take time."

"Okay, well that's positive."

"I think she was just trying to cheer me up." He brought his left arm up – a jerky motion – until the hand was in front of his face. The fingers were all curled up. "I can only move the thumb now. So actually I'm getting worse."

"That horse ride didn't help," Alisha said quickly. "You really do need to take things easy." That was said with a very pointed glance at Noran, who raised his hands in surrender.

"I will," Frazer said, sounding tremendously earnest.

"Hmm," Alisha narrowed her eyes and gave him a thoughtful stare. "I think it'll be for the best if you just sit and listen to Noran explain things for a few days. The Captain knows, he can talk for that long without a break. Then we can see about you being a little more active."

Frazer nodded enthusiastically. "All right."

Alisha had what she called her archaeology study on the seventy-second floor. It was a big room, with long tables holding a clutter of pre-Mutiny items. She'd written plenty of notes on whiteleafs saying what each of them were, or what they might be. "Half of them I really have no idea," she admitted sadly.

There were so many things on the tables. Weird coiled brass funnels with knobs and tiny levers on the outside. "Musical instruments," Alisha said. "You blow through them. But they don't sound too good. There's got to be some trick to it we haven't quite fathomed out yet." Narrow boxes with glass balls the size of my thumbnail. "The labels in the box suggest they're full of something, but I can't work out what."

I held a glass ball up to the window. "It's perfectly clear," I said.

She shrugged.

There was an entire table of beautiful, intricate jewellery – bracelets, rings, necklaces, earrings, odd-shaped trinkets that I couldn't work out where they'd go. The pieces of time jewellery were fascinating. They were ornate bracelets of metal with a glass-covered disc showing a circle of twelve numbers and needle-like pointers. Some were very elaborate, like works of art.

"You wear them on your wrist and they tell the time," Alisha explained. "Twelve hours in a day, see, and the pointers turn round the numbers to show which hour it is."

"Really?"

"Yes. But they're historical ornaments, probably family relics. I'm pretty sure they came from Earth before the *Daedalus* was ever built."

"Why do you say that?" I asked, examining one. It was surprisingly heavy, inset with tiny pebbles of sparkly glass.

"Because every *Daedalus* machine is electrical. These are mechanical. You need to see Karval – he got one working. It's never off his wrist, he's so proud."

"How did he make it work?"

"It took him years. He used smaller versions of the instruments you saw in Noran's workshop. Once you get the back off them, they're filled with tiny metal cog wheels and a coil that you can tighten up. It makes the little cogs turn as it unwinds. They turn the pointers."

"That's amazing."

"Like I said, it took him a long time to figure the mechanism out. He must have gone through a dozen before he fixed his."

I nodded absently and moved on. "Are these screens?" I asked.

"Yes. Much smaller than the one I remember in Ixia village hall. There were plenty more on the walls here, but they've all been smashed."

"Does the Electric Captain appear on these?"

"No. We don't know how to get them working yet – just wiring them up to the electricity in the induction strip isn't enough. There's something missing. Noran will work it out eventually, I'm sure, if he has enough time."

I looked along the tables with all their ancient treasure. Two of them were laden with artefacts that Alisha said nobody could even guess the purpose of. "Where did all this come from? I thought the Mutineers smashed anything valuable along with the machines."

"They certainly tried. But you've seen how big Tressaco is – we don't even know exactly how many rooms it has, and it's only one tower mountain out of seventy. They emptied most of the homes, and set fires in a lot of places, but destroying everything would have been impossible – there's just too much. Scavengers from the villages still come here for a couple of hours every now and then. They collect a few items from the lower floors to replace stuff that's been broken or worn out. But they're too afraid to search further up. While we've been here for decades; so we can afford to be thorough searching out more interesting items." She smiled and picked up what I thought was another time-piece bracelet. It was odd, with a circular section like the other versions I'd seen but made out of some shiny black substance. I knew it wasn't glass but it looked like it was. And the strap was fat but could never be worn on a wrist – the loop was too small; you could barely get two fingers into it.

"This one," Alisha said, "is our biggest mystery. It's also a perfect example of how the captain's loyalists hid stuff from the Mutineers. Karval and Mortos found it in the water tank when they were fixing the system."

"What system?"

"The water system, my dear." Her eyebrows went up expectantly, as if I knew what she was talking about. "The one that feeds the toilets and the showers? Tressaco has big tanks every five floors, which fill up out of pipes leading down from somewhere above us – presumably the same water that gets pumped from the aft ring lake up to the rain sprinklers in the sky. Then smaller pipes bring it from the tanks to individual homes. The plumbing was all clogged up and broken when the first of us came here, but twenty years ago they cleaned out this section and got water flowing again up here." She gave the unusual bracelet an impassive look. "This was wrapped in layers of plastic, sitting on the bottom of a tank where it was blocking an outlet. Somebody went to a lot of trouble to save it."

"So it must be important, then?" I asked.

"Yes. Unfortunately we don't understand exactly what it is, other than it's an electric-powered machine of some kind."

"That's a machine?" I didn't see how it could be. The bracelet was too small to do anything.

"Yes." She grinned. "Noran figured it out, of course. It fits the smaller charging pads." She picked up a small pad with a circular indentation and stuck its nub to the induction strip.

"Ah," I said, looking from the bracelet to the pad. "It uses electricity."

"Well done." She put the circular section of the bracelet into the pad's indentation. Right at the top of the black hoop, a tiny circle of red light shone brightly. "Red means it's charging."

Like the torch, the bracelet machine took a few seconds before the light turned green.

"Now what?" I asked.

"Now we don't know." She slipped her finger into the loop and plucked it off the pad. "The charge lasts about twenty days, so it must be using electricity somehow. We just can't see how, which is incredibly frustrating given how important it has to be." She gave it a last wistful glance and put it back down.

There were so many artefacts spread out on the tables. "None of them look old," I said as we went along, examining the curiosities. "Dad said the Builders' machines made things tough."

"He's right, they made everything to last. And not just things; we have their clothes, too."

"Clothes?"

"Yes. There are wardrobes full of clothes in every Tressaco home. We don't make these," she said, gesturing at the long blue dress she was wearing. "And they wear well; it takes years and years of washing and daily use before these fabrics start to thin out or fade."

"But—" I stared down at what I'd assumed were deerskin trousers.

"I just went to our stockpile and pulled them out for you," Alisha said with a small smile. "You wait till you see what else we've got. My dear, you're in for such a treat. Some of the dresses are simply dazzling. If I envy the early *Daedalus* generations anything, it's the parties they must have had. There's no other reason to have clothes like that."

"Sounds great," I said, recalling my green Cycling Day dress. I was pretty confident nothing could ever match that, no matter what fancy fabric the machines had produced once upon a time.

After the archaeology study, she took me out into a high circular stairwell that stretched up three floors with a panoramic window covering one side. The air was hot inside.

"That side's a huge auditorium," Alisha said as we stood at the top of the grandiose curving stairs, "which is why the stairs are here. There aren't many like this in Tressaco, but it's useful. It's a perfect place for my air-pressure measure."

"Your what?"

"This." As we walked down, she gestured to a slim transparent pipe that was standing vertically up the middle of the stairwell, held in place by several ropes. It must have been twelve metres long. "See the big basin at the bottom? It's full of water."

"Okay, yes."

"So is the tube." She pointed. "Can you see the top of the water?"

I could. The water filled maybe two thirds of the length of the tube. Then I looked down into the basin again. The bottom of the tube was open underwater. "I don't understand. How is the water staying up in the tube?"

Alisha grinned. "The tube is sealed at the upper end, so the only thing holding the water up inside it is air pressure."

I did get the principle – that air pressure exerted a force on the surface of the basin's water – but I never realized it was so strong. The column of water in the pipe must have been over seven metres high. That's a lot of water to be holding up. "That's so clever," I said. Alisha must be where Frazer gets his brains from. "Did you work out how to build the measure yourself?"

"Yes. I set it up a year ago, when I started noticing the air was getting a bit strange."

"Strange how?"

"For a start, the higher up the tower you go, the harder it is to breathe. Then boiling water seemed to be cooler somehow, which is so peculiar I thought I was imagining things, or at least hoped I was. But I've measured the water height every couple of days since then. The level keeps falling, which means there's less air pressure keeping it up. At this rate, the atmosphere will be gone in another five or six years. Not that we'll live that long. There won't be enough left for us to breathe after three years at the most if it keeps reducing at this rate."

"The Swirl!" I gasped. "It's leaking out through the Swirl."

"What swirl?"

"Above Akebia village. I saw it myself a few weeks ago. When the moonlight's on, you can see the mist sink away up into the sky. They said it started right after the Jolt, three years ago." For some mischievous reason, the memory of Rell popped up into my mind, his arms fitting snugly round me as we danced, face close to mine. In fact, very close. Any nearer and we might have kissed. It all seemed like it happened a decade ago now.

"I need to go there," Alisha said bluntly. "I need to see it."

"I wanted Mayor Fininen to ask the Electric Captain about it," I said. "Dad told me she used to answer questions. I was going to ask for a vote at the next village meeting. But… I'm here now."

"Three of us went to try and warn Ixia," Alisha said softly. "They thought they could talk to their families, that at least they'd listen."

"No!" my hand came up to cover my mouth. "We Cycled them. The Regulators said they caught them stealing sheep."

"That's a lie," Alisha said. "You've seen how much food we have."

I thought I might start crying. "What have we done? Why are we living like this? Why?"

Alisha put her arms round me. "It's all right. They knew the risks."

"But they're dead!" I sobbed. "I was there. I was the flower girl."

"Ah," Alisha said. "Is that how you knew where to find me? I did wonder."

I nodded miserably. "The woman whispered to me that you were in Tressaco. She said you knew about the habitat losing air. I never told the Regulators."

"That was Bethal. She helped me build this air-pressure measure – tied all the ropes in place. I'm hopeless with knots. She was a good friend. We had a lot of laughs together over the years."

"I'm so sorry."

"Don't be. She brought you to me. That would have made her so happy."

I wiped my eyes and stared at the pressure-measure tube, fearful of what it revealed, that I'd been right all along. "What do we do now?" I asked.

"I need to talk to a few people. We can never seal up a hole in the sky by ourselves. Somehow we have to get the attention of the remaining thinking machines on the *Daedalus*, the ones still keeping us flying. They may be able to help."

"How?" I asked "How do we get their attention?"

"I don't know."

(7)

I didn't realize how tired I was until the moonlight came on. The walk to Tressaco had taken a lot out of me. Mind you, Noran had been right about the lift winch; turning the wheel to get up and down seventy-odd floors several times a day was going to toughen me up considerably. A couple of weeks of doing that and I'd have muscles like Makkus.

Frazer and I had supper with Alisha and Mortos. Naturally Frazer insisted on using the microwave oven to heat the water; it was so much quicker than the ovens back in Ixia. I'd spent my whole life having communal meals in the village hall. Just the four of us chatting around a table, responsible for our own food, felt peculiar – but rather nice. Alisha had plenty of stories from her life in Ixia. It didn't sound much different to my time there. Nothing changes in the *Daedalus*. I guess that's the point of village life – just keep everything going until we reach the new world.

I went to bed, comforted by Alisha's promise to visit the clothes stockpile tomorrow before she had her big meeting with everyone about how to deal with the Swirl. I thought I'd sleep straight away, but I didn't. My head was whirling with everything that'd happened, all the things I'd been introduced to. Image after image kept materializing in my mind's eye. With that came questions.

Why did the survivors of the Mutiny abandon the tower mountains to live in villages? Even without electricity, the homes were so much better than our cabins. And how many people had there been at the time of the Mutiny? We had a hundred villages with roughly a thousand people in each. There were seventy tower mountains, with a hundred floors each.

Okay, so not every floor was given over to homes – maybe eighty levels in total, but there were twenty-five homes on each of those. Would the families be four people, like ours, or more? I know there had been terrible fights between Loyalists and Mutineers. How many had died? At school they always said the majority of adults on both sides were killed in the fighting, but the numbers were starting to scare me. I shivered beneath the warm bedcovers.

Everything I'd always wanted to know, everything I didn't understand about our voyage, it all came flooding through my skull. And Chief Atov had to know Bethal and her friends weren't stealing sheep. He'd lied, with the support of Fininen. So what was happening to Mum and Dad–

I woke with a start at my usual time, half an hour before the daylight came on. I had slept, but it was a fitful night. My questions and dreams had wound up merging.

When I got up, the first thing I did was have a shower – the second water revelation of Tressaco. The water that sprinkled out was cool, but nothing like as cold as the canal. Mortos said Noran was working on getting some of the old house water heaters wired in to the induction-strip circuit, so we could have hot water any time we turned on a tap, but he was being cautious as water and electricity is a bad combination, apparently.

A shower of warm water to wash in whenever you wanted! I couldn't really imagine that happening. Maybe he was joking.

After the shower I went to Frazer's room and helped him get dressed. He didn't stop talking. He was full of plans for fixing motors and pulleys to his chair. An enthused Mortos joined in with him at breakfast, the two of them discussing batteries and gearing, what tools to use, maybe a different chair Mortos remembered down on floor fifty-three which had larger wheels.

Alisha and I sat there listening to them, exchanging smiles every now and then.

"Frazer, you're supposed to be taking it easy," she chided eventually.

"I will, Gran," he insisted. "I have to learn about electrics from Noran before we can begin making the actual devices. But I can draw up plans at the same time, can't I?"

"Well, yes..."

I grinned into my fruit bowl. I could see how delighted she was at being called Gran. And just like the rest of my family, she was being carried along by Frazer's gusto.

"It wouldn't hurt for you to get a piece of time jewellery working," Mortos told Frazer. "It's work that would keep you sitting still." That was directed at Alisha. "It's not physically demanding, although you have to concentrate hard. And it would give you practical experience with our tools, as well as learning everything there is to know about gearing."

"Great!" Frazer exclaimed. "Will you teach me?"

"Karval's the time-jewellery man. I'll ask him."

"Can I start today, do you think? Which piece can I fix?"

"I have several in my study," Alisha said. "Hazel, be a dear and fetch one, would you? As soon as you get back, we'll swing by the clothes stockpile for you. Then it'll be time for the meeting. We can all start thinking about how we tackle the Swirl. Okay?"

I finished my grapefruit. "Sure."

I took the stairs up to the seventy-second floor. Even that left me breathing hard when I got there.

Inside the archaeology study, I stared down at the pieces of time jewellery. It was hard to get my head around Alisha's belief that they had been made back on Earth. If she was right, they were a thousand years old, at least. That would make them so incredibly precious, the only items I'd seen on board all of *Daedalus* that truly connected us to the world we'd come from.

And Frazer was going to take one apart. Frazer!

Now I just felt guilty having to choose one. After looking at them again, I picked up the one that looked the least elaborate, so surely the least valuable?

I gave all the other amazing relics a long look, enjoying the knowledge that people could build such wonders. We just needed to learn how again – something the villages would never do; the way they lived their lives gave them no time to study electricity or gears. My gaze stopped at the odd bracelet machine that had spent five hundred years hidden in a water tank. Its tiny green light was still shining. And I couldn't even begin to guess what it was.

I slipped my finger through its hoop, picking it up. The little light turned purple.

"User DNA sequence confirmed as a descendant of Captain Ashleigh Kruger. Function access restriction discontinued."

I squealed in shock and dropped the machine. It had *spoken!* I wanted to run from the archaeology study, but my legs had frozen. All I could do was stare down at the floor where it was lying. The tiny light had turned back to green and was now pulsing like a slow heartbeat. "What?" I realized my throat was so tight I'd probably not actually spoken out loud. "What?"

"Please specify your question," the machine said. It was a calm, melodic voice. Hard to tell if it was male or female.

"What are you? Are you alive?"

"I am an artificial intelligence program operating within a neural processor module. My primary function is a bond-adaptive personal interface to *Daedalus* systems and cybots for my user."

I kept on staring at it, still unable to move. "What?" I repeated.

"To determine an appropriate explanation level, please could you tell me what education grade you have achieved?"

"I've left school. I know reading and writing, and I can do maths, too. I was learning to look after chickens, but that's not really what I want to do with my life, especially not now I'm here in Tressaco. There's so many more important things I'm going to help Alisha with."

I might have been imagining it, but the green light pulses seemed to take a short pause. "I am unable to detect any *Daedalus* network nodes. Local environment decay indicates a considerable period of time has elapsed since I was last active. What is the ship's current status?"

"Well, *Daedalus* is kind of okay because we're still flying to the new world though the Swirl is bad news but apart from that everything's good oh actually I think Chief Atov lied so he could execute the three Cheaters but that's not what you asked is it so um we found you well okay my great-grandmother found you no actually it was her friends anyway you were in a water tank we think you were hidden there during the Mutiny oh that was five hundred years ago so yeah it's been five hundred years since you talked to anyone I guess." I knew I was babbling, but the initial shock was fading, allowing me to feel real excitement rising inside me. I could barely keep my hand still. I wanted to dance with joy.

I took a breath and made an effort to calm down. If I started to jig about, the machine would probably think I was crazy. It might have been right.

"Please confirm there has been a mutiny?" it asked.

"Yes. Five hundred years ago. Do you remember it?"

"No. My memory store only contains basic ship and encyclopaedia files. All previous user files were erased when the function access restriction was implemented."

"You mean you were locked up?"

"Effectively, yes. A security Level One access restriction to all independent AIs was enacted by the captain. Such an order would only be given in the most extreme circumstances. It must have been done to prevent abuse by those involved in the mutiny."

"So... why have you come back to life now? Alisha and her people have been charging you up for twenty years."

"A subsystem analysed your DNA when you touched me. You are descended from Captain Ashleigh Kruger. That contact authorized my full functionality. In effect, you are the key to unlock me."

I'm not sure how long I stood there with my heart yammering away in my ears. Quite a while. "What? No, forget that. I have to stop saying that. Okay, I don't know what deenay is, but are you seriously saying I'm related to the captain?"

"DNA is the terrestrial genetic code. In simple terms, it is the part of your biochemistry that carries traits such as skin colour, hair colour, blood type, height and so on. You share many traits with Ashleigh Kruger. You are directly descended from her."

"No way!"

"DNA analysis of this nature is infallible."

"Oh. Wait, Alisha has been touching you for years, and she's my great-grandmother. Why didn't you unlock for her?"

"If her DNA did not trigger the release, she is not related to the captain. Therefore the connection must be through the other side of your family."

"Mum!" My hand reached up to pat my hair. "She has red hair too. Oh, sweet Captain, what is she going to say when she learns who our ancestor is?"

"Do you have an instruction for me?"

"What? Sorry! Um, what do I call you?"

"My identification name is normally assigned by my user. It can be whatever you wish. Once decided, I will then respond to that."

"Right. How about John? That was my grandfather's name on Mum's side of the family. I really liked him. He Cycled when I was quite young. Would you mind that?"

"I do not mind any name. Please be aware that, at this stage of adapting to you, I have not created a repertoire of appropriate emotional response routines to match your personality. They will develop over time as I learn your demeanour."

I wasn't entirely sure I liked the idea of that, but whatever. "Okay, John it is. Pleased to meet you, John."

"I am pleased to meet you, too." The machine's voice deepened slightly, becoming more male. "Are you going to tell me your name?"

"Oh!" I blushed. "I'm Hazel."

"Hello, Hazel."

I squatted down next to the machine – John! "What happens next?"

"Users normally wear a unit like me on their wrist as a bracelet."

"I don't think you're going to fit. That loop isn't big enough to go on my wrist."

I saw it happen. I actually saw it! The black loop changed. It thinned out, expanding. But there were no moving parts; it was solid. "How did you *do* that?" I gasped.

"My external structure is a matrix of active metamolecular strands. I can change shape to accommodate my user's dimensions."

I had the silliest smile on my face as I picked John up. Slowly, I slid my wrist into the loop. Sure enough, it contracted around my skin.

"Is that comfortable?" John asked.

"Yes." I stood up and admired the black bracelet. "I'm dreaming."

"I assure you, Hazel, you are not."

I tipped my head to one side. "John, can you see me?"

"Yes. Audio and visual sensors are embedded in my structure."

"You asked for instructions. What sort of instructions do people normally give you?"

"Ordinarily I provide personalized access to other machines. This can include direct access to information and the use of cybots to serve you. However, I cannot currently detect the ship's communication network, nor any other functioning machines."

"The Mutineers broke all the machines on board."

"All of them? Are you sure?"

"Well, yes, I guess."

"Hazel, that is a great many machines."

"I know." I sighed. "We're supposed to be reaching our new world soon as well, but the Electric Captain never tells us when we'll get there."

"What is the Electric Captain?"

"It's the original captain, Ashleigh Kruger. When it looked like she and the Loyalists were losing, she cast herself into the biggest thinking machines in *Daedalus*, the ones that control the ship's flight. The Mutineers couldn't get her out without destroying those machines, and if they did that, they'd kill the *Daedalus*." I gave John a sheepish look. "That's what they taught us in school, anyway."

"That is plausible," John said. "The captain and some senior crew were equipped with a direct neural interface to the command AIs. Hazel, if the Mutineers broke all the other machines, how do you feed yourselves?"

"We farm the habitat."

"How many humans live in the *Daedalus* now?"

"There's a hundred villages, and we each have about a thousand people."

"Villages?"

"Yes. We built them."

"Do you not live in the existing tower-mountain homes?"

"No."

"Why not?"

"I'm not sure. There was a lot of damage and the lifts don't work because there's no big electricity on anymore. I guess it was easier to live next to the fields. That's where the Electric Captain told us to live after the Mutiny."

"But you are here in Tressaco."

"Oh yeah, but this is where the Cheaters live."

"What are Cheaters?"

"People who didn't want to be Cycled." I drew down a deep breath and explained the Cycle we lived by.

"Self-sacrifice is extremely unusual behaviour for a human society," John said when I finished. "There is no equivalent in history."

"We don't have any choice. *Daedalus* is finite. The Electric Captain worked out this is how we can keep going."

"And we are currently flying to a new world?"

"Yes. It's supposed to take five hundred years. Roughly, anyway."

"And the Electric Captain does not keep you informed of progress?"

"No."

"Hazel, this is not an optimum situation."

I shrugged. "I know. And on top of that, the air's leaking out of the habitat. It has been for years."

"What repair methods are you using?"

"I think it's about time I took you to meet Alisha."

Frazer, Alisha and Mortos were still sitting round the table when I walked back in.

"I was wondering what had happened to you," Alisha said in a light-hearted tone. Then she caught my expression.

Honestly, I had no reason to feel guilty. Yet Alisha and her friends had spent so long trying to work things out. Decades.

I held out my arm, showing them John. "I picked it up. I'm sorry. But..."

"Good morning, everybody," John said.

Alisha let out a squeal of shock – just like I had. Mortos gave the bracelet a startled look, jumping to his feet as if he was about to run to safety. And Frazer? Frazer went, "Oh my dayz, that is *so cool!* What is it? How does it work?"

"It's an artificial intelligence," I said, trying to sound blasé.

"It gives its user access to all the ship's machines. That's me. I'm the user."

"I may be the last functional independent artificial intelligence on the *Daedalus*," John said. "And there are no machines left to access."

"It works," Alisha said in shock. "You got it to work." She came over and held up my wrist, staring at John. "And it's changed shape – the strap got bigger. How did you do this?"

"Um, well…" I gave Frazer a huge grin. "Turns out Frazer and I are related to Ashleigh Kruger."

"No way!" Frazer cried.

"Hazel is correct," John said. "Ashleigh Kruger placed restrictions on my use. Only one of her descendants could reactivate me."

"All it took was me touching it," I said. "John knew my biochemical traits belong to the captain's family straight away. It can analyse them." I ignored the amused scorn on Frazer's face as I explained. It sounded to me like I knew what I was talking about.

"Why were you hidden?" Alisha asked.

"I have no direct knowledge, so I deduce it was a tactical procedure," John said. "There were tens of thousands of units like me in use at the time of the Mutiny and the ship's electronics department could produce as many more as were required. From your descriptions of the Mutiny, it is likely that AIs were being targeted for destruction by Mutineers. My user wanted me to survive."

"Do you know how to repair the broken machines?" she said.

"My memory has schematics for eight thousand different machines on board, including many types of buildbots."

"What are buildbots?" Frazer asked.

"Machines which produce requested items on demand, such as clothing or food. The more sophisticated buildbots are even capable of reproducing themselves."

"So essentially buildbots are like super carpentry shops?"

"That is the principle, yes."

"What about basic knowledge?" Alisha asked. "Can you teach us science and our history?"

"I have files containing all the scientific knowledge humans had discovered up to the time *Daedalus* left Earth. Historical and cultural records are also available."

Alisha sank down into her chair, looking dazed and out of breath. "This is what we've been waiting for. Sweet Captain! We can rebuild it all, get the pre-Mutiny machines working again, relearn all the knowledge we lost. This must be why you were hidden, so you'd survive the Mutiny and help us."

"Yes." John sounded hesitant. "I cannot determine the circumstances that have prevented the Electric Captain from initiating a full rebuild operation. The *Daedalus* was designed with multiple redundancies specifically to withstand extreme disasters."

"Well, you can ask the Electric Captain yourself," Mortos said. "We just have to take you to a village screen."

Alisha flinched at that. "We could, but there's a lot of politics involved. The villagers still consider us Cheaters, remember. Right now all we are to the Regulators is walking guano. I'd like to see what we can achieve for ourselves here first. Perhaps John can tell us how to get Tressaco's big electricity circuits working again. That should go a long way towards convincing the villages to listen to us."

"My memory contains schematics of the tower mountains and their utility systems," John said. "I should be able to offer some guidance."

"Thank you." Alisha gave me a contented smile. "But people are going to be arriving for the meeting now. I'd like to introduce you to them."

Alisha had called the meeting in a long room on the seventy-ninth floor. As we had Frazer with us, we had to use the winch platform to get up there.

Alisha and Mortos shone their torches ahead while I pushed him along the corridor. I didn't mind; his six-wheeled chair and the perfectly flat floors made it easy. It was just steering, really.

"Why aren't you walking?" John asked Frazer.

"I can't. Not anymore. I had an accident which damaged my spine. But hey, I'm going to put motors on this chair so I can be independent. Can you help with that?"

"I will provide whatever details you require."

"What did people like me use to get around in before?"

"They did not. A damaged human spine was always repaired, either with micro-filament surgery or vectored gene therapy to regenerate the broken nerves."

I stopped right there in the middle of the corridor and brought my wrist up so I was looking straight at John. "You mean doctors used to be able to fix this sort of injury?" I asked it incredulously.

"Yes."

"There's a medicine machine in our village hospital. It was damaged by the Mutineers so it only makes a few types of medicine now – biotics, painkillers, that kind of thing. Do you think you could tell us how to mend it properly so it makes more – maybe the kind that you said, for nerves?"

"I don't understand," John said. "You say it is a functional pharmalogical processor?"

"We call it a medicine machine. Is that the same thing?'

"I would assume so, yes."

"Okay, well the Mutineers smashed bits of it. They did the same thing to all the village medicine machines."

"Hazel, a pharmalogical processor is a very complex device. If it is physically damaged, it will cease to function entirely. There can be no state where it produces some medicines but not others."

"But that's what it does," I insisted. Even so, I couldn't help a satisfied smile; I'd always thought how oddly convenient that was.

"This is a strange paradox," John said. "A pharmalogical processor cannot operate in this fashion, yet you claim it does."

"Yes."

"If it's not damaged," Frazer said, "what else would make it work like this?"

"Someone would have had to install a prohibition routine in its processors, restricting its output."

"The Mutineers," I said. "It has to be."

"I thought you said the Electric Captain established the villages and the Cycling life after the Mutiny?" John asked.

"She did."

"Paradox," Frazer said flatly, enjoying the word.

"Could you remove the prohibition?" I asked.

"Possibly. It depends on the level of sophistication involved."
"What does that mean?"
"That I cannot guarantee success."
"I don't care. We have to try." I gave Frazer a timid smile. Right then, curing him meant more to me than the air leak.

(8)

About twenty of Alisha's friends turned up for the meeting. I'd met most of them the previous day. They were expecting to talk about the air leak and what we could do about it. Instead they were confronted by John.

The questions they put were quite sweet, almost timid.

"Could the food machines really make any kind of meal?"

Answer: yes. Which is sort of obvious, I thought. If you can build machines that make food, then why wouldn't they make every type?

"Did people travel by canal boat before the Mutiny?"

No. Apparently there's a whole load of underground roads in the habitat, with electric carts that drive themselves. They're fast.

"How fast does *Daedalus* fly?"

Ten per cent of the speed at which light travels. I didn't get that at first, so John went on to explain that light is not instantaneous but *very* fast. The figures he gave were ridiculous. But Dad always said you learn something new every day. So far I'd burned through about ten lifetimes of new, and it was only mid-morning.

"What powers the engines?" Frazer asked that one, of course.

Antimatter, which blows up if it touches ordinary matter, so the explosion pushes the ship along, accelerating it.

"Are there any other arkships?"

Daedalus was the third to leave Earth. Another five arkships were being built when it launched, with more planned. Over a hundred automated explorer starships had been launched in the century before the *Daedalus*, to explore star systems and send back the results. Some carried seeds and eggs, so they could turn empty lifeless worlds into planets like Earth, allowing us to live on them if we ever reached them.

I was watching Frazer when John told us about the other ships. I thought he might cry from happiness. I so got that. Knowing there really are other people out there somewhere, living wondrous, interesting lives, was profoundly reassuring.

"What sort of music did they listen to?"

John surprised me. It didn't just tell us; it played some. Right there on the seventy-ninth floor, looking out over the lush curving landscape, I heard a song from Earth for the very first time. It was written fifteen hundred years ago. I didn't understand half of the words, but you didn't need to – it was about coming home. And the music that accompanied those poignant lyrics was fun and funky and wonderful. It was called "Sweet Home Alabama".

I will never ever forget it. If I practised my guitar every day for a century, I could never play it as well as those musicians from a world lost so far behind us in time and space.

After that John played some orchestral music, which was completely different and utterly awesome in its own way. I wanted to listen to "Sweet Home Alabama" again. And I knew Alice would just love it.

"What is this?" Narline asked in a firm voice. She held out a large whiteleaf on which she'd finished sketching something out in charcoal. Narline is the oldest person in Tressaco – a hundred and fifty nine, which probably makes her the oldest person on *Daedalus*, end of.

I brought my arm up so John could get a proper look at the drawing. Narline's hand shook slightly, but her ancient face had a very determined expression. The question had come out almost as a challenge.

I stared at the image she'd drawn. At first I thought it was a flower, a very elaborate one, with thin petals that ended in long twirling fronds. Then my perspective shifted, and I realized it was supposed to be some kind of animal. It had a bulbous egg-shaped body with curling limbs sticking out around the circumference. I didn't know if they were arms or legs; it looked like they could be either. There were no hands or feet.

"That image is not in my memory," John said.

I could hear a number of sighs from across the room – the only disappointment of the day.

"Are you sure?" Narline said.

"I'm afraid so, yes."

"What is that?" Frazer asked her curiously.

Narline shook her head. John's inability to identify the drawing seemed to be a bitter disappointment. "I saw this picture once," she said. "Over a century ago now, when I was living in Mallux – that's a tower mountain near the forward endwall. A whole row of pictures had been drawn on a wall deep inside. Someone hadn't just tried to wipe them off, they'd practically shredded the wall to get rid of them, but there was enough of this one left to make it out. And underneath whoever drew it had written, 'Yi, type two'."

"I've never seen anything like it in the school's book of animals," I said.

"Nobody has, my dear," Narline said. "That's why I was hoping your new friend here could tell me what it was."

"It may be a work of art," John said.

Narline gave me a look that was almost pitying. "You didn't see that wall. Whoever destroyed it was savage. There were skeletons, too, in the rubble underneath. Very old ones. People who never got Cycled."

"A Mutiny fight," I said.

She shrugged. "Maybe. We'll never know now."

"How do we go about sealing the leak?" Mortos asked.

"I would suggest we find out which command AIs are still functional. If there is a working engineering section, it will have specialist cybots they can deploy to effect repairs," John said. "Once the leak has been stopped then the atmosphere reserve tanks can be opened, and the habitat air returned to standard pressure."

"You mean there's a tank with enough air to refill the whole habitat?" Frazer asked. He sounded very dubious.

"Several, yes. The air is stored in liquid form to reduce volume."

"You can liquidize air?"

"At extremely low temperatures. It is called cryogenics."

"How low?"

"We'll deal with those sort of things later," I said quickly. Frazer would clearly go on asking science questions for years if I gave him the chance. To be honest I was quite interested myself, but we had to prioritise. "How do we find out which of the command AIs is still working?" I asked.

"As the ship's network is no longer operational, I would suggest direct contact."

I felt a little thrill at that, suspecting what John's answer would be to my next question. "Okay. So where are the command AIs?"

"In the forward compartments. The *Daedalus* requires many specialist divisions to maintain it. Each department is divided up into independent sections under the control of a command AI which can be physically sealed in case of emergency. Given the habitat remains intact and functional, one or more must have survived the Mutiny."

"In the forward compartments?" Alisha said. "You mean the ship behind the forward end wall?"

"Yes."

"Cool," Frazer said. "That's where the captain made her last stand. Nobody's been there for five hundred years."

"It was blocked off," Alisha explained.

"Blocked off how?" John asked.

I looked round the room, and all I saw were confused faces. "We don't know," I admitted. "We don't even know where the doors to the front section are anymore."

"I do," John said. "I have full schematics for the ship."

"Can you get us through?"

"It depends on the nature of the barrier. If the doors have been locked electronically, I may be able to open them. If not, I will advise on the best method of breaking through. I do not believe every access route is closed – there are hundreds of secondary corridors and cybot access passages."

"We need support from the villages," Alisha said firmly. "We can't just wander round the end wall looking for a way in. They'd cause all sorts of trouble for us evil Cheaters."

"Surely John is enough to convince people we're doing the right thing?" I queried.

"Hazel, the mayors and Regulators have a vested interest in keeping things just the way they are."

"But the air's running out!"

"We need to have something big, something they can't conveniently ignore while they try to Cycle us. Something that everybody will understand."

"The big electric circuits," Noran said. "Switch the whole of Tressaco back on – lifts, lights, everything."

People were nodding in approval at that. It's not that I didn't want the tower mountain switched on, but my priority was different. And I was John's user.

"Is there a hospital in Tressaco?" I asked John.

"Yes. There is a major medical facility on the twenty-fifth floor and two smaller clinics, one on the second floor, the other on ninety-three."

Everyone had fallen silent, watching me.

"Will they have medical machines that can heal Frazer?"

"They were originally equipped with advanced pharmalogical processors. We would have to discover if they are still functional."

"If Frazer walks back into Ixia, nobody will be able to ignore that," I told everyone. "They'll have to listen."

"Hazel, even if the processors can be reactivated, the therapy will take several days to repair his nerves," John said.

"Fine," I said. "As soon as Frazer has the medicine, we can concentrate on getting the big electricity back on. Hit them with both miracles."

Alisha gave me a sly, admiring smile. "Aye aye, captain's daughter."

The clinic on the ninety-third floor was a wide corridor leading back into the rock of the tower mountain, growing darker the further down you went. John said the rooms on both sides were treatment rooms. I pushed Frazer along with everyone from the meeting following, chatting away eagerly as they shone their torches to light the way. Quite the party. Optimism was contagious.

I'd thought just getting to Tressaco and finding Alisha was amazing, but since then my life had honestly been fantastic.

The fifth room on the left should have a diagnostic scanner, John told us. He was right. There was a large bed in the centre, covered in dust and cobwebs, with a wide semi-circular hoop over it.

"Nothing appears damaged," John said. "Noran, we will need to remove the unit's casings and inspect the power supply. You will have to wire it directly into the induction-strip circuit. There should be enough current."

"I'll get my tools," he said.

While he was gone, we went deeper into the clinic. The fifteenth room had a medicine machine very similar to the one in Ixia. "This will also have to be wired in to the induction strip supply," John said. "Once the processor core has power, I will be able to talk to it directly."

"How come the induction strip still has electricity?" I asked.

"The induction strip has a reserve power feed'" John said. "Its supply cable enters the tower mountain from the grid on the habitat's floor. However, Tressaco's main power supply comes from the primary power grid, which is above us on the sky. It supplies the sunstrips and the irrigation pipe pumps with electricity, so it is obviously functional. I deduce Tressaco's feed has either been switched off or the cables have been cut. Either should be relatively easy to rectify."

"Okay," I said as we wheeled Frazer back to the diagnostic room. "If the power is on, will the machines work properly?"

"They should do. The buildbots use an enhanced molecular alignment process to construct items, which creates a very strong material. All the *Daedalus* systems were built from it so they would remain operational for centuries."

"Like you," I said.

"Like me."

"But not us."

"When *Daedalus* left Earth, genetic techniques had increased the average human lifespan to over a hundred and seventy years."

"We Cycle at sixty-five," I said grimly.

"Hopefully that will end when we bring the *Daedalus* systems back online."

"Oh, I'm going to make very sure of that. Trust me."

Noran returned carrying two bags bulging with practically every tool from his workshop. He and Mortos started removing various panels along the bottom of the bed while the rest of us shone torches on them to illuminate the task. I had to hunch down beside them so John could see what they were doing and issue more instructions. It might have been selfish, but I wasn't going to take the bracelet off so someone else could use it.

"I am unfamiliar with that cabling," John said. "Hazel, please move me closer."

I pushed my arm further into the rectangular hole Mortos had opened while Noran shone his torch in. When I squinted into the gap, I immediately knew what John was talking about. I've seen animal intestines in the abattoir, the way everything is packed together. This was like a geometrical equivalent, with all the machine's glossy components collected in a tight three-dimensional layout. Slim bundles of coloured cables came up through a small circular hole in the floor and split into bands that disappeared into the metallic guts. But there were other cables there as well, slim milky-white strands that coiled round the components in an untidy tangle. It was odd, but they reminded me of plant roots.

"These white fibres are extraneous," John said.

"What do you mean?"

"They are not part of the original machine. I have a small number of sensors, which are showing me they're organic in nature."

"Like a plant?" Frazer asked.

"It would appear so. Their biochemical structure is unusual. I do not know what they are."

"But they're inside the machine," I said.

"Yes. They appear to have grown up through the conduit and followed the main network cabling into the processors. That is strange. I am unable to deduce where they have come from."

"Well, what are they doing?"

"Also unknown. However, from the nature of the infiltration, I would deduce it is not beneficial."

"You mean the Mutineers planted them?"

"Possibly. Noran, I would suggest removing them if possible. Can you try cutting one, please."

"No problem," Noran replied, and picked a very sharp knife out of his tool collection.

I held John as close as I could as the blade sliced through the slim fibre Noran had chosen. A tiny drop of viscous dark yellow liquid glistened on the severed end.

"Definitely organic," John announced, "though the fibre itself seems benign. Noran, please sever the remaining fibres."

I watched him cut through the rope-like frond where it came up from the conduit hole. You'd think he'd been doing it all his life, slicing it as deftly as if he was filleting a fish. His blade was smeared with the yellow liquid when he was finished.

"I'm not sure how that's affected the processors," John said, "but let's see what happens when we boot up. Noran, I now need you to remove the casing on the third yellow block."

Noran began following John's instruction, exposing various terminals inside the machine and attaching lengths of wire to the metal tabs. At the same time, Mortos and Karval started using slender instruments on the room's induction strip, removing the surface to uncover the wiring inside.

Within a quarter of an hour, the diagnostic scanner was wired into a power supply.

"I'm not saying it's dangerous," John said, "but it's probably best if we all stand back while I switch it on."

"How are you going to switch it on?" Noran asked.

"It went into standby mode as soon as we applied power. I can detect that, and I have established a link with its general network node. Here goes."

Small purple lights came on inside the hoop. Then the hoop itself started to move, sliding along the length of the bed, then back again until it was poised at the head.

"It's ready," John announced.

Mortos and I lifted Frazer onto the bed. I noticed the lights in the hoop had changed. Most of them were now green with some ambers, while a couple shone red.

"Is it okay?" I asked.

"There is some impairment, obviously, after so much time inactive," John said. "However, it is seventy-two per cent functional. That is sufficient for this scan."

"What about the fibres? Does it remember who planted them?"

"The scanner processors do not run that kind of AI. It does not think like you or I. However, it has clearly undergone extensive degradation in its processing core. I determine this may be due to the fibre tips breaching its physical integrity. The damaged areas occur primarily around the connection nodes. Its operating routines are compensating as best they can."

"But it won't harm Frazer?" I insisted.

"No. That's not possible."

I stood beside the bed to offer what support I could while the hoop slid down the length of Frazer's body and back again. Frazer didn't even notice I was there, so mesmerized was he by the hoop and its lights. Something about how smoothly it moved, how efficient it was, kindled a great deal of confidence in me. This was from the era of the Builders. And they really knew what they were doing.

"Scan complete," John said. "The damage appears to be treatable."

I couldn't help it – I let out a small sob of relief. Behind me, Alisha and her friends were applauding. Frazer was trying desperately not to show any emotion, but I knew exactly how much hope was rising behind his deadened expression. For a moment, that troubled me – it was such a fragile hope, the opinion of a broken nine-century-old machine. I couldn't bear the idea of that hope being taken from him – and me.

"The diagnostic software has produced a formula for a genetic vector," John said.

"What's that?" I asked wearily. I was more than happy that John thought we could heal Frazer, but I didn't like not understanding all the terms he used, terms which my pre-Mutiny ancestors must have known all about. So why hadn't the Electric Captain made that part of our schooling?

"A genetic vector is the medicine this type of treatment requires," John said. "To produce it, we must now try and restore power to the pharmalogical processor."

We put Frazer back in his chair and everyone trooped along to the room with the pharmalogical processor. This one took a lot longer to wire up to the induction-strip electricity.

John wanted small panels removed from all over the casing. Once the innards of the machine were exposed we could all see the dull white fibres again, more extensive this time and growing up from the conduit hole in the floor as before.

"There must be a lot of this stuff in the conduits," Alisha mused. "Is it a fungus? I know fungus grows in the dark."

I glanced at John, but it remained silent.

It was a long wait but eventually Mortos and Karval and Noran finished doing as John told them. As before, we all stood back while the machine was switched on. We all gasped in surprise and admiration. Half of its surface crawled with strange lines of light. Blocks of green and yellow writing rolled down small screens.

"That's smoke," Frazer exclaimed in alarm, pointing with his good arm.

Sure enough, tiny wisps of smoke were curling up out of a couple of the open panels.

"The electricity is charring the organic fibres," John said. "Don't worry, it was inevitable."

"Is it dangerous?" I asked.

"Only for the fibres. The pharmalogical processor is rebooting."

"What does that mean?" Noran asked.

"The program – its thoughts, if you like – is coming out of storage and returning to the processors which control its functions."

I watched the coloured lines and words as they danced across the machine's surface. It was mesmerizing.

Finally, John said, "The machine is ready. I'm transferring the vector formula to it now."

Nothing happened for several minutes. Then I watched numbly as a small circle opened to reveal an alcove. There was a white collar resting inside.

"Take it out," John told me.

When I picked it up, I was surprised by how light it was. It was also very flexible.

"Put it round Frazer's neck."

I had to stretch it slightly to get it over his head. Frazer tried to focus on it as I tugged it down.

"I am activating it now," John said. "Frazer, it will stick to your skin. Do not be alarmed."

"Okay," Frazer said nervously.

I kept staring at him, holding his gaze as I smiled with a reassurance I didn't really feel. The collar tightened up and he flinched in silence.

"So how does it work, then?" he asked when it was fastened to him.

"It is inserting the vectors into you," John said.

Frazer ran his forefinger around the collar. It moved with his skin, as if it had become part of him. "How does it insert them? I've still got sensation in my neck but I can't feel anything happening."

"Micron-level filaments have penetrated your skin and are feeding the vectors into your blood. When they reach the damaged nerve cells, they will begin to regenerate the impaired sections."

I glanced down at John. "How long will that take?"

"Frazer should begin to regain feeling within a day. It will be mild at first, like a tingling or itch. Regaining full nerve function can take anything up to a week. I would recommend as much rest as possible during this time."

"Okay," Frazer nodded enthusiastically. Then his expression changed. "Oh my dayz, I think I'm going to–" His cheeks bulged. I just managed to push his torso forward in time. He threw up on the floor.

"You may experience some nausea during the treatment," John said.

"No kidding!" I snapped.

"Let's get him home," Alisha said.

We wheeled Frazer back to the lift and down to the sixty-seventh floor. He didn't protest when we lifted him back into bed. Alisha brought a big bowl from the kitchen and some towels.

"I'll sit with him," she said. "You go with Mortos and the others, see if you can switch the big electricity back on."

"Frazer?"

"Go," he said. "I'm fine. And I seriously want to see Tressaco with the electricity working."

I went back to the lift with Noran, Mortos and Karval.

"Where do we go?" I asked John.

"The top floor."

We took it in turns to wind the winch and the platform slid smoothly up the shaft. Once again, I was seriously out of breath when we got to the top.

The hundredth floor was different to the others I'd seen, a place of dark empty rooms with slit windows and long corridors leading back into the heart of the tower mountain.

John guided us down one that didn't seem any different to the others. At the far end was a tall, featureless metal door. Closed.

"Now what?" Karval said. "There are many doors like this in Tressaco. We can never get them open."

"Above the lintel is a small hole," John said. "It is the manual release. One of your screwdrivers should fit."

We all shone our torches at the top of the door. Above it was a small metal circle with a hole in the middle. It must have been over two and a half metres up.

"I can't reach that," Mortos said.

So Noran wound up giving me a piggyback. He tottered up to the door and I tried to shove a screwdriver down the hole. The first one was too big, so Mortos swapped it for a thinner one. I pushed it in until it stopped, then shoved hard like John told me. There was a soft *click*.

"Nothing's happened," I said.

"That was just the lock," John told me.

I got down and watched as Karval and Mortos forced more screwdrivers into the tiny gap down the middle of the door and used them as levers. After they strained away, the two segments finally shifted apart a few centimetres. They could just get their fingers round the edges. I know John said everything on *Daedalus* is built to last, but that door had been shut for five centuries – it was seized up good and proper. Mortos, Karval and Noran tugged and grunted and swore for an age. Eventually they had a half-metre gap, wide enough to squeeze through.

The darkness inside was so profound it even managed to somehow diminish the light from our torches. And the cool air smelt strange too; it was so dry, like it was sucking moisture from my mouth. I hoped the others wouldn't see how intimidated I was.

John called it the power utility management room. It was big, larger than the village hall back in Ixia and twice as high. We walked along aisles between grey cubes taller than me. They had fat black pipes rising from their upper surface to vanish into the deeper darkness shrouding the ceiling.

Right at the centre of the room was a smaller chamber with glass walls. The control centre, John said. Inside that were desks with a multitude of buttons and screens – all dead.

"What do we do?" Noran asked.

"I was expecting the standby systems to be on," John said. "I would have been able to establish a datalink to them."

I had the strangest impression that its voice was sounding sheepish.

"So there's no electricity at all?" Noran asked.

"It may have been cut at the top of the tower, where it branches off the main power grid."

"Can we get up there?"

"There is an access stairwell on this floor. But it is a long climb."

I walked out of the control centre. After John's success with the machines in the clinic, this had come as a severe disappointment. I'd expected to switch on Tressaco and have everyone in the villages see the rooms blazing with light all night long. Then we'd go into the forward compartments. The cybots (whatever they were) would repair the leak and John would open the reserve air tanks. After that, we'd fix everything the Mutineers had wrecked. And with working food machines, there'd be no more Cycling. I would live to see the new world.

Silly how you let dreams take over.

I shone the torch round the silent cubes, turning so it shone across the black pipes, then lifting the beam. "John," I said, my throat suddenly dry and tight. "What's that?"

(9)

There are some facts you don't learn at school, small strands of knowledge that have survived the Mutiny and get passed on, normally within the relevant professions. For instance, Dad told me that walnut wood used to be the most expensive timber on Earth. It's because of the grain pattern, he said. Certainly the bowls and platters our artisan, Jason, crafts are all the richer because of the walnut's elegant texture of whorls and burls.

I'd been with Dad several times when the carpenters cut down a walnut tree. I watched as they sawed through the trunk, then set about lifting the base, where the roots emerge – that's the wood that has the most intricate grain shapes, the part most valued by crafters. The roots flare out from the stump in a completely random fashion, bending and twisting round each other, forking again and again as they spread out.

That same kind of intricate, haphazard tangle was growing out of the power utility management room ceiling, emerging from the central hole where the black pipes vanished. But this growth wasn't brown and grey like walnut roots; it was a sickly white with skin that looked soft, as if it were flesh. The main trunk, just where it came out of the ceiling hole, was as thick as my torso. Then it began to split again and again and again, each frond thinner than the last as they wrapped themselves tenaciously round the black pipes like ivy strands until finally worming their way into the top of the grey boxes.

Mortos, Karval and Noran came out of the control centre, shining their torches up along with mine.

"That's the same as the threads we found in the medical machines," Noran exclaimed.

"But bigger," I replied softly. Something about the growths made me shiver. They weren't *right*. Certainly not in here, this sanctuary of the Builders' perfect engineering.

"Is that what's keeping the power off?" Mortos asked.

"I deduce it is," John said.

"Where's it coming from?" Karval asked. He was craning his neck, trying to look up the hole in the ceiling.

"Above somewhere," Mortos said. "The Mutineers must have planted it at the top of the tower mountain. This is how they shut down the *Daedalus* machines."

I stood on tiptoes so I could see the top of the grey cubes. The white fronds followed the pipes down, then vanished into the casing at the junction. "What's in these cubes?" I asked.

"They house the transformers and secondary distribution circuits," John replied.

"Simpler, please," I chided.

"The high-voltage cables from the main grid above go into them. The power is reduced and divided into smaller cables for each floor and the major utilities."

"So there's more cables coming out of the bottom of each cube, and travelling all the way through the tower mountain?"

"Yes. The conduits form a comprehensive network throughout the tower mountain."

I looked up at the thick white trunk and its chaotic gnarl of strands, the way they divided. "That's how it grew into the clinic," I said. "It follows the power cables. Sweet Captain! It must be *everywhere*."

"But it starts here," Noran said thoughtfully, staring up at the trunk."

"I know that tone," Mortos said. "What are you thinking?"

"That we do here what we did in the two medical machines. Cut through the brute."

"Er... John?" I queried. "Should we do that?"

"You're on a starship that's leaking air, where parents have to suicide so they don't over-consume their children's resources, all because the machines have been sabotaged. What have you got to lose?"

I gave the bracelet a startled glance. That had sounded like anger to me. I hadn't considered that machines could become angry.

Mortos and Karval helped Noran up onto a cube. From there he shimmied along one of the black pipes so he could get close to the white trunk. He brought up the biggest blade from his tool kit and gave us a grim look.

"Do it," I said, fortified by John's attitude.

I was right. The white skin was nothing like as tough as bark. The knife cut in easily just above the first knot. Thick yellow fluid began to dribble out of the slice. Noran set to enthusiastically.

It took him nearly a quarter of an hour, but eventually he hacked and sawed right through the trunk. It wasn't a single growth, rather a bundle of finger-thick fibres. Below the cut, the huge tangle of entwined fronds sagged, individual strands twisting and snapping. The yellow fluid splattered onto the roof of the control room, running slowly down the glass.

Noran slowly clambered down. He was sweating profusely from the exertion and breathing hard, with more of the yellow fluid sticking to his clothes. "That stuff reeks," he complained. "Kind of like salt, or fresh meat. Urrgh." He gave an exaggerated shudder and wrinkled his nose.

"John?" I asked cautiously. "Has it made a difference?"

"Let's go back into the control room."

I gasped as soon as I walked through the door. There were small red lights shining on all the desks. "What does it mean?" I demanded.

"It means the transformer relays are open again. We just have to reset the cut-offs."

I gave the black bracelet an exasperated look. "Once more: what does it mean?"

"It means the electricity is now available. There are switches on the outside of every transformer which have to be manually reset."

"Show us."

The cubes all had a series of five black circles on the side. They didn't light up, but they did change colour when you pressed them. John told us the sequence. First, Standby, which made the others all turn amber. Then Reset, Charge Test. If that turned from amber to green, you ignored Clear and touched Activate. We went round the power utility management room, switching them all back on.

The teachers used to read the Sleeping Beauty book to us at school, which was my absolute top favourite back when I was ten. Switching on the transformers was like the grown-up version. I could hear the cubes start to hum and buzz as the Activate circle turned green. Sometimes when Charge Test went from amber to red, we'd have to press Clear and start again at Standby. There were five cubes that we simply couldn't get going no matter how many times we ran through the sequence. John told us to move on.

As well as the growing noise level, the lights came on before we were even halfway through the task of switching on the cubes. They flickered a pale violet for a few seconds all across the ceiling, then quickly built up to a dazzling white. I had to blink moisture from my eyes, they were so bright. Somehow it made the power utility management room seem warmer. And strangely, safe.

I'd been all nerves when we forced the door open. Now I felt ridiculously confident – Sleeping Beauty was wide awake and happy.

Back in the control centre, all the screens were alive with the kind of writing that had appeared on the pharmalogical machine, but there was a lot more of it and I didn't understand more than one word in ten.

"I have access to the main utility processor array," John said. "The reboot is running."

"So will all the lights come on?" I asked eagerly.

"Now Tressaco has power again, individual systems will have to initiate a full diagnostic review to determine what functions are still valid. Those that have maintenance routines will activate them prior to restoring full operational mode."

I held the bracelet up level with my face. "John."

"Yes?"

"You need to give me shorter, simpler answers, okay?"

"Understood."

"Just until I learn what all your descriptions of machines and how they work mean. Then you can babble on about technology as much as you like."

"Very well. Most of the lights should come on fairly soon."

I winked at the black bracelet. "Thank you."

"The lifts may take a while. Remember how stiff the door into here was? All moving systems are going to be suffering like that. They'll check themselves over and do what they can to get working again."

"And the hospitals and food machines?"

"The same. But unless they're physically damaged, they will return to active status. More thorough repairs will require engineering-department buildbots to fabricate new components and cybots to install them."

"But first we have to fix the leak," I said forcefully.

"Absolutely."

The four of us left the power utility management room. We were all eager to see what was switching on in the rest of the tower mountain. As we left, the door slid shut behind us.

"Did you do that?" I asked John.

"I ordered the door mechanism to bypass its diagnostic routine and just close. Was that basic enough for you?"

"Cheeky," I replied with a grin.

The corridor lights were all on.

"They liked everything really bright, didn't they?" Mortos remarked as we walked back to the lobby.

"Internal lights in all public areas are designed to be as bright as the habitat sunstrips," John said.

"Why?"

"Studies determined that sunlight contributes to human health and happiness."

"Seriously?" I asked.

"Yes."

"The Builders had time to study stuff like that?"

"Yes."

"Wow." Back in Ixia, we barely had time to do anything after work. I was always struggling to find time to practise my guitar, and these people used to wait and watch to see what sunlight did to their body. Incredible.

In the lobby we all turned to the corridor that led back to the lift-platform shaft.

"Wait," John said. "I'm calling a lift for you."

"They're working?" I exclaimed. "Already?"

"Eleven lifts are beyond self-maintenance. Twenty-three are becoming operational. Five are ready for use."

A *ding* sound came from a set of lift doors. They slid open. Things moving automatically was such a buzz for me. I wasn't quite sure what a lift would look like, but it wasn't quite as impressive as I'd been anticipating. The five centuries of grime was to be expected, but the rest – a metallic box of a room four metres to a side, three of the nine ceiling light panels shining? Ah, well.

We went in and the doors shut.

"Now what?" Karval asked.

"Which floor do you require?" the lift asked.

"John! It's just like you," I said.

"It most certainly is not."

Does an artificial intelligence unit have feelings? Can they be hurt? Certainly sounded like it.

Mortos smiled. "Level sixty-five, please."

All of us gasped as the lift floor moved. For one nasty moment, I thought we were shooting down the shaft so fast that we'd take off and slam into the lift's ceiling. Then the floor was shoving up against my feet. The doors dinged and opened.

"I can get used to this in no time at all," Noran announced contentedly.

Frazer swore his sickness had eased. He certainly didn't look so pale. Alisha had propped him up with pillows, but all he looked at was his room's ceiling, where slim curving light strips were laid out like a flower. They glowed with a soft gold radiance that changed the whole room, turning it warm and rich.

"It's amazing," he said. "You did it, Hazel."

"Yeah. Well, John did," I admitted.

"No, it's you," he insisted. "You're the captain's daughter."

That fierce insistence coming from Frazer was unusual, and slightly unnerving. "Not really. We have a lot of grandparents between me and her."

"Hazel. You started this. You brought me here. You had the right blood."

Alisha put her arms round me and hugged tight. "You're a miracle, my dear. An absolute miracle."

I sniffed and had to wipe my eyes. So much dust in the air. "I want to switch everything back on," I told them earnestly. "All the tower mountains, and the buildbots in the forward section. That way everyone can have a machine like John again. Okay?"

"Oh, I believe you," Alisha said wryly.

I told Alisha I could look after Frazer for a while so she could see her friends and find out what else was switching on. She promised to come back with a meal for both of us.

"Hazel, Frazer, I am glad we are together now," John said after she left. "I need to speak to you both. It is urgent."

"What is it?" I asked.

"It concerns the growths we have discovered in the conduits."

"What about them?" I asked.

"They are not terrestrial."

"Simpler," I told him firmly.

"They do not have DNA. My sensor revealed their genetic molecule has a different chemical base. They did not come from Earth. They are alien."

"Alien?" I repeated dumbly. "How could they be alien? The Mutineers planted that stuff. You said so."

"No. I agreed they were the cause of the *Daedalus* being in its current state. I did not mention their origin because I did not want to alarm everyone unduly."

"Well, you're alarming me!"

"You are my user. I have to report my concerns to you."

"Oh, sweet Captain. So did the Mutineers have alien help?"

"I do not know. It is difficult to understand how they obtained such a biological weapon."

"The root thing is a weapon?"

"I believe so, yes. It targets the data network and restricts the electronic processors. That is not something that can evolve naturally. It was designed to do this."

"But how did the Mutineers get an alien weapon?" Frazer asked.

"You said the *Daedalus* arrived at the original planet as planned?" John enquired.

"Yes."

"Then logically, that is where the bioweapon came from."

"But the aliens they found there weren't intelligent," I protested. "That was the whole point of the Mutiny – the Mutineers wanted to go back and claim the planet. So how could they have made this?"

"It is possible that human scientists sympathetic to the Mutineers could have genetically manipulated samples of alien biology," John said. "If so, this bioweapon is their creation."

"It doesn't really matter where the Mutineers got it from now, does it?" Frazer said. "The question is, what do we do about it?"

"It will have to be eliminated in order to restore *Daedalus* to full operational status," John said.

"We can do that," I said. "We've already cut it off from this tower mountain."

"I am concerned by how deeply it has infiltrated the network."

"They were scared of you, those Mutineers," Frazer said. "You can teach us how to deal with the bioweapon. That's why the Mutineers tried to destroy all the independent AIs, and it's why the Loyalists hid you. You're our counter-weapon."

"No," I said. "Not quite. Knowledge is our counter-weapon. That's what the Mutineers were most afraid of."

"You are correct," John said.

I sat with Frazer for most of the afternoon. We talked with John to start with. Learning basics, John said, like how most machines were voice activated even if they weren't AI-level smart. And our heritage – Earth with its ancient national conflicts and eventual unification. How our ancestors' science finally gave them unlimited energy and opened up the resources of the solar system so they could evolve into what they called a post-scarcity civilization – the one that built *Daedalus*.

After a while, Frazer started to doze off – whatever the vector things were doing to his body, they absorbed a lot of his energy to do it – so I curled up on a pile of cushions close to my sleeping brother and listened to John quietly playing more songs from Earth while I tried to absorb every utterly momentous thing that had happened since I arrived in Tressaco. The day had been so overwhelming – my thoughts were like butterflies caged inside my head and it took a long time for them to calm.

We ate in Frazer's room that evening. Alisha and Mortos brought the food in. I could see how tired Frazer was by then, but he managed a boiled egg. When we finished our meal, he was fast asleep.

"Is that normal?" I asked John.

"Perfectly. Don't worry, he will be tired throughout the procedure. It is a good sign."

I tucked the covers up round him and kissed his forehead lightly before leaving. Even though I knew John was smarter than ten of me, I was so scared the treatment wouldn't work. Our hopes were being raised to such a giddy height, any crash now would be devastating.

"Are you all right?" Alisha asked kindly when we were back in the living room. "It's been a phenomenal day."

"It has," I said weakly.

"We've been busy," Mortos said with a huge grin. "There's seventeen lifts working now. We've visited every floor and turned on all the lights in the rooms with a window. Tonight, Tressaco is going to shine across the whole length of the habitat. Twenty villages will see us at least, maybe more."

"That's fantastic," I told him.

There was a party planned. Everyone was going to go outside and celebrate the tower-mountain lights beaming out into the night. "Oh, I can't leave Frazer," I said.

"We'll take it in turns," Mortos said sympathetically. "I'll stay with him now. You go down and see the lights for yourself. The daylight will switch off soon."

Alisha and I walked to the nearest lobby, which had two of its five lifts working. The lift took us down to ground level – *fast*. There were dozens of people hanging round outside the big entrance hallway. Bottles of fruit vodka were being handed round. I took a sip of the raspberry one, which burned its way down my throat and made me feel wide awake. The warmth lingered.

"More?" Alisha asked. She held up another small glass, a wicked smile on her face.

"Maybe just one," I said.

She filled the glass to the top and handed it over.

Standing right beside those gnarled old fruit trees, looking up at Tressaco, the electric lights didn't seem to make any difference. Karval kept looking anxiously at his watch.

"Do you think they'll see it?" I asked Alisha.

"I'm sure they will, yes."

"I really hope so." I drank another of the small glasses. "It's going to be wonderful when everybody sees the lights. They'll know we're right about everything. Nobody will ever be Cycled again. There's a fantastic life right ahead of us."

"Uh-huh," Alisha was giving me a curious look.

"This is good stuff," I told her, and held out my glass so she could refill it.

"It certainly is." She poured out more raspberry vodka. "Why don't you save that for a toast when the daylight goes off?"

"Righty-ho."

Karval gave his watch another glance. "Three minutes."

"I'm going to see Mum and Dad again," I said happily. "But I'm so glad I found you," I told Alisha, and put my arm round her.

"Me too," she agreed.

Karval started calling out how long we had. Then everyone was doing a countdown with him.

I joined in, excited and jubilant. This was a day not even the wildest kind of dream could ever match. "Five. Four. Three. Two. One."

Turns out Karval was a few seconds fast. We waited in breathless silence. Then the daylight switched off, and the moonlight took over.

I stared up at Tressaco, and my jaw dropped. It was amazing. Each floor was like a ribbon of enticing rose-gold light wrapped round the tower mountain. From where we were standing, the windows seemed to reach all the way up to the sky itself, and together they made Tressaco so bright, casting its welcoming radiance across the forest to crown the ancient, noble fruit trees.

I hugged Alisha tight as everyone cheered and drank their toasts. "Sweet Captain, that is so lovely," I exclaimed, and downed my glass in one. "I want to dance!" I shouted. "John, can you give us some music? Music to dance to?"

"I believe so. I can access the audio system in the vestibule to play it for you."

"The what where?"

"The ground-level entrance hall to Tressaco."

"Whatever. That'll do for sure."

I dragged Alisha over to the big vestibule, giggling as I remembered stumbling into it for shelter the night I arrived.

What would poor old Bronwyn make of it now? Admittedly, the lights inside weren't perfect – several were glimmering away in random colours, and some didn't work at all. "Actually, this is perfect for dancing," I decided.

Alisha and I took another drink together, her smile as broad as mine. "I want a good dance song, now," I warned John, "else you'll be back in the water tank."

"I have one I believe to be appropriate."

"Hit it!"

The vestibule's audio system was louder than I was expecting, but that was okay. A song about a dancing queen started playing. Sweet Captain, but I love Earth music. It was fast and exciting, sweeping me along with its easy beat. And I had all the moves for something so lively. Alisha was laughing wildly as she bopped away with me, both of us singing along with the chorus at the top of our voices. And everyone else was joining in, jiving away together. Having the time of your life, just like the song said.

The whole habitat spun round me, and I must have tripped on something. As the song ended I found myself sitting on the floor, Alisha's face looming over me.

"Time for bed," she declared.

(10)

I woke and knew I needed to get to the pharmalogical processor on the ninety-third floor. Fast. I had to get Builder-era medicine to counter whatever was killing me.

I tried to talk but all that came out was a groan.

"Good morning, Hazel," John said.

I peered at the black bracelet on my wrist. "What happened?" I croaked.

"Alisha and Noran brought you home."

"I don't remember."

"That is because alcohol disrupted your primary neural functions."

"What?"

"You were drunk."

"No. I only had a couple of glasses."

"You had seven."

"Really?"

"Yes. In a very short period of time. Your blood-alcohol content spiked at point zero nine."

I winced as I raised my head. "Is that bad?"

"I am still gathering data on your basic metabolic levels, but to summarise, yes."

"How do I make my head stop hurting?"

"Fluid, vitamin C, and I'd suggest a shower as well."

"What's vitamin C?"

"Plenty of orange juice, basically. If we visit the pharmalogical processor, I can get it to synthesize some aspirin. Or a more traditional hangover cure is a large fried breakfast."

I made it to the bathroom just in time.

* * *

Alisha and Mortos were ready with sympathetic smiles when I walked into the living room. There was a large glass of orange juice standing on the table.

"For you," Alisha said, giving it a grand gesture.

"Thank you." My hand was trembling slightly as I picked it up.

"How are you feeling?" Mortos asked.

"Better now I've had a shower," I admitted. Actually, it had been a huge step up. Standing under water warmed to perfect body temperature, it seemed to be washing the alcohol out of me. And it didn't just sprinkle out of the nozzle like before; now the plumbing pumps were working, the little jets positively fired out as if they were trying to push me onto the floor.

I gulped down some of the orange. "I'm really sorry."

"What for?" Alisha asked. "We were just partying. After all you've done, there was shipload to celebrate. Even Narline was dancing, and her arthritis plays up badly."

"The raspberry drink. I didn't realize."

"Yeah, it's a killer, that one. Tastes good, though. And you needed to loosen up, my girl. It was a hell of a day."

I wanted to ask if she really was Dad's grandmother. Clearly not all attitudes were transferred down the generations by DNA.

"You need to go and see Frazer," she said firmly when I finished the juice.

"Oh, sweet Captain, yes!" How could I have forgotten that? I'm never going to drink again, even if I live to be two hundred.

He was sitting up when I went into his room. "What's the matter?" I asked. His expression was unreadable, even for me. And *oh*, do I know my brother.

"They're there," he whispered.

"What are?"

"My toes. Hazel, I can feel them. They really itch. And look!"

I stared at his feet. His big toe moved. Not much, a slight bend, but it moved!

"Did you do that?" I gasped.

"Yes." His lips scrunched up, and tears leaked out of his eyes.

I flung my arms round him. "We did it! John, did you see that? Did you see?"

"I saw."

"Oh, thank you! Thank you. Thank you, so much!"

"It was a simple process. I merely–"

"Shut up and take the praise," I told him happily.

"Well... if you insist."

Artificial intelligence does have feelings. Really.

I stayed with Frazer for half an hour. It was amazing – we could practically see his body recovering. He was joyous as he told me the feeling was creeping back across his left hand. Then I had to hold back tears as he started to move his fingers again. He couldn't clench his fist or anything, not immediately, but he really was healing. The vector-medicine stuff worked.

By the time Alisha came in, he could flex every toe.

"I never dreamed that even the Builders could accomplish something this wonderful," she said.

"Everyone will have to listen to us now," I said proudly. "Are they coming yet?" Alisha's friends had been on lookout ever since the daylight switched on.

"Not yet," she said. "Which just gives us time to find you something decent to wear before they arrive."

"Oh, right." After everything else that had happened, I'd clean forgotten about the clothes – and I'd been looking forward to seeing them. I turned to Frazer, but he'd dozed off again.

We took a lift up to the seventy-first floor. Alisha led me into one of the homes.

I thought she'd been exaggerating about the stockpile of clothes. She wasn't. They were using the rooms as a giant wardrobe for all the pre-Mutiny clothes they'd found. There were piles on the chairs, on the tables. Then they'd run out of furniture and just started building big piles on the floor, which had merged together.

"We tried to sort them out at the start," Alisha said sheepishly, "but there were so many."

"Sweet Captain," I groaned. My hands were stroking the mounds of fabric. I picked up a tiny black dress that was all glitter. At first I thought it was for a child, but then I saw how it stretched, and the cut. I blushed at how revealing it would be.

A one-sleeve asymmetric dress in intense sapphire, which was delectably slinky – I wished I had the courage to wear *that* to an invitation dance. A scarlet skirt so vivid that none of our berry dyes could ever come close to such a colour. Long skirts, short skirts, dresses, blouses with and without sleeves, fabrics in a hundred textures and every colour imaginable, bold geometric prints, simple prints, trousers, shorts, boots...

"Oh, wow," I whispered. The *shoes!* The shoes were crazy. Some of them had heels that were little more than spikes, five, ten centimetres high. I didn't even know how you could stand up in them, but I really wanted to try. "Are they real?" I asked John.

"Completely. Some were considered extremely fashionable."

"Which ones?"

"Fashion is subjective. It can take time to build a style which suits you."

I grinned at Alisha. "I have to bring Alice up here."

"You will. But for now, what do you want to try on first?"

The next hour was dressing-up time. I knew I'd never wear them in public, but I had to try on some of the really fancy dresses – the asymmetric one for a start. John said the small ones were cocktail dresses – I had to make him explain what that meant. Elizabeth Bennet never went to a casual event like that, but I thought they sounded quite fun. Then I needed more explanations about the difference between ball gowns, party frocks, formal evening dress, work suits... I found a more ordinary looking deep-purple dress with emerald sides that fitted perfectly. I gave it a sad glance in the mirror. "It's a bit short," I said. The mock-ragged hem didn't come down as far as my knees.

"Don't play the modesty routine," Alisha said firmly. "You look great in that and you know it."

"But–"

"You're the captain's daughter. You're about to be the centre of attention for the whole habitat. Dress exactly as you deserve to dress. Be striking! Be bold!"

"Okay."

Alisha can be quite formidable at times.

We found a black jacket to go with the dress. It was like leather but thinner and lighter. Whatever the fabric was, it flowed like silk. When I looked at myself in the mirror, I couldn't help smiling.

"You look very elegant," John said.

"Thank you."

"We need some shoes to match," Alisha said thoughtfully. "Nothing too fancy. Perhaps some ankle boots."

Just as we turned to go through one of the shoe mountains, Noran hurried in. "Someone's coming," he announced.

Everyone turned out to form a welcome committee along the edge of the harbour pool. Caylin had seen the man heading towards Tressaco, jogging along the canal path.

"Just one?" Alisha asked her in a puzzled tone.

"That's all I saw."

"Probably really keen to know what's happening," Karval said. "Wants to be first."

"Or they're being cautious," Narline said. "Something like this is going to be pretty momentous for the villages. I bet they were up all last night wondering what to do about the lights."

I tried to picture Mayor Fininen being decisive and failed spectacularly.

Ducks along the canal began to flap their wings, scooting away from the bank, calling out in alarm. The running man came into view. I frowned. He seemed familiar.

"He looks exhausted," Alisha said.

The runner caught sight of us and staggered to a halt twenty metres away, panting heavily, his ebony hair stuck to his sweat-soaked forehead. Even his small beard was damp and flattened. He stared forward in confusion; clearly the last thing he'd been expecting was a big group of elderly people to be waiting calmly for him.

I peered at him, then took a couple of paces forward. "Rell?" I croaked. "Rell, is that you?"

Rell gave me the strangest look, like he couldn't believe what he was seeing, yet delighted to see it at the same time. "Hazel?"

"Rell!" I just ran at him.

He opened his arms and I hit him full on.

"You *did* come to visit me!" I gasped. My voice was all shaky and my vision blurred.

His arms hugged me tight, and it felt utterly wonderful. "You're okay," he sounded so surprised. "I was really scared when I heard what you'd done."

"Oh, Rell, I'm so much more than okay."

He looked me up and down. "You look sensational," he blurted.

I blushed and grinned at the same time – and Frazer always claimed I couldn't multitask.

We kissed. Right there in front of everybody. I didn't care. Rell had come to see me, just like he promised he would in his letter (yes, I kept it). He cared. He really did.

I broke off and scowled at him. "You took your time. Where've you been?"

"I'm sorry."

I looked back over my shoulder. Everyone was watching us intently. And there was Alisha out in front, a huge smug smile on her face.

"Ah..." My blush returned even hotter. I cleared my throat. "Everyone, this is Rell. Rell, this is Alisha, my great-grandmother. And this is Noran, and–"

"Hazel," he gripped my arm. "I'm sorry, but we have to go. Now!"

"What?"

"You have to leave here. Everyone does. They're right behind me."

"Who's right behind you?" Alisha demanded.

"The Regulators."

"That doesn't matter anymore," I told him brightly. "We've changed everything." I held up my arm, ready to show off John.

"You don't understand," Rell said. "The Electric Captain appeared on the screen yesterday afternoon. You're not just Cheaters anymore. She declared everyone living in Tressaco to be a Mutineer, including you and Frazer. The Regulators have orders to bring you in and Cycle you. All of you."

I shook Frazer awake. "What's up?" he mumbled.

"We're in trouble," I told him.

"What? Who's that?"

"This is Rell. He came to warn me – us."

"Rell? Oh, Rell, as in the Rell you grabbed at the dance?"

How the hell did Frazer know that? *Alice!*

"Hi," Rell said.

"Yes, that Rell," I conceded, and my cheeks turned all hot again. Frazer sniggered.

"The Regulators are coming," Rell said.

"That's great," Frazer said. "We can show them what we've done."

"No, it's very not great," I told him. "They're going to Cycle us because of what we've done. The Electric Captain declared us Mutineers."

"She can't do that."

"She did do that," Rell said. "Not just on Ixia's screen but all of them. The Regulators from five villages have joined together. Their chiefs also deputized another hundred and fifty men to help. They're going to search every room on every floor in Tressaco to find you. Do you understand? They will not stop until they have captured everybody."

"That's going to be difficult," Frazer said. "Tressaco is big. They'll give up and go home by tonight."

"No," Rell said. "I've never seen people so agitated. Chief Atov and his deputy are obsessed with this. It is personal for them – they won't rest until they have you and Hazel Blessed on the Cycling platform."

"It's going to be difficult," Frazer repeated firmly, "because they don't know how many people are here."

"Oh."

"Do they?"

"No," Rell admitted. "I was surprised myself when I saw so many Cheaters."

"Nobody is a Cheater, Rell," I said. "Cycling is wrong. I'm going to stop it."

He gave me a desperate look. "How?"

"We'll repair the food machines along with everything else on *Daedalus*, everything the *real* Mutineers took from us."

"Hazel–" Rell began.

He was going to be kind, I could tell. Explain to me how that was just a stupid dream, how I had to concentrate on saving myself.

"No," I snapped. "I will. We've already switched Tressaco back on, or hadn't you noticed?"

He gave me that endearing smile of his. "Every village in this section of the habitat noticed that last night. It caused a lot of arguments, I can tell you. I was there when your parents stood up in the Village Hall and denounced the Electric Captain."

"What happened?" Frazer asked breathlessly.

Rell shrugged. "They split the village. A lot of people supported them. In the end, Chief Atov ordered them to be locked up. That's when Tanari hit him."

"She did?" I asked. Actually, I wasn't that surprised.

"Yes. So she got locked up, too. I think there's about ten of them in the cells. After that, a lot of the men refused to be deputized, which is why Atov had to turn to the other villages for help."

"Did they lock up Alice?" Frazer asked.

Rell grinned. "Oh, yes. Right after she kicked Elijah."

I laughed in delight. "That's Alice."

Alisha came in and looked at us all in surprise. "I don't know why you three are so happy. Caylin has seen the Regulators. She says there's about a hundred of them. They're in two groups, coming along both canal paths. We've only got a few minutes to get away."

"That's wrong," Rell said. "Atov had assembled nearly two hundred men when I left Ixia."

"The missing ones will be spread out in the woods," Alisha said grimly. "Waiting for us to run."

"Smart move," Frazer said.

I looked at Rell, holding his gaze as I raised my arm. "John, we need to get everyone out of Tressaco without using the forest. Are there any alternative routes?"

"Yes. The lifts can take you down to the subway stations. The tunnels lead to the other mountain towers and park stations."

Rell froze in shock, staring at the black bracelet.

I licked my lips, enjoying his incomprehension. "Thank you, John. Can you stop the Regulators from taking the lifts down there?"

"Once everyone has reached the stations, I can issue a general shutdown order to the lift-control network. That should work."

"Who?" Rell asked weakly, pointing at the bracelet.

"Oh," I said as nonchalantly as possible. "Rell, this is John. He's my personal link to the *Daedalus* machinery."

"Where is he?"

"I am this unit," John responded.

"And he only works for Hazel," Frazer said maliciously. "Wanna know why?"

"Uh. Yes."

"Because she's a direct descendant of Captain Ashleigh Kruger."

"What?"

"That is correct," John said.

"Okay, boys," I said. "Stop ganging up on Rell. He came here to warn us, remember." I offered him a kind smile, but he was still staring at me in dumb wonder. "And you – snap out of it. Get Frazer into his chair, please. We really need to move."

"That chair," Frazer said helpfully, pointing.

"What do we take?" I asked Alisha.

"You," she said bluntly. "You are the most important person in *Daedalus* now. You have to be kept safe. Nothing else matters."

"Okay." I realized I was still in my fancy purple-and-green dress. "Give me a minute. I'll meet you by the lifts."

I dashed back to my room. No time to change, but I stuffed my more practical clothes into my bag and turned to leave. The crossbow was propped up against the wall. I grabbed it and ran for the lifts.

I heard voices as I sprinted along the corridor – angry shouting voices up ahead. One of them struck me like I'd run into an invisible wall. I staggered to a halt.

Elijah!

"No," I whispered fearfully.

"What's the matter?" John asked.

"That's Elijah, the deputy Regulator from Ixia. He hates me."

The lights went out, and I was back in the same darkness I'd known that first night we'd arrived.

"What just happened?" I grunted.

"I switched the corridor lights off," John said. "He won't be able to see you now."

I stood perfectly still, listening to that horrible voice.

"Where is she?" Elijah demanded.

"Who?" Frazer replied, as insolent as only he could be.

There was the sound of flesh striking flesh.

"You leave that child alone!" Alisha yelled. "What kind of filth are you? Hitting an invalid."

"Hauer, cover the old cow," Elijah snarled. "If she says another word, shoot her."

"Yes, sir," Hauer said.

"Now don't you smartmouth me again, boy," Elijah shouted. "You think we're stupid? Then how come we're here, huh? My advance party came through the trees. We got here before the daylight came on. I knew you'd try to run as soon as you saw the main party arrive. And you, traitor! You warned them."

"Traitor to what?" Rell asked.

I brought the crossbow up and started to creep forward.

"Traitor to the Electric Captain."

"She's not the real captain of *Daedalus*, not anymore," Mortos said. "Hazel is."

"Guano-eating Mutineer," Elijah said, but he sounded shocked at the heresy Mortos had spoken.

Up ahead, the light of the lobby shone down the corridor. I could see them all by the lift doors. Frazer in his chair with Rell standing behind him. Mortos and Alisha holding hands together. Elijah, Hauer and another Regulator, all pointing their pistols at them. They were only a couple of metres apart. At that distance, a shot would be fatal.

I could probably shoot Elijah with the crossbow. Probably. I've only ever used one a couple of times. Dad thought me missing the practice target was very funny.

Even if I crept a little closer and did hit him, the other two would fire a barrage of pistol shots down the corridor.

"What do I do?" I asked John frantically.

"From a tactical viewpoint, we are at a disadvantage."

"No kidding," I snarked.

"We need reinforcements."

"But we can't *get* reinforcements. Everyone's running. I don't even know where Karval and Noran are. By the time I do find them, the rest of the Regulators will be here. And we don't have any pistols, either."

"That wasn't the reinforcements I was considering. One moment."

"Now tell me," Elijah snapped. "Where is your sister?"

I lined the crossbow up on him, taking soft steps forward. He was *not* going to hurt Frazer.

"They're ready," John said quietly. "Almost sixty per cent activation achieved."

"Who's ready?"

Along the corridor, small doors slid open. I'd never even noticed them before – they were flush with the wall and the same colour. Cylinders rolled out, barely a metre high, with a smooth metal casing. There must have been ten of them trundling silently across the corridor floor.

"What are those?" I hissed.

"Cleaning cybots."

"Cleaning?" I spluttered. "You mean they wash up?"

"They suck up dust and remove general litter. They also polish surfaces."

"What the guanoing use are they?" I growled at him.

"Hazel, think. The Regulators don't know what they are. To them, the cybots are anything they say they are."

"Oh. Yes. Right."

"Last chance," Elijah said, and jabbed his pistol's muzzle against Frazer's forehead. "Where is she?"

The lights in the lift lobby began to dim. Elijah glanced up at the ceiling. As the lights finally went out, all the cleaning cybots moved forwards at once. Strange slender beams of light flashed out from them; they were an incredibly dense ruby red, and they sparkled as they cut through the air.

"We are Tressaco law-enforcement machines," the lead one said in a guttural voice. "Unauthorized weapons detected."

As they slid silently into the darkened lift lobby, their red beams opened out into fans and swept up and down the startled Regulators. "Weapons confirmed."

"No, no!" a badly startled Elijah shouted. "We're Regulators. We're allowed weapons."

"Negative. You are not authorized. Cease and desist. Put your weapons down." More beams aligned themselves on Elijah as the cybots encircled the Regulators.

"No. You don't understand. These people, they're Mutineers. We're here to arrest them."

"You have ten seconds to comply."

"But... but... the Electric Captain ordered this!" Elijah shouted furiously.

"Authority not recognized. Put down your weapons or we will use deadly force."

Hauer dropped his pistol and put his hands up. A cybot slid forward; it rocked about as it rode over the pistol. Loud metallic crunching noises filled the lift lobby and it shook violently. Then it was still.

"Weapon neutralized."

Seven red beams were now concentrating on Elijah's face. He was squinting into the powerful light. "No!" he yelled, and fired at a cybot.

The dart made a dull clanging sound as it ricocheted off its casing. Everyone ducked.

"Terminate the criminal weapon carrier."

"All right! Stop!" Elijah said. "Okay. Putting it down now. Look. See? Down." He lowered his arm and let his pistol fall to the floor. The remaining armed Regulator did the same.

Cybots rolled over their pistols. The crunching sounds burst out again.

"These people are criminals," Elijah said desperately. "You're law enforcement. You have to arrest them."

The overhead lights came back on – dazzlingly bright. Elijah winced, blinking furiously. Then he focused on the crossbow that was now being held ten centimetres from his face. He looked behind it and saw my expression. His whole body tensed in fright.

"You!"

"Me," I replied icily.

"She has a weapon!" he cried out. "She's not authorized. Stop her!"

Nothing happened. He glanced down in confusion at the stationary cybots ranged around him.

"The captain's daughter is authorized to do whatever she likes," a cybot said.

I smirked. "Oops. And Elijah, the next time you threaten my brother... that will be the last thing you ever do."

"I will find you," he growled. "You can't hide, not forever. However long it takes, I will find you. Justice will be done."

"Lift doors: open, please," I said.

Out of the corner of my eye I saw them side apart. Hauer gave them a bewildered look, which he transferred to me. "Captain's daughter?" he asked.

"My sister," Frazer said. "And don't you forget it."

"Let's go," I said.

I kept the crossbow levelled on Elijah's head as we went in. At my side, Frazer waved – using his left arm. Elijah frowned.

"Subway station level," I said.

The lift doors slid shut.

(11)

Everyone started talking at once. I sagged against the wall and my knees gave out. I slithered down. "Oh, sweet Captain!" I gulped. The crossbow dropped from my numb fingers. I couldn't believe what I'd done, the way I'd faced Elijah down.

Alisha crouched down beside me, giving me a hug. "It's okay," she said soothingly. "It's over now. You did good."

"Good?" Frazer exclaimed. "Oh my dayz, Hazel, that was fantastic! John, did you get the law-enforcement machine things working?"

"I did."

"Are there any more of them? We could maybe use them to arrest all the Regulators."

"That will not be possible. They are actually cleaning machines."

Frazer gave a delighted laugh. "Brilliant."

Alisha waved him silent. "Take a breath, sweetheart. Come on. Deep breath now."

I pulled air down into my lungs, as she said. My body spasmed as if I hadn't tasted air for a week. My vision blurred as water filled my eyes.

"I thought he was going to shoot you!" I blabbed. "I was so *scared*."

"*You* were scared?" Frazer exclaimed.

"What the sweet Captain is wrong with that man?" Rell asked. "He seemed… I don't know. Obsessed."

I sucked down another breath. "I told you back at the dance, remember? His brother…"

"Yeah, but – wow."

"I know."

"Zawn isn't so bad," Frazer said. "Quite nice, actually."

I gave him an evil look, which he didn't even notice.

"After what just happened, Elijah is going to be real trouble," Alisha said. "That is one twisted mind."

"I'm sorry."

"Hey." She kissed my forehead. "It's not your fault."

Which wasn't being entirely honest, but I did appreciate it.

The lift slowed and the doors dinged as they opened. Alisha and Mortos helped me to my feet again.

We came out into some kind of hall. The ceiling was low compared to how long the place was – it must have been over a hundred metres from end to end – and the lighting was strangely blue. There were four big archways in the wall opposite us with signs above them: BLUE LINE FORWARD. RADIAL LOOP NINE SPINWARD. BLUE LINE AFT. RADIAL LOOP NINE ANTISPINWARD. Each arch opened onto a set of broad stairs leading down.

"Where do we go?" I asked John. I couldn't muster much enthusiasm. In truth, all I wanted to do was stop everything and go home. I wanted Mum and Dad, their hugs and support. An hour ago, we'd all known we'd return to the villages in triumph and repair the Swirl hole. Now I was running for my life.

"Blue Line Forward," he replied.

"What about everyone else in Tressaco?" Alisha said.

"The lifts are still working," John said. "They will be able to reach subway stations. If they are quick."

I wondered if I was the only one who caught the doubt in his tone.

"How many stations does Tressaco have?" I asked, glancing back at the four lifts.

"Eight."

"Switch these lifts off. We can't let Elijah follow us down here."

"Confirmed."

Rell pushed Frazer's chair over the grimy hall floor to the Blue Line Forward arch.

"How did Elijah get up to our floor?" I asked. It was starting to bother me. A lot. "He said he arrived before daylight."

"He's a smart one, that Regulator," Alisha said. "I don't suppose it's too difficult to work the lifts out."

"But Tressaco has a hundred floors. How did he know which one I was on?"

"Everyone knows where my home is," Alisha said sadly. "All he had to do was ask someone while he was threatening them with those nasty pistols Regulators are always waving round. That's not the kind of thing that many of us could resist."

"I suppose not," I agreed, though I couldn't see Narline ever telling Elijah anything, no matter what he threatened her with.

"The lifts have reactivated," John announced.

"What!?" I spun round. All that registered was the trail the chair wheels and our footprints had left in the grime, from the lift doors to us as we stood at the top of the Blue Line Forward stairs. "Oh, sweet Captain. Why have they come on again?"

"The lift-control network restarted them. It must have interpreted my shutdown instruction as an error."

"Well... shut them down again. Use a better instruction this time."

"Confirmed."

I stared at the tracks on the floor. Nothing in *Daedalus* had ever seemed so incriminating. If Elijah got down here – actually, make that *when*, because he was never going to give up, not now, even if he had to run down every flight of stairs. He'd know exactly where we went. And we'd never be able to stay ahead of him, not with Frazer.

"Are there any cleaning cybots down here?" Frazer asked. He was staring at the tracks too.

"Yes."

"Activate all of them. Get this floor cleaned."

"Yes, do that," I exclaimed. "Good idea, Frazer."

My dear brother gave me a pitying look as Rell and Mortos lifted him out of his chair and started to carry him down the stairs. Alisha and I picked up the chair and followed. I saw a line of cleaning cybots snaking their way over the hall floor.

The stairs must have taken us down another twenty metres. It was slightly unnerving; for a start, I had no idea how far down the lifts had brought us.

"John?"

"Yes, Hazel?"

"How thick is the habitat floor? You know, till you reach space."

"Two thousand one hundred metres."

"Ah, okay." So I stopped worrying about being near the outer shell and putting my foot through into space and nonsense like that.

There was another wide corridor at the bottom. It was fifteen metres long, ending in a slab of metal.

"That is the emergency door," John said.

"Why is it shut?" Rell asked.

"Unknown, but all contingencies were planned for. The station and tunnel could be in vacuum, or flooded. There may have been a fight during the Mutiny. Or it may have been closed simply to deny your post-Mutiny society access to the subway lines."

"Can you tell what's behind it?"

"No."

I blew out a long breath and glanced at the others. "Can you open it?"

"There is power to the actuators, so yes."

"What do we do?" I asked, fearful of what might be on the other side. I glanced back at the stairs. A trio of cleaning bots had emerged from their small doors in the wall to start scouring the grime off the floor, and our tracks with it.

"We really don't have a choice," Rell said.

Alisha and Mortos looked at each other and shrugged. "Do it," Alisha said.

"Okay. John, open the door, please."

"Very well. I suggest you get ready to run."

There were some large clunks from the metal.

"What was that?" Rell asked nervously.

"Lock mechanism disengaging," John said. "The actuators are now drawing power."

I stared at the door, which was obstinately refusing to budge. Then I jumped in shock as it emitted a tortured groaning sound.

"Did it just move?" Frazer asked.

"I don't think so," Mortos said.

"Yes, it did," Rell said.

"John?" I asked.

"The actuators indicate they retracted one point three centimetres."

"Really?"

The door yowled in protest again. This time I caught the movement.

"It's working," I said.

"Any water coming through?" Rell asked, looking up and down urgently.

"No."

"What about air being sucked in?"

"Nothing."

A constant low growling began, and the door started to slide open slowly – very slowly. A black crack appeared along one side. I braced myself.

No flood of water. No air being ripped away.

I let out a relieved breath.

"The lifts are working again," John said.

"*How*?"

"The control system is continually overriding my instructions. I am trying to access a deeper level of its management routines and load a shutdown order."

"John, just stop them!"

"Working on that."

The noise from the door was increasing. It slid another few centimetres.

"There is another set of instructions entering the lift-control system," John said.

"What do you mean?"

"Something else is sending instructions into the control system to counter mine."

"Something else? What something?"

"The Electric Captain," Frazer said.

We all looked at him.

He shrugged. "Well, who else? She's the one who declared us Mutineers and sent the Regulators after us."

The emergency door had opened maybe ten centimetres – not wide enough for me to slip through, and certainly not big enough for Frazer's chair. The gap was growing, but agonizingly slowly. I gripped the crossbow anxiously.

"Now what?" I asked.

"There is one other override I can try," John said.

"Do it!"

A piercing wail started up. Half of the ceiling lights started to flash a garish red. And somehow it was raining – underground. Cold water came pouring down from above. I was soaked in seconds.

"Sweet Captain!" I shouted above the racket. "What is that?"

"I triggered the Tressaco general fire alarm," John replied. "It takes priority over everything that's hardwired in to the whole network. The lifts will all shut down and open at whatever floor they've reached."

"Nice work!" Rell yelled.

I stood there next to the emergency door as it crept open, all hunched up against the icy deluge; my black jacket was waterproof but the water was still running down my neck. I started to shiver from the cold. Water was sloshing all over the floor. At least we wouldn't have to worry about tracks any more.

The red light vanished. The terrible sound cut off. The water stopped.

"Let me guess," Frazer said. "The Electric Captain switched off the fire alarm?"

"Correct," John said. "However, the lifts did stop. It will take a little while for them to resume operation. We must hurry."

"I think I can get through now," I said. The gap was just wide enough. It was pitch black on the other side, which was daunting. There was just no way of knowing what waited for me – I guess I'm not quite the intrepid explorer I thought I was. I opened my bag to take out the torch. At least the clothes inside were reasonably dry.

The door was still complaining with screeching sounds as it continued its sluggish slide open. I hadn't realized it was so thick – more than a metre. I had to squeeze into the gap, with the metal squashed up against my chest and face, the rim hard against my back. It kindled a wickedly strong claustrophobia.

"Can the Electric Captain make this door close, do you think?" Frazer asked.

I squealed and wriggled frantically to get through. Came stumbling out on the other side and nearly fell, my legs were so shaky. "Frazer, you complete guano-for-brains! That's not funny!"

"What did I say?"

"Idiot." I heaved down a breath and switched on the torch. The corridor continued to an archway twenty metres away. "Nothing here," I called back. The door was still moving. It seemed to be slightly quieter now. Then it emitted a nasty crack and stopped moving altogether.

"The actuators have switched off," John said. "They were overheating from the strain. Their safety limiters cut in."

I just knew it wasn't wide enough for Frazer's chair. "You have to come through," I said. "It's not going to open any more."

Alisha forced her way past the huge metal slab, muttering all the way. "The lifts have started again," John said.

"Hurry," I called.

Mortos came next, holding on to Frazer, with Rell on his other side. Between them they hauled Frazer through.

"Can you shut it?" I asked John.

"I can reset the limiters," he said. "One moment."

In the silence, I heard the faint *ding* of a lift opening. "They're here," I whispered.

The Regulators would only be able to squeeze through the gap one at a time. And if we assaulted the first one, they'd realize how bad their position was. But that would mean one of us staying here and dealing with anyone that came through the gap. That wasn't good. I didn't know if I could actually fire the crossbow at a person – Elijah, yes, no problem, but the others? Besides, they were in the wrong, they just didn't know it yet. When this was over, everybody in *Daedalus* would have to come together. If we wound up shooting Regulators with crossbow bolts, that healing would never happen. There would be too much anger and hatred to overcome.

"Closing," John said.

"Wait–"

The door resumed its harsh snarling. I stamped my foot in aggravation – that would lead the Regulators straight to us. The door began to close, moving a lot quicker than it had when it was going the other way.

"Here!" Elijah was yelling. "This way. Come on."

I peered through the shrinking gap. Elijah and several other men came racing down the stairs. He saw the door closing and roared in anger, sprinting forwards towards me. The gap was too small now, and he knew it. He brought a pistol up, firing wildly at the gap.

I jumped out of the way fast as darts slammed into the wall. Then the gap closed, leaving us in silence. I knew he'd be pounding on the metal in frustration. That made me smile.

"I have done my best to disable the actuators," John said. "I believe they shorted out."

"Thank you," I said.

Mortos hoisted Frazer onto Rell's back.

"Can you manage?" I asked. I worried about the weight. Frazer's young, yes, but he's almost my height. Giving him a piggyback for a couple of minutes is fine, but the forward endwall was twenty-seven kilometres away, and that's if you go in a straight line.

"Easy," Rell said.

He was lying, and I admired him for that.

We walked down the corridor, shining our torches ahead. It opened out into what John told us was the station, a cylindrical chamber with a platform along one side. Both ends had a tunnel mouth. I expected them to be completely dark, but there was a row of tiny blue-green lights along their apex, spaced several metres apart. The meagre glow illuminated the stream of dank water running along the floor of the tunnel.

"Did we restore electricity to the tunnel lights as well?" I asked.

"No," John said. "They are the secondary lights, which are on a completely different circuit to Tressaco. They must have come on when the emergency doors were shut originally."

"They've been on the whole time?" I asked through chattering teeth. "Five hundred years?"

"It would appear so. It is a shame the drain pumps are not equally active."

"Yes." I eyed the water below the platform, not liking the idea of having to walk through it. Still, at least it didn't look too deep, maybe ten centimetres.

"I'm just going to put some dry clothes on," I said. Four resentful faces turned to look at me. "Won't be a moment." I scurried along the platform and stripped out of the jacket and the soaking dress.

Back in my deerskin trousers and purple shirt, I felt a lot more confident about tackling the tunnel and getting into the forward compartments. I put the jacket back on and stuffed the dress into my backpack.

"They're working faster," Frazer said when I went back to him.

"What are?"

"The vectors. I can feel how cold my legs are, and look." He moved his ankle.

"That's brilliant." I squeezed his hand.

"That is extraordinary," Rell said. "I talked to your doctor, Marana. She said the damage was permanent."

"She never said that to me," Frazer exclaimed.

"Of course not," Alisha said. "She's a doctor. They need patients to keep a positive mental attitude."

"True. That's the first thing they teach trainees," Rell said with a grin. His humour faded. "It really hurts me to think that every medicine machine can produce these vector things. How could this happen?"

"That's something I'm starting to question very hard," Alisha said. "The more I think about it, the less sense the Mutiny makes."

"And why did the Electric Captain declare us Mutineers?" I asked. "That's what I don't understand."

"The Electric Captain is a program," John said. "A less adaptive one than me, I suspect. It has one job – to maintain the status quo in the habitat. We changed that when we switched Tressaco back on. So the program responds by running down its list of options and selecting the one which it determines will accomplish the task of restoring equilibrium with the smallest amount of energy expended."

"But the Electric Captain didn't respond when people saw Tressaco's lights were back on," I said. "Rell, you said she was on the screens yesterday afternoon, right?"

"Yes. I'd arrived in Ixia the previous evening. I had to spend a couple of hours with Chief Atov convincing him I didn't know where you were. Then the next morning I met your parents and Marana. The Electric Captain appeared on the screen after lunch and told us that you and Frazer were in Tressaco with the Cheaters."

"How did she know that?" I asked uneasily.

"There may still be sections of the network that remain active," John said. "*Daedalus* has a great many internal sensors."

"You mean the Electric Captain can *see us*?"

"I would assume so. It would explain how she knew you were in Tressaco."

"Can she see us now?" Frazer demanded.

"I consider it very unlikely. I can detect no active network in this tunnel."

Which wasn't exactly the reassurance I was looking for. "Okay." I turned back to Rell. "What else did she say to Ixia?"

"That the Cheaters in Tressaco were attempting to damage the *Daedalus* and stop its flight to the new world. As such, she declared you all Mutineers. Which was when all the arguments started."

"So you didn't see Tressaco light up until the daylight went off?"

"No. And that shocked most people. Your father said, how can getting the lights back on be causing any damage? Atov told him that questioning the Electric Captain was also a form of Mutiny and to shut up."

"But he didn't, did he?" I said with a twitch of my lips.

"No."

"Did the Electric Captain mention me and Frazer?"

"No." He gave me a rueful smile. "I just guessed it would be you. Who else makes this kind of impact?"

We shared a long smile before I turned back to Mortos. "You know what we were doing yesterday afternoon, don't you?"

"Cutting that big fibre trunk in the power utility management room."

"How did the Electric Captain know that?" Frazer asked.

"The obvious assumption is that she was responsible for the fibres," John said. "That she is connected to them."

We all stared at the black bracelet on my wrist. Just listening to John say that seemed like Mutiny itself.

"But she's guarded us for five hundred years," Rell said. "Without her leadership and knowledge, our ancestors would have starved to death and the *Daedalus* would be a lifeless chunk of hollow rock lost between the stars."

"There is a saying that comes from Earth," John said. "History is written by the winners."

"Yes, and the Electric Captain won."

"Somebody did," Alisha said slowly. "Somebody who calls herself the Electric Captain. But how can we really be certain which side she was on?"

"We know because we didn't go back to the first world and steal it from the aliens living there," I said.

"No, you didn't go back," John agreed. "But that's not what I'm saying. To me, the Electric Captain does not appear to be acting with your best interests as her core program."

"Look, figuring out what's happening isn't our immediate problem," Mortos said. "We need to get away from here. This platform can't be the only way to reach the subway tunnels. Elijah and his people will find another route. He'll be searching for it right now."

"He's right," Alisha said, and gave Mortos a quick kiss. "Come on, we need to move."

"I'll take Frazer first," Mortos said.

"It won't be for long," Frazer said earnestly. "I can feel so much more of my legs now. I'll be walking by tomorrow, I'm sure."

"You heard what John said," I told him sharply. "It'll take a week for you to heal properly, and you're to rest as much as possible."

"That was before," Frazer said simply as he put his arms round Mortos's neck. "And if they do chase us then you're to leave me."

"I will not!"

"Think about it, Hazel," he said confidently. "They know I can't move my legs, that I'm a useless cripple just like Elijah says. They won't guard me the same way as everyone else. So the first night – *zam!* I'll run off. Simple, see? I'll actually be a lot safer than you, especially if you're stumbling round the forward compartments with Elijah and the Electric Captain hunting you."

I opened my mouth to argue. No words came out. I'm glad Frazer is smart, but sometimes I'd like to be right too. "Whatever!"

Frazer smiled his victory smile.

We climbed down off the platform. The water was cold and black. It came up to my ankles. My boots were good, but not completely waterproof.

"Which way?" Alisha asked.

"To your left," John replied.

We started off down the tunnel. It was a monotonous trek. Mortos and Rell swapped over carrying Frazer every ten minutes so they didn't get too tired. Rell was doing well enough, but I could tell Mortos found my brother heavy. It must have been so tough on him – he was a hundred and seventeen, after all. It made me grateful that Alisha had someone so decent devoted to her.

That thought diverted my gaze back to Rell. He and Frazer were talking quietly as they trudged along. The Electric Captain alone knows what Frazer was telling him about me.

Rell let out a short laugh, and his shining eyes glanced at me. Heat came to my cheeks. But it wasn't mockery or disgust I saw on Rell's face. More like approval. I risked a quick smile back. Having him with us made me feel really comfortable inside. Mind, he really ought to shave that beard off. It was so wispy, it did nothing for him. Why had no one told him that? But then I wasn't entirely sure I'd told him how grateful I was for him warning us. He risked everything for that one impetuous act. By running to Tressaco, he became outcast like me, a Cheater, a Mutineer. He must have known there would be no turning back.

And we'd kissed. That was something my thoughts kept returning to as we walked along. What happened directly after was so frightening and hectic that I'd put it out of my mind, but now... I'd just instinctively kissed him, I'd been so delighted to see him. And he'd kissed me back, equally urgent.

"What?" Rell asked. His expression was quizzical.

I may have been staring at him. "Uh, I was just trying to work out how far it is to the forward endwall."

"If we remain in this tunnel, we have approximately thirty-one kilometres to go," John said.

"And no food," Alisha chipped in. "Or drink. We need to watch that."

"What's the next station?" Mortos asked.

"Kotheo Park," John said. "One and a half kilometres."

"Kotheo is a village," I said, then thought about it. "And Ixia village hall has a notice saying it's the Blue Line station."

"Ixia is also an old park station," John said.

"What about Akebia?" Rell asked. "Our hall says we're Green Line."

"Another park station."

"So the Loyalists used the park stations as the centre of each village," Rell said. "I wonder why?"

"Cycling," I said, as my earlier comfort drained away. "The bodies all get taken under the ground on the Cycling platform, right? I always thought they went into something like a big sewer pipe that washed them all the way to the composter machines." My gaze was drawn to the tunnel apex, with its tiny blue-green secondary lights. They formed a line ahead and behind us before the distance swallowed them up. And the subway tunnels linked everything together. I started to wonder if having the secondary lights on was a coincidence after all. "Maybe the bodies go through these tunnels."

"How?" Rell asked.

"Some kind of cart?" I guessed. I hadn't exactly worked out every detail in my head.

"What pulls the cart?" Frazer asked straight away. "What puts the bodies on the cart?"

"You're the one with the brain," I countered. "You tell me."

"The Cycling lift platform is a fixed mechanism, so if you put a cart in the right place, it might just tip the bodies onto it."

"And what pulls the cart?" Rell asked.

"Only one thing it can be, a cybot of some kind. Some of the machines still work, remember."

"All that is possible," John said. "We would need more information to determine the actual operational nature of the Cycling procedure."

"What sort of information do we need?" I asked.

"One thing at a time, Hazel," Rell said, and stopped. Mortos took Frazer from him. I saw the strain on his face as Frazer linked hands round his chest, but of course Frazer didn't see that.

"It can't be much further to Kotheo," I said. "We'll take a rest there."

"Did you hear that?" Frazer asked suddenly. "I heard something."

We all froze.

"What?" Alisha whispered.

"I'm not sure."

Those tiny intermittent lights along the tunnel that had helped us see our way suddenly seemed detrimental. If they were ordinary lights like we'd switched on back in Tressaco, we'd be able to look along the tunnel and see if anything was there. Of course, if anything *was* there, it'd be able to see us too.

"Which direction?" I asked. "Where was the noise? Ahead of us or behind?"

Frazer frowned in concentration. "Behind, I think."

I locked eyes with Rell, and both of us knew exactly what the other was thinking. Then I heard it too, a faint voice gusting down the tunnel from behind.

"Elijah," we said in unison. Any other time and that might have been rather sweet.

(12)

"Let's move," Alisha said.

Mortos gritted his teeth and began walking fast. All of us were kicking up sluggish ripples as we hurried forward.

"John, what's up ahead?" I asked. "Is there any way out of the tunnel before the station?"

"There are several access hatches," John replied. "However, it is impossible to know how much earth is now on top of them."

"Sweet Captain!"

"However, Kotheo station is a triple intersection; it has a radial loop as well as the Blue and Purple lines. Knowing which tunnel we took will be difficult for any pursuers."

"Unless there's fifty of them," I said glumly.

"Fifty would be making a lot more noise," Mortos said. "I'll guess that your friend has just gathered a few equally devoted fanatics to give chase down here."

"So what do we do?"

"We can't simply carry on down this line and hope they take another," Frazer said. "Elijah was smart enough to arrive ahead of the others at Tressaco. He'll have worked out we have to hide somewhere the Regulators would never normally look for Cheaters or Mutineers. And there's only one place we can do that."

"Beyond the endwall," I muttered. Elijah would never have the courage to venture there – would he? The Electric Captain was very clear that people had to stay away from the remaining machines, the ones which keep *Daedalus* flying straight and true.

"We need to lay a false trail," Alisha said. "I can do that."

"What do you mean?" I asked uneasily.

"I go down one of the other tunnels or, better yet, carry on along this one and make some noise. Meanwhile, you take a different route."

"No!" this time it was me and Mortos in unison.

She gave me a lopsided grin. "It can't be you. It can't be Frazer. It can't be Rell or Mortos. Who does that leave?"

"But–" I looked at Mortos for support, and saw from his haunted expression he knew she was right.

"John."

"Yes, Hazel?"

"You said these tunnels are for electric carts. Could we charge one up?"

"There is a maglev rail running along the bottom of the tunnel which the subway cars use for propulsion. It is inactive. I suspect the water will have penetrated most of it by now."

"There must be something we can use?"

"We can check the garages when we arrive at the station. The maintenance cars have auxiliary power, and wheels."

Rell soon had to take Frazer from Mortos, who was exhausted from trying to hurry. It took us another quarter of an hour to reach Kotheo. For the last couple of minutes, we could all clearly hear whoever was pursuing us. They weren't walking like us but were jogging along, talking as they went, their boots splashing in the water, making a constant and growing racket. I was really hoping the tunnel was making the sound carry a long way.

Kotheo station was almost identical to the one at Tressaco, a platform with a wide archway halfway along. We shone our torches down it, seeing the big emergency door cutting off access to the stairs beyond.

"Keep going straight through," John said. "There is a service tunnel ten metres beyond the platform."

It was smaller than the main tunnel by about half a metre, but we ducked down it. Twenty metres on there was another junction, then one with three tunnels, all of which rose upwards at a gentle angle to leave the water behind. When we reached them, the little overhead lights went out.

"What happened?" I asked.

"I switched them off," John said. "Hopefully our pursuers will be unwilling to check a lightless tunnel. They may also consider it unlikely we would have ventured down it."

"Good call," I admitted.

We only used one torch – mine. The tunnel we were walking up opened into a big chamber that John called the garage. So I finally got to see what subway cars looked like. White metal bubbles – that was my first impression. White bubbles with a flat base and big round windows that bulged a bit like eyes. There were dozens of them laid out in rows. When I shone the beam through the windows, I could see padded seats inside, four of them, all facing each other.

"Cool," Frazer murmured. "How do they work?"

"You tell them where to go and they take you there," John said. "It's a simple system."

"Where are the maintenance cars?"

"At the far end."

These cars were elongated metal bubbles with blue and red stripes down the side. The windows had no glass, and each of them had four wheels.

"No power," John said in a disappointed tone.

"Can we charge them up?" Frazer asked.

"It would be difficult. I can detect very few active systems in here."

"What about that?" Frazer asked, and nodded.

I looked where he was looking. At the end of the row of maintenance cars was a trolley, just a simple metal rectangle with four wheels and some kind of mechanism underneath, but nonetheless absurdly simple. I could almost imagine Dad building it in Ixia's carpentry shop.

Mortos went and shoved at it. The wheels were stiff but he moved it easily enough. One of the wheels emitted a faint squeak. "That'll work," he said.

Rell lowered Frazer onto it. And finally I could help move my brother. Rell and Mortos were exhausted from carrying him, poor things.

"Time for me to go," Alisha said.

"What? No!" I said.

"Don't," she warned. "Elijah has to be led away from you. Hazel, you have to get into the forward compartments. You have to talk to the engineering-section machines. And I can give you that chance." She stepped forward and hugged me. "This way you can give everyone hope again."

I just nodded. I don't think I'd realized until then just how much responsibility I'd taken on. And all because I'd picked up an old machine, purely out of innocent curiosity. That and having the machine discover who I was.

I wondered what it must have been like for Ashleigh Kruger in her last moments, locking all the AIs before she cast her mind into the command thinking machine in one last desperate attempt to thwart the Mutineers. It was such an incredible act of faith, believing her children would somehow emerge from the shadows to rebuild the *Daedalus* and restore everything the Mutineers had ruined. But I suppose everyone believes their hopes and dreams can live on through family. What's the point of life otherwise?

"I won't let you down," I told Alisha, but really I was promising Ashleigh Kruger, because for her sacrifice she really deserved a person better than me to accomplish something so momentous – someone much better. But I'm what she wound up with. As Dad always says, you just have to work with the tools you've got.

"I'm coming with you," Mortos said.

Alisha protested straight away. "No. You need to keep Hazel safe."

"And I can do that best by distracting Elijah. With you."

The love I saw in his eyes made me all teary again.

Alisha gave me an anxious glance.

"Go," I urged.

Her face was haggard with uncertainty, so I said it again. "Go, get them away from me and Rell and Frazer. We can take it from here. It'll be easy now with the trolley."

"Be careful, Gran," Frazer said.

She kissed him. "You too. And hey, next time we meet, you'll be walking."

"I will," he said earnestly, and raised his left arm up high to prove it.

I walked back down the service tunnels with them. When we got back to the main Blue Line Forwards, Elijah and his group were making a lot more noise.

"They're close," I said quietly.

"Oh, we are going to have fun playing with them," Alisha said. She hugged me again. "Take care of him. He's a good lad."

I patted the crossbow. "Nobody's going to hurt Frazer."

"Oh yeah, him too." Alisha winked. Then they both hurried away down the main tunnel, holding hands as filthy water splashed up from their boots at every step. I stared after her. She was talking about Rell, not Frazer.

The noise of the pursuit was growing a lot louder – the squelch of feet in the water, heavy panting, Elijah's occasional barked words. I shrank back down the service tunnel, allowing the blackness to claim me.

I was right about the tunnels amplifying and carrying sound. I'd really thought Elijah was close behind us; I actually had to wait another few minutes with my nerves getting even more frayed as they just kept getting louder and louder.

They came out into the station, then I heard someone shout: "There!"

"Where?"

"Did you see it?'

"No, what?" That was Elijah.

"A light. I saw a light down there."

"Straight ahead?"

"You sure?"

"Yes. It was like one of those tiny cylinder lanterns the Cheaters had."

"It's not there now."

"It was only on for a second."

"Okay, let's go. Come on, run. If we can see their lights, we're really close."

They ran past the end of the tunnel. Elijah was in front, his face slick with sweat, holding a pistol. The others followed, not so enthusiastic-looking, red-faced and breathing hard. I'm pretty sure none of them had been expecting a chase like this.

I stood there waiting until I was sure there were no Regulators trailing after the main group. I'd underestimated Elijah already today. I wasn't going to do that again.

Back in the garage, Frazer and Rell were getting anxious.

"Now who was taking their time?" Rell said in that annoyed yet relieved tone people have when they've been expecting the worst.

"Just making sure," I said.

"How many were there?"

"Seven counting Elijah. They didn't look happy."

"Good!" Frazer said. He was sitting on the trolley, hugging his legs. But still, he was upright without any support for his back.

"How's it going?" I asked.

"I'm not so cold anymore."

"Well, that's a start." I dropped my bag on the trolley next to him, then held out the crossbow. "Do you think you can use this?"

"Oh, yeah!"

I kept it out of his reach. "It's not a toy, Frazer. This can seriously hurt people."

He cocked his head to one side. "You mean as badly as forcing us to drink the Blessing?"

That surprised me. Frazer doesn't often get angry; when he does, I find it kind of alarming. With that brain of his wrongly applied, the potential damage he could inflict is huge. "Yes," I said calmly. "So let's not stoop to their level, okay? We're the good guys. This is a last resort."

"I get it."

I let him take the crossbow. Then Rell and I gripped the trolley handle. "It'll be easier to pull, not push," I explained to him.

"Yeah, everyone knows that," he said simply.

I gave up. "John, which way?"

"Back to the junction first," he said.

We started pulling. The wheel let out its constant squeak as we moved forward. I took a guess that I'd be quite tired of that noise before long. There were a lot of service tunnels winding round under Kotheo, connecting garages to other big chambers containing broken machines and cybots. John said they used to be engineering shops where the machines repaired parts for cars and rails. Frazer so wanted to stop and examine everything.

John guided us out onto the Purple tunnel and we set off, heading forward again. The water was only a few centimetres deeper than back in the Blue Line tunnel, so we could keep a walking pace going. But the constant exertion from pulling Frazer along was giving me a headache, and I could barely feel my poor saturated feet anymore. I knew I couldn't last much longer. Frazer sat with his back to us, the crossbow resting on his lap, keeping a vigilant watch on the tunnel behind.

"I haven't said how grateful I am," I told Rell. "What you did, warning us – that was such an amazing thing to do."

"Thanks, but let's face it, compared to what you've done…"

"That was just luck, and being in the right place."

"Don't be so modest. You set out to save your brother, and it turns out you're going to save all of us."

"I think you're over-estimating me by about a million per cent."

He turned and smiled softly at me. "No, I'm not. Hazel, I've never met anyone like you before. You just… the way you go through life, you do what you want to do, and you're always right to do it. It's like you're the only complete person on the *Daedalus*. The rest of us, we might as well be sheep"

I could feel my cheeks warming. When I glanced back to check on Frazer, to see how much he was gloating, I saw he'd fallen asleep again. "I thought you weren't coming," I confessed. "Alice gave me your letter. Then days and days went by and I was so caught up helping with Frazer. It was a miserable time, that's all."

"I'm sorry about the delay, I really am. We were busy in the hospital. A couple of the younger children came down with bad coughs, more like a fever."

I pictured Rell helping to tend sick children and felt a burst of guilt. We'd danced one evening, that's all. Then I went and piled up all these expectations on him in my head, mainly because I'd felt so desperately sorry for myself. "That was very noble of you."

"I lost my brother a long time ago," Rell said. "He got sick when I was young, maybe four or five. I don't remember much of him now but I'll never forget the doctor, how hard he tried to save him. He was so frustrated that he could do so little. But the effort he made helped us all deal with it. After that, well, I knew that was what I was going to do, to help people." He shook his head ruefully. "And now I've found out that the medicine machines can do so much more for people. And you're the one who gave that to us."

"It's really Earth knowledge – it belongs to all of us. I was just a key to unlock it, that's all."

"Yes, but it was *you*. After the invitation dance, I looked at the Swirl every night. You were so angry about the way people just accept everything, so determined to do something to put it right. I couldn't get you out of my head." His lips quirked. "I didn't want to try."

Before he could say anything else, I leant over and kissed him. The trolley came to a stop, and with it that tiresome squeaking. I hadn't realized how easily his lips would fit against mine. Nor how warm they were, how snugly his hands pressed against my spine, holding me closer still. My own hands closed around his shirt, twisting the fabric as my fingers curled up tight. And I barely had to lift myself up on my toes at all.

Then we were both smiling at each other, and I knew, right down there at the centre of my mind, I really had found someone special. I've kissed boys before – I know when it means nothing, when it's part of the sweet moment at a dance like it was with Scott, or supposedly for fun like Zawn; but this time it was the real thing. Elizabeth Bennet finally sees past her own prejudice. That wasn't feverish imagination, or self-delusion, not even just the physical connection that Alice makes. Rell was genuine, my Mr Darcy. And that kiss – well, I also knew it wasn't one-sided.

He gestured round the gloomy tunnel with its dank water, his smile widening. "Some setting, huh? It's romance all the way with me."

"I don't know," I replied with playful disdain. "Two Mutineer fugitives on the run. It has a certain excitement about it."

"We're not Mutineers."

"No?"

"No. I think I prefer rebels. Now that's proper exciting."

"Rebels it is," I agreed.

We picked up the trolley handle and resumed our walk down the tunnel. I was convinced the squeaking wheel was louder now.

"Do you think people will listen?" I asked. "Once we fix the Swirl, I mean?"

"Listen, if we can find some cybot that repairs the hole in the ship, and switch it on, they'll make you Mayor of every village."

I laughed, but at the back of my head I wondered just how Mayor Fininen would react to the old machines being rebuilt, the change it would make to everyone's life. How his authority would weaken. Him and Chief Atov.

"How did it happen, do you think?" Rell asked, suddenly serious.

"What?"

"That *Daedalus* started to leak?"

I brought my wrist up and gave John a quizzical look. "Yes, how did that happen?"

"Probability," John said. "Space between the stars is not as empty as it appears. There are meteors, particles of ice and rock, interstellar gas, dust clouds. However, the probability of encountering an object large enough to penetrate all the layers of defence the *Daedalus* has is extremely small."

"Ha! That's our family for you," Frazer said. "We're like bad-luck magnets."

I sneaked a glance back at him. Just how long had he been awake?

"The universe is too big to hold a grudge against you," John said. "Although it is unusual for the *Daedalus* to be damaged like this in interstellar space, it is not impossible – especially given how far the ship has travelled and for how long. Probability cannot be ignored; the odds of a major impact fall for every light year travelled."

"But if the Builders knew that…" Frazer said.

"They took precautions. Very good precautions. Firstly, there is a plasma shield around the *Daedalus*."

"John–" I began wearily.

"Plasma in this case is a gas that is charged with electricity, like static. That means it can be contained and shaped by magnets. It is tenuous, but it forms a cloud that surrounds the *Daedalus* for over a hundred kilometres. So if we fly towards something – say, the size of a pebble – friction will vaporize it in a millisecond, and nothing happens."

"So whatever we hit was bigger than a pebble," I said.

"Indeed. But don't forget we are flying at ten per cent of the speed of light. Even if it was only a chunk of rock the size of your fist, the kinetic energy of its impact would be phenomenal – like a bomb going off. That is why the forward section of *Daedalus*, beyond the endwall, is twelve kilometres thick."

"It is?" I asked. The only real dimension I knew was the length and circumference of the habitat – fifty-five kilometres by thirty-four point five, which is just about the first thing we all learn in school. I marvelled at just how much more of *Daedalus* there is beyond the part we can see.

"Yes, and the first eight kilometres of that is another kind of shield, a dense layer of carbon foam, designed to absorb the impact of anything that gets through the plasma shield."

"So whatever we hit got through the plasma and the carbon foam?"

"Yes. It then carried on into the main structure. You should know that a collision of that size will have destroyed a significant number of the forward compartments."

"Not the ones with the repair cybots?" I asked in dismay.

"In the Engineering Department, there are twenty separate independent sections. Anything big enough to damage all of them would have destroyed the entire ship. If they survived the Mutiny, one will have the resources to fix the leak."

"Okay then," I said, relieved.

As we trudged on, I tried to banish the idea that we were still being followed. I guess I could only worry about one big problem at a time, and the hole in the sky had to be the biggest.

It took us a couple of hours to reach Cobaea station. I knew that tower mountain – it was one that had a guano spill pipe. A lot of the barges that supplied Ixia village loaded up in its canal pool.

"We need to see if there's a way out here," I said. "I've got to have a break and something to eat, otherwise I'm just going to fall over." As if to emphasise the point, my stomach gurgled. The only thing I'd had that morning was a glass of orange juice. My mouth was dry, too – not enough to make me try drinking the water we were walking through, mind. Dehydration was making my headache even worse.

"Good idea," Rell agreed.

John guided us down a service tunnel near one of the station platforms. As before, it branched several times and we pulled the trolley through various garages and chambers, winding up in a smaller room containing smashed machines.

"A great deal of violence was used here," John remarked as we parked Frazer's trolley in the middle.

I turned a slow circle. The machines used to be cubes or cylinders, most of them about my height, some a bit taller. But their casings were all buckled, with long gashes exposing interior components which had also been smashed and broken. Something had repeatedly hammered away at their guts, reducing them to mangled scrap.

"What could do this?" I asked.

"I am uncertain as to the exact implement," John said. "Best guess would be an axe."

I tried to imagine how long it would take someone – or a whole team of people – with an axe to do all this. Worse was the amount of anger that must have been unleashed to achieve it. I wasn't looking at a methodical attack; this was unthinking rage. And this room was just one of hundreds, probably thousands, where the machines which tended us and helped people live their grand lives were destroyed. How the Mutineers must have hated Ashleigh Kruger's decision to leave the first world behind, how fanatical their opposition became. It wasn't just violence they used but treachery too, planting their alien bioweapon to sabotage the machines they couldn't reach. It scared me to think that anyone could be so zealous that they'd risk the lives of everyone on board to achieve their goals. It would be like facing a whole village populated by Elijah.

"Big axe," Rell murmured. I guessed he was having the same troubling thoughts as me.

"We need to get outside," I said. "John, how do we do that?"

"It will be difficult for all three of you. There are stairs."

"That's okay. I'll stay here with Frazer."

At which Frazer burst out laughing.

"What?" I demanded.

"How is John going to guide Rell outside if you're in here? Sweet Captain, Hazel, you can be so dumb at times."

Oh yeah, he was definitely getting better. I thought about how throttling him then and there, before his legs improved any more, would have been easy. Really very easy. "Fine. We'll just leave you here by yourself, then."

I got the victory grin again. "That's okay," he said. "I'm still tired. I'll take a nap while you two are off doing *stuff*."

I narrowed my eyes to give him a suspicious glare, but all I could see was innocence. "Are you sure?"

Frazer gestured round. "Elijah doesn't have a clue where we are. I really do need to rest. We need food. What's your counter-argument?"

I sighed and looked at Rell. "Come on then."

"We need to see if there is a manual door-release rod somewhere in this room," John said. "It will make life easier for you."

So we spent the next five minutes searching through metal cupboards and the small cases and the piles of trash for what John basically described as a stick of metal, not helped by Frazer going, "Oh, bring that one here," every two seconds when I picked up some old tool or bent piece of junk. So what we really succeeded in doing was rearranging half the rubbish into a pile beside Frazer's trolley, where he started lovingly examining each item as if it were more precious than John. My only disappointment was not finding any oil to deal with that guano-damned wheel.

Thankfully, Rell found the door-rod thing John wanted, which to be honest didn't look much different to the screwdriver I'd used to get us into Tressaco's power utility management centre. "Take care," I said to Frazer as John told us to open an ordinary-sized door on the back wall. "And try to rest. We'll be back in an hour."

He was sitting on the edge of the trolley, shining his torch on some piece of dirty treasure. "Yes, yes."

I rolled my eyes then stood on tiptoes to slide the rod into its tiny hole above the door. There was a soft click. Between us, Rell and I managed to slide it open.

(13)

There were many corridors underneath Cobaea, definitely more than had been at Kotheo station. It was uncomfortable to think that this whole labyrinth world had existed underneath my feet my whole life and I'd never known it was there.

We had to open three more doors before we reached a broad hallway with stairs at the far end. Daylight was shining down them. I hurried forwards.

"Hazel," Rell called. "Let's just take it easy, shall we? We don't know what's up there."

"Oh, yes. Sorry.'

Somehow my hand found his as we walked cautiously up the stairs. I didn't know which I was happier about, being out in the open again or holding hands.

We peeked over the top stair. There was a large vestibule ahead of us, the same size as the entrance in Tressaco but with a different decor. This one was all dark red with gold edgings spiralling round pillars. It must have been quite majestic before the Mutiny. All I could see beyond the huge open archway was an extensive wall of bulky old tree trunks. Just like Tressaco, Cobaea was surrounded by a wild forest.

"Let's go," Rell said. His voice was rich with excitement. I knew how he was feeling – with Elijah off chasing Alisha, our goal of fixing the Swirl was now all that mattered. Once that was done, we could start a real challenge to the Electric Captain.

Just being back out in the fresh air and daylight banished my headache. The trees were pressed up close to the curving base of the tower mountain. They were all fruit trees, of course. I picked a big apple that was a deep burgundy colour, looking about as perfect as an apple can be. When I took a bite, it was so sour I had to spit it out.

"Always the way with these ancient trees," Rell said. "The fruit starts to sour after a century or so. We really should clear them away and plant new ones."

"I need something to eat," I said plaintively, and flinched inwards at how bad that sounded. For all that I treated village life with bored disdain, I did get three meals a day there – as my stomach kept reminding me.

Rell gave me a look of mild surprise and gestured round at the forest with its web of grape vines loaded with full clusters, and every branch bent from its heavy crop of fruit. "I'm sure we'll find you something."

I blushed. Then Rell was grinning, and put his arm round my shoulder to give me a quick hug. How did he get to understand me so well? We'd probably not spent more than eight hours together in total – it just seemed like weeks.

"Maybe if we look *really* hard," I proposed.

Laughing, we made our way round the edge of Cobaea. I could hear birds scurrying through the forest's undergrowth. Between the tangle of thick boughs, there were fast flickering movements as wings flapped.

"Can you shoot some ducks or a turkey?" Rell asked. "I'm pretty good at starting a fire. We could cook them."

I glanced down at the crossbow, then up at his earnest face. "Um, it would take time to cook a bird. We told Frazer we'd only be an hour."

"Right."

"It would need plucking and gutting, too. We don't have a knife."

"You can't shoot, can you?"

"No."

He chuckled. "Did Elijah know that?"

"I was standing right beside him! Even I couldn't miss from that distance."

"Good to know."

So Rell was a teaser? Good to know.

We came out of the forest and stopped abruptly. The canal pool in front of us had two longboats tied up at its wharf. One of them was filling up with guano from the pipe that emerged from the side of Cobaea while the other waited its turn.

"Now what?" Rell asked.

I studied the scene, seeing the two bargemasters sitting on the prow of the one being loaded – I even recognized one of them: Dakiki, who visited Ixia regularly. They weren't part of Elijah's mad hunt.

"We're young," I said quietly.

"Yes?" Rell said cautiously.

"So we're clearly not Cheaters. We're just lovers who wanted some time alone together. What could be more innocent and believable than that? It's just a shame we forgot to bring any food when we sneaked out of the village."

"Innocent, huh? I hope you can act better than you can shoot."

The bargemasters looked up as they saw the two of us emerge sheepishly from the cover of the trees. Dakiki smiled at what was clearly our impetuosity. He waved at us.

"Hello, Hazel. It's a way from Ixia isn't it?"

I shrugged. "Not really."

He introduced Randorf, the other bargemaster, who smirked at us. "So have you two been exploring?"

"Some," Rell agreed.

"Interesting rooms up there if you've got the energy to climb the stairs," his hand gestured at Cobaea's cliff of balconies rising above us. "Plenty of them still have the old furniture. Beds and the like."

"And clothes," Dakiki said. I realized he was studying my dress and jacket.

"But no decent food," I told them.

Dakiki smiled again and beckoned us to follow as he went into his longboat's little cabin. We were handed a pack that had sandwiches wrapped in whiteleaf and a flask of fruit juice. "Keep the flask," Dakiki said. "It's a long walk home. You're going to need it. Fill it up from the canal, just not near here." His thumb jerked back at the pipe which was splattering its rank sludge into the cargo hold. "Go upflow."

I nodded my gratitude.

"How's your brother?" he asked.

"Doing okay," I said.

"I'm glad. It never seems right to Cycle someone that age."

We went back out and sat on the prow of the longboat, my legs dangling over the edge. After the fear of the Regulators coming for us, and the hours spent in the wretched tunnels, such tranquillity felt slightly unreal.

"So why did you come here?" Randorf asked. "Tressaco is a lot closer to Ixia."

"We're heading to Kilda," Rell said. "That's my village."

I didn't question the lie. If Dakiki and Randorf told a Regulator they'd seen us, Kilda would be a good misdirection. "Did you see Tressaco last night?" I asked. "It was all lit up."

"Everyone saw Tressaco," Randorf said. "Didn't you hear? The Mutineers did that."

"There are no Mutineers anymore," Rell said.

"I was in Pelang this morning," Randorf said insistently. "The villagers said the Electric Captain told everyone a whole new batch have grown up out of the Cheaters. Regulators deputized a bunch of people to help catch them. Good job too. Nobody wants to go back to the bad days. You need to be careful walking round by yourselves until they've all been Cycled."

I was getting uncomfortable with Randorf. His thoughts were too closely attuned to those of Elijah for my liking. How can people go through life without questioning what they see? Dad was always telling me to be objective and look at all the facts before making a decision. "But it's good, though, getting the lights back on," I said. "If we can do that, we might be able to get other machines working again."

"Why?" Randorf asked, sounding genuinely puzzled. "We don't need the old machines anymore. Everything works just fine as it is."

"Medicine machines," I said, ticking them off on my fingers. "Food machines. Clothes machines. They can all make our lives so much easier. We spend our whole time working. Wouldn't you like to be able to stop and have time for yourself?"

Randorf gave Dakiki a what-can-you-do look. "Stop and do what, exactly? I like what I do. It's important work, it keeps me busy, and I get to visit all the villages in the habitat. There's no finer job than being a bargemaster in *Daedalus*. You youngsters, you don't know how lucky you are."

"Ignore him," Dakiki said. "He's so old and set in his ways he wouldn't know a new thought if it bit him on his arse."

"I'm a year younger than you," Randorf protested.

Dakiki tapped a finger on the side of his head. "Not inside here you're not," he chortled.

I didn't even need to glance in Rell's direction to know there would be a warning expression on his face. Just for once I managed to clamp down on my impulse to explain to Randorf how wrong he was. Instead I bit into a cheese-and-tomato sandwich, the sort I'd never really enjoyed before. It tasted delicious. "Nice," I mumbled round a mouthful. Then the irony got me. It was only three weeks ago when I'd been saying to Alice how I might like being a bargemaster. What would it take for someone like Randorf to think in a different fashion? That would be a huge problem for us once the Swirl was fixed and we cleared away the Mutineers' bioweapon. People have their view of the universe and the way things are because they genuinely believe that how they live is right and normal since they're the ones doing it.

Randorf's pale grey eyes were staring at me, as though he could sense my feelings about him.

Rell finished his sandwich. "Thanks," he said. "We'd best be getting on."

"Say hello to your father for me," Dakiki said to me. "He's a good man."

"I will, and thank you."

He held my hand to steady me as I got up. "Be careful out there."

"I... Yes," I stammered. I was pretty sure he wasn't talking about getting lost or running out of food.

I remembered to fill the flask up away from the guano pipe, then Rell and I walked back round Cobaea's curving base. "Do you think Dakiki knew?" I asked as soon as we out of sight.

"That the Electric Captain called you a Mutineer? Most likely," he said.

"Randorf will tell the first Regulator he sees that we were here."

"I know."

"Doesn't that bother you?"

"No. He's got to load up his barge with guano, which is going to take hours. Then he'll have to reach a village – probably tomorrow. We'll be in the forward chambers by then."

"Do you think so?" I asked, and suddenly the notion of more endless tunnels didn't bother me so much.

"We'll make it. You're an unstoppable force."

I grinned. "I wonder what Randorf's going to think when he sees what we do."

"I'm not sure his brain can take that many new ideas. It'll probably melt out of his ears."

"Is there a medical term for that?"

"Yeah: stupidity."

We retraced our route through Cobaea's basement levels. Frazer wasn't sitting on his trolley. I saw the torch shining on the other side of the room.

"What are you doing?" I demanded. "And how did you get over here?"

He was sitting with his back resting on the wall. One hand was holding some kind of hemispherical tool against an induction pad. "I walked," he said with immense pride.

"Frazer! Are you all right? You're not supposed to try that for another day."

"I know. It was hard, but I did it. My legs work! I can walk again, Hazel! I can walk!"

"It would be wise not to exert yourself while the nerves are still being repaired," John said.

"Come on," Rell said, and signalled me. Between us we hoisted Frazer back up. His arms went round our shoulders, and we helped him carefully back to the trolley. I watched him closely as we moved. His legs really were taking small strides. He collapsed back onto the trolley with a grateful expression. Sweat glinted on his forehead.

"I know," he said, fingering the white medical collar. "I'll take it easy now."

"You certainly will," I scolded.

"Can you bring my tools back, please?"

"I don't suppose you found any oil, did you?" I asked.

"No. Sorry."

"What are all these?" Rell asked as we carried the devices back to Frazer.

"Not sure about all of them," he said in a disgruntled tone. "They were the ones that looked intact. I just charged them up. I was going to start switching them on in a minute and make some notes."

"The dark cylinder with the display panel is a rangefinder and contour mapper," John said.

"Uh?"

"Touch the yellow button for three seconds."

Frazer's thumb found the yellow button. A beam of the brightest emerald light stabbed out of the cylinder, slicing across the room just like the red light on the cleaning bots.

"What kind of light is that?" I asked. "It doesn't spread out like the torch beams do."

"Laser," John said. "They can be made very powerful. With enough energy, they can cut through metal. This one is harmless, but do not look directly into it. You would damage your eye."

"Cool," Frazer said, swishing it about. "What's this?" He held up a hemisphere.

"A morphtallic programmer, of course," John said.

I gathered myself to scold John, then stopped as I stared suspiciously at the bracelet. "Big one or small one?" I chuckled. So AIs have a sense of humour. Interesting.

"Small. Morphtallic is a metal substance that can be programmed – moulded – into whatever shape you want. It is used by engineers who want a quick fix for something. Ordinarily the cybots would use it to create a temporary patch for the Swirl hole until a full repair can be initiated."

"Is there any morphtallic in here?" Frazer asked quickly, looking round.

"I have not seen any," John said.

Frazer sighed and held up a knife. The blade was about fifteen centimetres long, with a square end instead of a tip. I wouldn't have thought it was a powered tool, but Frazer had obviously worked it out. There was a small green charge light glowing on the handle.

"Be careful with that," John said. "It's a disassociator blade, or D-blade for short. When turned on, it can cut through anything."

"Anything?" Frazer said eagerly.

"It's not a challenge," I told him quickly.

"How do I switch it on?"

"Twist the top quarter of the handle. Do not put your fingers anywhere near the blade."

Frazer twisted the top of the knife. The whole blade lit up scarlet. Frazer jabbed it into the casing of a wrecked machine. The blade sank in up to the hilt, so fast it was like he was still shoving it through the air. "Coolest cool!"

Rell was nodding in approval. What is it with boys and things that cut or smash or shoot?

"This?" Frazer asked after he'd switched the D-blade off. He was holding up a metal tool that was a slim rectangular box with a chunky handle loop. "It took a long time to charge."

"That is an e-beam welder. Welding is how two pieces of metal are joined together."

"Okay," Frazer was flicking the row of switches on the back of the handle.

"Don't—" John began.

Frazer squeezed the handle. A needle-thin beam of blinding white light stabbed out from the end of the welder with a loud screeching sound. It struck the roof, and a burst of sparks exploded downwards. Several tiny embers landed on my jacket and I squealed, slapping them out with my palms. "Sweet Captain!" I shouted angrily at Frazer. "What is wrong with you?"

"Hey, I didn't know it was going to do that. That's how you discover new things, by trying them!"

"I would advise more caution with electrically powered items until I can inform you of the consequences when activated," John said.

"Good point," Frazer croaked, and for once he was subdued. He was still staring at the welder in a kind of shock. I took it out of his unresisting fingers. "I'll take care of that," I told him, and put it into my bag.

Rell was smirking. "Come on, let's get going."

We grabbed the trolley handle and started pulling.

It was a long haul through the tunnels that afternoon. Frazer ate the sandwiches Rell had saved for him then fell asleep. I don't know how, but that squeaking wheel was even louder than before. We passed through another four stations without incident. Then, just after Janth Park station, Rell suddenly stopped. He squinted into the darkness ahead, frowning. "Something..." he grunted, sounding puzzled.

"What is it?" I asked. We'd been making such good progress that this sudden interruption was raising goosebumps on my arms.

"I don't know. I thought I saw something moving up ahead."

It was my turn to squint. The tiny lights along the top of the tunnel stretched on and I had no sense of how far ahead I could actually see. But I certainly couldn't make out anything moving.

"Hold me up," John said.

I raised my arm, so the black circle on the bracelet was facing along the tunnel.

"We have a problem," John said. "Rell is correct. Something is coming this way. I can see the infra-red signature approaching."

"The what?"

"My visual sensor extends into the infra-red spectrum. Essentially, I can see heat. That includes the kind of heat given off by a human or animal body."

"Really?" Frazer asked. "That's brilliant."

"It is useful on occasion. Right now we need to go back. Fast."

The way John's voice stayed so level only made it seem even more urgent. Without a word, Rell and I pulled the trolley round in a U-turn and started back the way we'd just come.

"There is a side tunnel in four hundred and twenty metres," John said.

"Okay," I muttered. "Did you see who it was?" I just couldn't believe we'd been so unlucky that Elijah had found us.

"The infra-red signatures are small," John said. "I'm not sure they are people."

"They?" I asked. "What do you mean, they?"

"There is more than one heat source."

"But they're not big enough to be human?" Rell queried. He sounded calm, but we exchanged a glance that acknowledged how alarmed we both were.

"The sources are smaller than I would expect from an adult human," John said. "Do you still have dogs?"

I glanced behind nervously. Frazer was holding the crossbow up ready. We were moving quickly now, feet splashing heavily, that wretched squeaky wheel going round so fast it was almost a constant squeal.

"We still have dogs," Rell said. "The shepherds use them to control their flocks. Sometimes families have them as pets."

"We can't outrun dogs," I said anxiously. It would be just like Elijah to use dogs to hunt us. Though I wasn't sure how he could have got them so quickly.

"Hold me up again," John said.

I did it as best as I could without breaking pace.

"They are not travelling fast," he said.

"How fast is not fast?"

"About the same as human walking pace. We are pulling ahead of them."

"Sweet Captain," I muttered. I could feel the sweat on my forehead. My legs and arms were starting a dull ache from the effort of running with the trolley, and that same effort had brought my headache back worse than before.

"How many can you see?" Frazer asked.

"At least five," John said. "There may be more. It is difficult to be sure – they are in a line."

"Five," Rell grunted. I knew that had scared him. It certainly unnerved me.

"Maybe dogs run wild down here?" Even as I said it, I knew that was just so much guano.

"The temperature is also several degrees cooler than a human," John said.

"Do dogs have a lower body temperature than humans?"

"No. Typically it is higher."

"Then what are they?"

"Sheep?" Frazer suggested.

"Sheep also have a higher temperature than humans," John said.

"Let's just get to the side tunnel," I panted.

It took us another five minutes, by which time my lungs were burning and every leg muscle was a red-hot thread, while every heartbeat delivered a throbbing pain behind my temple. We pulled the trolley into it and kept going to the first junction. John immediately turned the side tunnel's lights off.

We rolled the trolley a few metres down the junction, then Rell and I crept back to peer back down the side tunnel. Without the little overhead lights, the darkness had become oppressive, a solid shadow gathering itself around me. A patch of dull grey haze marked the mouth of the main tunnel, thirty metres away.

"Can you see them?" Frazer whispered in my ear.

I gave a huge start, every nerve tingling with shock. I have no idea how I managed not to yelp. Fear, probably. The glare I focused on him should have set him alight – mainly from shame. In the darkness he couldn't see it.

"How did you…?"

"I walked," he said simply. "It's easier now."

"Great," I grunted.

"So?"

"So what?"

"Can you see them?"

"No!"

"If they maintain their original speed, they will pass the end of the tunnel in approximately six minutes," John said.

"I brought the crossbow," Frazer said.

"Okay."

The three of us stood together on the edge of the junction. All I could hear was our breathing.

"Do you think they'll be able to see us?" Rell asked.

"I don't know," I replied. I hadn't thought of that – after all, there was no light around us at all.

"If they're animals, they're more likely to smell us," Frazer said.

"So what do we do?" I asked.

"Remain calm," John said. "In a worst-case scenario, and they come down the service tunnel, we have the e-beam welder to defend ourselves with."

He was right, and that did help slow my heart. The view down to the main tunnel was unchanging. My hand crept to my bag, fingers probing the outline of the welder.

"Three minutes," John announced.

"I can hear them," Rell said.

I strained. We were making a surprising amount of noise – my heart, breathing, the others rustling as they moved fractionally. But there, rising above that background, sounds came washing along the service tunnel. Something sloshed about in the water that trickled along the floor of the main tunnel. It wasn't footfalls, at least not like we made – more like a rope whipping the water. The sound grew louder.

In unison, the three of us shrank back round the edge. It was so dark I couldn't see Rell's face. And I wanted to. I needed the reassurance it would bring. My hand fumbled for him, and his fingers closed round mine, squeezing encouragingly.

The peculiar noises were at their peak. And I still had no idea what was causing them. Along with the sharper splashing was a slithering, as if things were being dragged along. Despite how scared I was, the temptation to peek was so strong I almost gave in to it.

Thankfully, some rational part of my mind kept me back. The sounds were constant, coming from the main tunnel. Nothing was coming along the service tunnel towards us. I didn't want to do anything that would risk exposing us.

Then the sounds were growing feebler. I put a palm on the wall and slid it along, feeling my way until I was looking round the junction. The tiny segment of the main tunnel I could see was empty.

"I think they've gone."

We waited another couple of minutes, then very slowly tugged the trolley back down to the main tunnel. I winced at every squeak from that evil wheel, sure that it was betraying us, but I still wasn't going to let Frazer walk. It was another seven kilometres to Akebia.

Back in the main tunnel, with the water gurgling softly round our boots, we looked both ways. I knew which way the things had gone, but I couldn't see anything moving down there. When I held John up, he said he could no longer detect their heat signature.

Rell and I started pulling yet again. The discomfort in my limbs had eased but my headache was relentless and I still seemed short of air. I kept telling myself that fixing the Swirl and pouring more air into the habitat would cure the problem once and for all. I just had to tough it out for another couple of days.

(14)

"Cheater children," Frazer announced after we'd travelled another kilometre.

"What?" I asked.

"Cheaters who were still young enough to have children when they left their village, or they took their children with them. Then they had children in turn. I'll bet one of the tower mountains has a whole Cheater community of all ages. That's what was in the tunnel. A bunch of kids."

"John said their temperature was wrong," Rell said.

"Their clothes would be an insulator," Frazer countered in that confident tone I'm way too familiar with. "John couldn't see all their heat."

Rell gave me a look, as if he expected me to step in and correct Frazer. I raised my eyebrow and carried on pulling. I was pretty sure it wasn't a group of children. For a start, they would've been chattering away, and there'd be at least one adult with them. But arguing with Frazer was too exhausting – and for the life of me I couldn't think what kind of animals they were. Nothing seemed to fit. That disturbed me as much as their existence. How could there be unknown animals living in the tunnels for *five hundred years*?

Something was bobbing about in the water ahead of us. A small pale patch. "Stop," I blurted. I walked over and picked it up.

"What is that?" Rell asked.

"Flowers," I told him in confusion. They were saturated with the grubby water, which was dripping down my hand. The petals were sagging, but they were all fresh. Freesias, irises, and some puffball fuchsias all clumped together with a few bay leaves tied round the stems by a reed. "A posy." I stared at it uneasily as recognition dawned. "A Cycling Day posy."

"Really?" Frazer asked keenly.

I nodded slowly, not liking the thoughts stirring in my head. Not at all.

"Then those things... " Rell trailed off, as disconcerted as me.

"Those things were dragging the Cycled bodies off to a compost machine." I brought my arm up, speaking softly to John. "Were they a type of cybot?"

"Theoretically that is possible," he said. "A biomechanical unit would have a similar heat signature, but *Daedalus* did not use biomechanical systems."

"Could the Electric Captain have made them?"

"Again, theoretically yes, if there are working buildbots. I cannot deduce why she would have done that. Many existing cybots would be more than capable of collecting and transporting Cycled bodies."

"Well I'm not scared to say it even if you are," Frazer said. "They were aliens!"

Rell gave a half laugh which trailed off nervously. "They can't be," and he turned to me to confirm that.

"I don't know," I said uneasily. All I could think of was that the *Daedalus* had visited the first world where our ancestors had encountered some kind of aliens. And the insidious fibres the Mutineers had planted – they were made from alien biology. So it wasn't completely impossible for another kind to be on board. "John?"

"We are dealing strictly in probabilities here. An alien is at least as likely as a new kind of cybot or an unknown animal species. Further speculation is pointless. We need facts."

"The Electric Captain introduced Cycling after the Mutiny," Frazer said. "So whatever those things are, they're working for her. And right now she doesn't like us or what we're doing."

"You really think they could be aliens?" Rell asked me.

"It's possible," I said simply, and just acknowledging that made it seem like the tunnel temperature had dropped several degrees.

As we resumed our trudge, I told him what we'd found in Tressaco when we'd tried to switch the medical machines and electricity back on. How the fibres had grown throughout the whole tower mountain, targeting the machines.

"The fibres had to have been planted by the Mutineers," Frazer said. "They were the ones who wanted to force Ashleigh Kruger to turn round by wrecking the *Daedalus*."

"So the Mutineers had their aliens," Rell said. "And... what? Ashleigh Kruger had hers?"

"We don't know," I said. "But I don't think the history that we learned in school is right."

"If the command AIs in the forward section are still working, they may have the answers we need," John said.

"We're going to be really busy in those forward compartments," Frazer said happily. "It's going to be so great."

"Yeah," I said. But I wasn't sharing his enthusiasm.

It was hours more before we finally arrived at Akebia station. By then I was so tired my limbs were trembling and my headache was producing little sparkles at the back of my eyes. Moving my head actually made it worse.

"Migraine," Rell said when I described the pain. "We all need to rest and get some food."

"I'm sorry," I said to Frazer as I sat on the edge of the platform and tried to inhale enough air. "I think you're going to have to walk."

He clambered off the trolley and gave me a big hug. That's so rare. I felt an equally rare lump in my throat.

"I can walk," he said quietly. "I'm never going to be a burden to you again, Hazel. I promise."

"You have never been a burden," I told him solemnly. "But no more tree climbing, okay?"

"Okay."

Rell was staring intently up at the curving ceiling. "It's up there," he said in a daze.

"What is?" I asked.

"My village. Everyone I've spent my whole life with." He stretched up his arm, as if trying to touch them. "It's so strange. We never knew this was down here. The tunnels. The maintenance chambers, garages..."

"We don't know a lot of things," I told him. "But we're going to find them out again."

"How do we get up there?" Frazer asked.

"No," I corrected him. "How do we get up there *quietly*, without anyone knowing." The main entrance to the station must have been sealed off somehow. I didn't like to think how much racket and disturbance we'd make if we broke through directly into the village hall.Rell described the lift platform Akebia used for its Cycling Day ceremony, where the bodies of the newly Blessed sank down into the ground. It was very similar to the one at Ixia.

"That will be the station's secondary maintenance access lift," John said. "It is in the loading bay."

"Lead on," I told him.

The service tunnels just outside the station led to the loading-bay room. There were no lights on inside it. We switched our torches on to see an empty chamber. No wreckage, no old machines. Just the lift rails running up the far wall.

"A clear path," Rell observed. "So the *things* can get straight to the Cycled bodies."

My torch beam illuminated two buttons set on the wall beside the rails. "It can't be that easy," I muttered.

Rell's arm went round my shoulder and gave me a little squeeze. "I think we're entitled to some *easy* after everything we've been through."

I pressed the button with the downward-pointing arrow on it. A soft whirring sound emerged from the deep shadows above. A metal platform slid down the rails until it was level with the floor.

"Told you," Rell said, grinning. "Easy."

We trooped on and I pressed the button with the upward-pointing arrow. The platform ascended. I shone my torch up in time to see the safety doors slide apart, revealing a square of moonlight. I hurriedly switched the torch off.

We slid up out of the ground, five metres from the back of the Akebia village hall.

It felt quite creepy, the way we emerged back into the habitat. Underground was where we sent our dead. I could well imagine how eerie it would look if living people had come up on Ixia's Cycling platform. It was almost like a form of sacrilege.

Thankfully, there was no one around to see us appear. It was night, and the platform was surrounded by the cherry trees I remembered planted around Akebia's village hall. Thin streaks of moonlight filtered through the leaves and blossom overhead, turning the air to a sweet mellow haze. If my head hadn't been quite so sore, I might have appreciated that.

"Now what?" Frazer asked as we stepped off the platform.

"My parents' cabin is five minutes away," Rell said. "Maybe longer – we'll need to be careful getting there. I don't want to draw attention to you."

"Nobody knows us here," Frazer said in annoyance.

"They all know me," I said.

"Yeah, but they don't know we're the ones that've been declared Mutineers; they'll just think it's romantic you coming back with Rell."

"And in this village, that news will take a good twenty seconds to spread to every cabin," Rell said.

I rubbed my fingers against my temple. "We'll go the safe way. But... Rell," I said with a glance to the Village Hall. "Are there any headache pills in there? I could really do with some."

"Of course. Come on."

As we moved off, the first thing I did was check the sky. Sure enough, the Swirl was still there, lurking between two light strips. I nudged Frazer and pointed.

"Oh my dayz," he muttered.

Rell led us round the village hall to a small door and peered inside. "It's clear."

We slipped in and closed the door behind us. Akebia's village hall was different to ours. The walls were all some kind of seamless black stone while the ceiling was a glass that shaded between colours. It kept transforming us as we walked along the corridor. I was watching Frazer's blond hair in front of me as it went from purple to green, then red and yellow and blue, then back to green. It was so tempting to get my torch out. The weird light effect wasn't helping my migraine.

Rell stopped outside another door, listening intently. "This is the hospital," he whispered. "I can't hear anyone inside."

Frazer was holding the crossbow. I saw his hand tighten on it and wished I'd got the welder out of my bag.

Rell opened the door and his shoulders dropped in relief. The walls and ceiling were different to Ixia's hospital but everything else was familiar – the beds, the cabinets full of herbs and bandages, the instruments.

"The medicine machine is along here," Rell said, leading us down a corridor with doors open on single bedrooms. There were patients in some of them – I could hear coughing and wheezing. One man was humming nervously. We hurried along as quietly as we could.

The circular room with the medicine machine had a glass ceiling that was half green and half purple. When I closed the door behind us, I was washed in pale green radiance while the machine bathed in cool purple.

"I know the sequence," Rell said confidently, and started tapping circles on a small screen.

"Wait," I said. "John, can you talk to it?"

"No, the network node is inactive."

I stared at the access panels on the base of the machine. "Do you think the alien plant is here, too?"

"That is the most likely conclusion."

"Should we cut it?"

"No!" Frazer said immediately. "If we do that, the Electric Captain will know we're here. She knew we'd cut the fibres in Tressaco as soon as we did it."

"Really? The alien plant fibres interfering with the machines are tiny. I thought maybe she noticed because we cut the big root in the power utility management room."

"I've just started to walk again," Frazer said forcefully. "I don't want to risk the Regulators catching us tonight, okay."

"All right," I agreed. He did have a point – cutting the fibres would be reckless. I'd just hoped that John could get the machine to produce something that would stop my migraine completely, that's all.

Rell started tapping the request circles again. A minute later, three pink pills dropped into the dispenser tray. I grabbed them and swallowed immediately. It wasn't the first time I'd used them, which is why I was so keen for John to coax the pharmalogical processor into producing something a lot stronger.

More pills popped out, and Rell took two for himself.

"Can we just check and see if the alien fibres are in the machine?" I said.

"I suppose so," Rell said. "How do we do that?"

I eyed the small rectangular access panels. "John, you said the D-blade could cut through anything, right?"

It was Frazer who did it, slicing the glowing red blade carefully around an access panel as if he were cutting the core from an apple. He was used to tools and cutting, so I guessed he'd make a better job of it than me.

We all bent down to look as I shone my torch into the hole. Sure enough, a slim string of white fibre had sprouted up through the conduit hole in the floor. It branched into a multitude of thinner fibres which wove chaotically round the internal components.

"The vile stuff is everywhere," I said. "It must control everything."

"We need to check the village screen," Frazer said.

"What will that prove?" Rell asked. He looked particularly disturbed. I wondered if he'd been humouring us, that he didn't truly believe we'd found an alien bioweapon that attacked the *Daedalus* machines. I couldn't be angry with him about that. I mean, if anyone had said the same thing to me three days previously, I would've laughed in their face.

"That the Electric Captain is allied with the Mutineers," Frazer said. "That we've been lied to. That we're in a whole lot more trouble than we thought."

He wasn't exactly subtle. But now he'd gone and said it, I knew I had to see if the screen was infected by the alien fibres.

"Okay," Rell said, nodding. "Yeah. I get that."

We left the hospital and sneaked along the corridor to the main hall. The doors had big glass windows in the middle; Rell peered through. "No one about. But we have to be quick – there's always someone in the kitchen. We have a night shift that cooks the bread."

We hurried past the benches and chairs to the screen on the far wall. For all I'd spent my life watching the Electric Captain on ours, I'd never actually paid any real attention to the screen itself. This one was maybe a couple of centimetres thick, two metres long and one wide. And it was fixed flat to the wall.

"The power and network cables are on the back," John said. "Their sockets will be inset into the wall."

Frazer pressed his head to the wall at the side of the screen; he closed one eye and squinted. "There's a tiny gap, maybe a millimetre." He shone the torch at it. "Can't see a thing."

"We need to take it off," I said.

"There are brackets holding it in place," John said. "It should just lift off."

"That's it?"

"Yes. Simply slide it up, then bring it forwards."

Rell and I shrugged at each other. I gripped the bottom corner, which wasn't nearly big enough to give me a decent grip. The edge dug into my palms. Rell took the other side.

"Ready?" I said. "Lift."

It didn't budge.

"John?"

"The screen is quite heavy, and it has been in place for at least five centuries. Apply more force."

If I could have spared the energy, I would have glared at him. I pushed harder, gritting my teeth at the way the edge was cutting into my hand. Then, finally, I felt it move a fraction.

"Yes!" Rell and I said it at the same time – we smiled at each other in unison.

Slowly the screen began to shift, sliding up the wall a millimetre at a time. The weight was far greater than I'd been expecting. I was straining as hard as I could. Every heartbeat produced a nasty thud behind my eyes. Then suddenly there was no more resistance and the screen was free – and I was losing my grip – and it really was too heavy for me to hold up. I bent as fast as I could, trying to put it down before I dropped it. Didn't quite make it. The screen fell the last ten centimetres, its corner slamming into the ground.

Rell got his side down and Frazer shone the torch on the screen. I'd been expecting all sorts of damage, but it was intact.

I let out a long breath of relief. "Sorry," I said meekly to Rell.

Frazer shifted the torch beam up. Just like John said, the screen had been covering a small rectangular hole in the wall with a row of black electrical sockets at the back. One of them had a plug inserted, with a coil cable that now stretched down the wall to the rear of the screen. Next to it, a white fibre had wormed its way out of a socket. Unlike the cable, it wasn't long enough to stretch down to the screen. It had snapped, and a single drop of dark yellow fluid glistened on its broken end.

"Oh, guano!" I groaned.

"Hazel," said a voice behind us. "I knew I'd find you here."

I yelped and jumped at the same time. Frazer swung the torch round wildly. My hand reached for my bag, though I knew I'd never get the welder out in time; the Regulator darts would shoot into me – then the torch beam swept across the three people who'd just come through the door. My heard did another judder.

"*Alice?*"

She smiled so gloriously wide, and opened her arms. "Ta-dah!"

"Alice!" My hand went to my chest where my heart was still quivering in fright. I thought my knees were going to give out. "Alice, what are you doing here?"

Alice ran over, her smile even wider and more than a little smug. She gave me a huge hug, which calmed a lot of my shakes. "I'm here to help."

"Help?" I said weakly.

"Me and the boys. You remember the boys, right?"

I looked over her shoulder to where Shao and Tamran were standing sheepishly. "I remember."

"Chief Atov and his deputy arse, Elijah, wanted to Cycle you. You didn't think I was just going to stand by and do nothing, did you?" she asked.

"No."

"It's really good to see you, Alice," Frazer said sincerely.

"You too. And now I'm here we're going–" She stopped, mouth dropping open. I don't get to see Alice startled very often. My lips twitched in a smile.

"Frazer," she said in wonder. "You're standing. You can walk again!"

"Yeah," he said modestly. "Hazel switched on some of the old medical machines in Tressaco. They cured me."

"*You* switched Tressaco back on?" she asked.

My turn for the modesty routine. "Yeah."

"She's the captain's daughter, you know," Frazer said. "That's why the Electric Captain has gone bananas."

"Huh?"

"Listen," Rell said. "It's wonderful you're here, but we all have to get out of the hall. Now."

"Oh." I flinched, and looked at the broken white fibre. The tiny drop of yellow-brown fluid amplified my guilt and worry once more. "He's right. We have to leave."

"People will know we've been here," Frazer said, and pointed at the screen. "We have to lift it back."

"Oh, right," Rell said. He beckoned Shao and Tamran. Between them they got hold of the screen and started to lift. Shao shot me a surprised look when he discovered how heavy it was, but as always he didn't say anything.

Alice linked her arm through mine, pausing only to pinch my sleeve. "Nice jacket."

"Thanks. Alice?"

"Yes?"

"I'm really pleased you came."

"That's what friends are for. Speaking of which," she pulled me a bit closer. "You and Rell?"

"Yes?" I asked cautiously.

"You did?"

"What? No."

"No?"

"Alice! I've spent the whole day running through tunnels being chased by Elijah."

"That sounds exciting."

I looked at Rell. The boys had got the screen up, but it was proving difficult to hook it back on the wall bracket. Frazer had his cheek pressed against the wall again, torch shining on the brackets, giving them directions. "No, it's not," I said. "Trust me."

"I didn't know there were tunnels under the habitat."

"Well, there are. And that's not even the bad part. But... how did you get here? Rell said you'd been locked up after you kicked Elijah."

"Certainly was. But then all the Regulators left Ixia to arrest whoever they could find in Tressaco. Our friends let us out ten minutes after they'd gone. Mayor Fininen was not a happy man. Your father threatened to put him in a cell."

"Really?"

"Yes."

"Then what?"

"I got straight on a horse and rode here. I knew Rell had gone to warn you – it was obvious you'd both head for Akebia – so as soon as I arrived I went and found Shao and Tamran. We've been waiting for you ever since. The three of us. Together. In Tamran's cabin."

I struggled against a mischievous smile. "Alice." I don't know why I'm scandalized by her anymore. Maybe I'm just comfortable in the role of the quiet friend.

"It was my idea you'd come to the hall eventually," she said. "I thought you'd be hungry."

"That's not good."

"What isn't?"

"If you worked that out, so will Elijah, eventually."

"I know. But you've got me and the boys now. We can all go and live in a tower mountain together. It'll be amazing. Hey, maybe you can switch another one back on?"

"That's… you were really going to do that? Leave Ixia? For me?"

She pulled me close again. "Absolutely. I've had more enough of village life, thank you. And you running off like that to save Frazer – I was so proud of you. Plus…" She glanced slyly at the boys, who were still struggling with the screen. "I can have me a tri-marriage."

"Oh, Alice."

"What? Plenty of people do these days. If we're going to live with a bunch of old people, I'll need to do something for serious fun."

"We're not running away to a tower mountain," I said solemnly. "Everything is different now."

"Got it," Tamran announced triumphantly.

The boys stood back to admire the screen. I may have been imagining it – I was very tired – but it could've been a tiny bit lopsided. Everyone's silence kind of confirmed they were all thinking the same thing.

"It'll do," Alice announced.

Which was good enough for me.

"You can stay at my cabin tonight," Tamran said. "I'm still doing it up but it's nice and isolated."

"Certainly is," said Alice, sharing a knowing smile with Shao.

"Just somewhere to sleep for a few hours," I said. "That's all I need. We'll have to leave before daylight switches on. I don't want anyone to see us."

"I'll get some food," Tamran said. "My sister is on the early kitchen shift."

We started walking towards the doors.

"Where are you planning on going?" Alice asked.

"The forward compartments."

"The... *what*?"

I grinned. That was twice in one night I'd managed to startle Alice. Not bad going for the quiet friend. I pushed the door open.

And a Regulator pistol was pointing at my head.

(15)

There were five Regulators standing in the corridor. I only saw Elijah. And his twisted smile was a lot more frightening than the pistol.

"You," I gasped.

"Me," he smirked. "I told you I would find you. And now you will face the Electric Captain's justice."

He advanced, and I backed into the hall. Alice and the others had their hands up. The Regulators kept their pistols on us. Hauer was behind Elijah, along with three Regulators from Akebia.

"Well, well," Elijah said when he saw Alice. "I might have known you'd be a part of this."

"Part of what?" Frazer asked in a voice rich with contempt. "Part of repairing the *Daedalus* and getting us all safely to the new world?"

Elijah frowned, looking Frazer up and down. "How are you walking?"

Frazer spoke clearly, making very sure the Akebia Regulators could hear every word. "When we switched Tressaco's electricity back on, the medical machines came on as well. They repaired my broken spine. Now, you tell me why that's such a bad thing?"

"You don't argue with the Electric Captain, boy," Elijah snarled. "Chief Sedilko, you heard the Electric Captain declare the Tressaco Cheaters to be Mutineers?"

"I did," said Akebia's chief. I'd seen him briefly at the invitation dance, a different *life* ago. He was in his late fifties, with thick silver hair and a heavily lined face, as if he was permanently sad. "But that doesn't include Rell, Tamran and Shao," he said.

"Rell was in Tressaco," Elijah said. "I saw him. Hauer?"

Hauer looked thoroughly miserable. "He was there."

"Rell was in Ixia when the Electric Captain was on the screen," I said. "He came to warn me about the lynch mob. You saw him when the Tressaco law machines disarmed you and told you I'm authorized to do whatever I want. Remember *that*, Hauer?"

"Don't you twist things!" Elijah shouted. "You Mutinied."

"Our boys stay here," Chief Sedilko said calmly. "I'll deal with them."

"Fine, whatever," Elijah said. He fixed me with a hot stare. "But these three come with me."

"Alice wasn't in Tressaco," I said. "How could she be? You locked her up in Ixia."

"Shut your mouth. You don't get to decide anything."

"Chief Sedilko?" I asked.

His face showed extreme uncertainty. He clearly wanted this scene to be playing out anywhere but Akebia.

"You said the Electric Captain declared us Mutineers?" Frazer asked in a level tone.

"Everyone knows it," Elijah said. "It was on every screen in the *Daedalus*."

Frazer cocked his head to look at Tamran. "Is that right? Was it on this hall's screen?"

"Yes," Tamran said unhappily.

"So you just do *what the screen tells you*?"

I could see Alice giving Frazer a curious glance. Once again, I marvelled at my brother's smarts. I'm sure I would have got there eventually.

"What's your point?" Chief Sedilko asked.

"Ask him," Frazer said, pointing at Elijah. "Ask him what the Tressaco law-enforcement machines said."

"Those machines were old and broken," Elijah snapped.

"That is not true, Regulator Elijah," a voice said from behind me. It was John's voice. It spoke as a pale radiance appeared, shining across the hall to banish the multi-coloured shadows.

I saw the shock on Chief Sedilko's face and slowly turned. The screen had lit up with a face. *Not* the Electric Captain. This was a man in his forties with a narrow chin and short hair.

His thin beard was perfectly trimmed and the collar of a smart uniform was visible. Somehow the face fitted John's voice perfectly.

"Who...?" Chief Sedilko grunted.

"How do you know my name?" Elijah whispered in astonishment.

"I am the *Daedalus* flight-command machine. The Electric Captain is responsible for maintaining the habitat and the people in it, but I am in overall charge of the ship. So of course I know your name, Elijah. The Electric Captain has reported it to me."

"She declared them Mutineers," Elijah said weakly.

"She was startled by Tressaco being switched back on and acted incorrectly. For that, she has apologized to me. Now, lower your weapons. The captain's daughter should not be threatened for doing what I told her to do."

"Captain's daughter?" Chief Sedilko said.

"Hauer?" I prompted.

His shoulders slumped. "That's what the Tressaco machines called Hazel."

Chief Sedilko gave him an incredulous stare, which then switched to me before finally turning to Elijah, anger building. "What is going on here?"

"Hazel is the descendant of Ashleigh Kruger," the face on the screen said. "I invited her into the forward compartments to discuss repairs that have to be made to the *Daedalus*. You do understand the Swirl above your village is a leak, don't you, Chief Sedilko? The habitat is losing air at a dangerous rate."

When the screen used his name, the poor chief looked like he'd been slapped hard across the face.

"That's what the Swirl is?" Tamran asked numbly.

"I told you," I said. "I told you all back at the dance. I have to get into the forward compartments where there are cybots – mobile machines – that can repair it."

"No," Elijah said. "No. This is a trick." He pointed his pistol at the screen. "You're a part of it. You're not a command machine, you're a Mutineer. You'll turn the *Daedalus* around and take us back to the first world."

"Regulator Elijah, stand down," the face ordered.

"No. This is wrong. Hazel ran away with her brother so he could Cheat. Now they're Mutineers. The Electric Captain said so. We all heard it!"

"Chief Sedilko, please restrain Elijah."

Elijah spun round, his pistol pointing at Sedilko, who immediately raised his, aiming at Elijah. They were standing barely two metres apart. The other Akebia Regulators hurriedly lined their pistols up on Elijah.

"Do the maths, Elijah," Sedilko said in a reasonable tone. "You can't win."

Elijah clenched his teeth, glaring at me. I found myself holding my breath as the two of them stared at each other for a couple of eternity-long seconds, then Elijah slowly lowered his pistol and holstered it. If anything, that seemed to make his anger even greater. "I believe the Electric Captain," he said, looking squarely at the screen. "Not you."

"I'm not your enemy," I said as earnestly as I could. "I just want to save the *Daedalus*. We have to seal the leak."

"Cheaters told her that guano about losing air," Elijah growled furiously at Sedilko. "Cheaters I caught. You can't believe her."

"Cheaters who risked everything to warn us," I cried back. "And you murdered them."

"See? See? This is what she's like!"

"The captain's daughter is correct," the screen said. "You will all die within two years if the damage is not repaired and the habitat atmosphere refilled."

Elijah whipped round. "Then why don't you do it?" he snarled. "If you're really what you say you are, what do you need *her* for?"

"The damage caused by the puncture impact destroyed my links to the cybots. The captain's daughter and her people will follow my direction and switch them on, as she did in Tressaco."

"Lies!"

"Enough," Sedilko said. "Take him out," he told his Regulators.

Elijah's hand went back to his holster. "You're not locking me up."

"Fine. Get back on your horse and get the hell out of my village. Tomorrow morning, I'm going to call a conclave of all the mayors and Regulator chiefs. This is going to be sorted out once and for all. And your behaviour, Regulator, will be the first item on the agenda."

Elijah gave me one last furious look and stomped out of the hall, followed by Hauer.

"Thank you, Chief," I said.

His thick eyebrow rose as he studied me. "Are you really the captain's daughter?"

"Yes. I only found out yesterday."

"Okay then." He made his decision and faced the screen. "What happens now, sir?"

"Please give the captain's daughter all the assistance she requires. Hazel, you need to have a full night's sleep. Tomorrow morning, please follow the route I gave you to the forward compartments."

"I will, sir," I said formally. "Thank you."

"I look forward to meeting you."

The screen went dark.

We didn't go back to Tamran's cabin. There was a whole ward in the hospital that wasn't being used, and it had decent beds.

It was also next to Chief Sedilko's office – and the Regulator cells. I think he wanted to keep us close. Just in case.

Tamran was sent to get some food from the kitchen.

Chief Sedilko asked me plenty of questions. I kept the answers as close to the truth as possible – without mentioning John, alien bioweapon fibres, and creatures in the tunnels. I figured the chief had enough new thoughts to deal with. Besides, I kept thinking of Randorf – he was a good man, an honest man, but his view of the universe was so narrow, leaving him resistant to any change. Maybe I did the chief a disservice with the comparison. Maybe not. I couldn't take the risk – there was too much at stake.

Frazer showed Sedilko the white collar that had merged with his skin, which the chief conceded was some kind of Builder technology.

"So what kind of assistance do you want?" he asked.

"Nothing much," I admitted. "The flight-command machine said there was an entrance to the forward sections in the endwall not far from here. It will open the door for us when we get there."

"All right. I'll escort you there in the morning."

"Thank you."

Tamran returned with a tray of food and milk. I hadn't realized how hungry I was until I saw it. It'd been too long since my solitary cheese-and-tomato sandwich.

"Get a good sleep," Sedilko said. "I'm going to explain what's happened to the mayor. We need to see about organizing that conclave."

As he left, I saw two of his Regulators standing guard in the corridor outside. I guessed he trusted me as much as I trusted him.

Alice and I started helping ourselves to the food. "What happened to Zawn?" I asked quietly. "The morning after Frazer and I ran away?"

Her gaze flicked towards Rell, who was talking to Shao. "You're kidding. You want to know about Zawn when you've got yourself a piece of that?"

Now it was my turn to glance at Rell – a guilty glance. "I don't care about Zawn, I just wanted to know what happened. That's all."

"Why?"

"Zawn was on duty when we sneaked out. I managed to dodge him. Did he get in trouble for it?"

"Yes. If you must know, Chief Atov suspended him – said if he couldn't even see a boy in a wheeled chair roll out of town then he probably doesn't have what it takes. Zawn was pretty upset. But that was nothing compared to Elijah. He and the chief had a blazing row. The whole kitchen heard it."

"Oh, no," I moaned. "So Elijah blames me for Zawn being suspended."

"Yeah," Alice said. She didn't sound upset about it.

"Zawn was so pleased he'd been chosen to be a Regulator." I remembered the smile on his face the day he was awarded probationary status. I was the first person he sought out to tell. The two of us had sneaked off to the cabin we used, and it wasn't even raining that night. Now that prestigious job of his had been put in question – because of me. Zawn must have known Chief Atov would react badly, yet still he let me go. I couldn't figure that out. How could his feelings for me still be that strong? I'd never done anything to encourage him – quite the opposite, in fact.

Losing his job was a rotten reward for helping someone.

When I got back to Ixia, I'd have to make sure Zawn was reinstated. Somehow.

Alice started on the cold chicken and bread rolls. "You have had such an amazing time. Captain's daughter. You!" She shook her head in amusement.

I drank down a whole glass of milk. "It's not as glamorous as it sounds."

"Don't be so modest." She sat on a bed next to Tamran and playfully fed him a grape. He responded by sliding his arm round her waist and kissing her. "Stop that," she said, without meaning it at all.

"So are you coming with me tomorrow?" I asked.

"To the forward compartments? Try and stop me," she growled.

"We can't wait that long," Frazer announced matter-of-factly as he peeled the shell off a hard-boiled egg.

I hated the way he said that. It meant he was more than likely right. And there I was just starting to relax. My muscles were so tired, I wasn't even sure I could move off the bed. "What do you mean?"

"We broke the alien fibre when we took the screen off the wall. *She* knows we're here."

I let out a hiss of distress. He was right. The fright of encountering Elijah had dominated my thoughts, I hadn't considered the consequences of that miserable little alien fibre.

"Who knows you're here?" Alice asked.

"The Electric Captain."

"But... the flight-command machine is in charge."

I winced, held up my arm so she could see the black bracelet. "That's not quite true. Alice, meet John."

"Delighted to meet you, Alice," John said. "Hazel speaks of you a lot."

Alice's jaw dropped, showing off a mouthful of chicken. "That's the same voice–"

"John linked to the screen," Frazer said. "He could do that once we broke the fibre. At least, that's what I assumed."

"Very astute," John said.

"So that man wasn't the flight-command machine?" Alice said.

"No," John said. "I created the image."

"So what are you?"

"An independent artificial-intelligence unit. However, the rest of it is all true. Hazel is the descendent of Ashleigh Kruger. The habitat is leaking air. We do need to switch on the engineering department cybots to repair the breach."

"And the Electric Captain isn't our friend," I finished. "We don't think she ever has been."

"If she follows the same pattern as before," Frazer said, "then right now she'll be on every village screen in the habitat telling the Regulators that Akebia has Mutinied. A whole army of Regulators will be here before the daylight switches on."

"With Elijah leading the charge," I muttered gloomily.

"Seriously?" Alice challenged, but without any of her usual confidence. Tamran tightened his arm protectively round her. Shao went over and sat on the other side of her. Her twin guardian angels. I was impressed by their devotion. Maybe it would work if she married them both.

"Very seriously," I admitted.

"We have to leave," Frazer said. "Everyone knows where we're going now. The Regulators will keep watch on the endwall. We can't let them stop us."

I looked at the ward's windows, long rectangles of clear glass set into the black stone wall at waist height.

"They don't open," Rell warned me.

"Of course not." I dug into my bag and produced the D-blade.

"Sweet Captain," Alice murmured as I sliced round the window, then let it fall outside. It landed on the grass with a dull thud.

I stuck my forearm through and held it vertically, sweeping it slowly from side to side. "John, what can you see?"

"There is an infra-red signature a hundred and fifty metres away. Adult human size, partially concealed behind a tree trunk. They're watching the village hall."

"Elijah?"

"I do not know."

"It'll be him," Rell said in a disgusted voice.

"Anything else?" I asked John.

"Some rabbits. Several birds nesting in the trees. No further humans."

"All right. Where's the nearest door to the forward compartments?"

"I deduce the main ones have been blocked. Therefore I would suggest a cybot access shaft which starts behind the waterfall."

"Behind the waterfall?" Tamran asked. "You're kidding."

"No. I do not kid."

"I never knew there was an opening there."

"Me neither," Rell said. He sounded troubled. "The waterfall is… powerful. Parents have to warn their children to keep clear when they swim in the pool."

"We'll go for the waterfall," I said.

"What are we going to do about our lurker friend?" Rell asked.

"We're going to stop being fearful and running, that's what we're going to do," I told him – and meant it. Elijah wasn't going to surprise me or wreck our plans anymore. What we were doing was too important. To emphasise that, I took the welder out of my bag.

Alice stared at it in trepidation. "Hazel, what's that?"

"A weapon. A real one."

"You're not going to–"

"To save the lives of everyone on board, I'll do whatever I have to."

She managed a meagre smile. "This is why I love you. Always a surprise. Okay then, boys. Let's go."

(16)

Rell went first, then helped Frazer through the window. I went next, followed by Alice and her loyal entourage. Everyone trusting and helping the other. A proper team. It felt really good, being a part of that. Belonging.

We moved silently through the cherry trees, walking at a reasonable pace so Frazer could cope. John watched Elijah for us. The Regulator was following us but not getting any closer as he slipped from one tree trunk to another. No doubt he thought he had the edge on us, that he'd finally be able to lead a team of Regulators to our Mutinous activities, exposing us at the very culmination of our treachery. Try as I might, I couldn't think how to turn that on him, to convince him of the truth.

All I could do now was hope that refilling the habitat with new air would swing the majority of people round to realizing I was right. It would be such a different life. We'd find out what those things were in the tunnels and understand what the Electric Captain was doing. There would be no more mysteries. Then I'd be able to spend some proper time with Rell. I couldn't quite imagine that, but I knew I'd enjoy it. I'd still not got John to play him any music from old Earth. That was going to be such fun, discovering all those ten thousand songs together.

It took us twenty minutes to circle round Akebia village to the edge of the pool. The noise of the waterfall thundering down, relentless and eternal, became more and more imposing as we approached. And somehow the endwall, that blank face of dark rock reaching up to the sky and stretching out on either side until the habitat's curve took it away, was far more daunting than any of the tower mountains.

I reached out and touched the rock, almost reverently. Beyond it lay the forward compartments and the answers to everything. And way, way up ahead, the new world was waiting for us. Our future.

I found it hard to concentrate on that. Rell had been right about the waterfall. Up close, it dominated every sense. It may have been because it was still night, but the sheer quantity of water pouring down was actually scary. I kept thinking what would happen if I slipped and fell underneath it. I'd be slammed mercilessly onto the bottom of the pool – which was all rock – and the force would probably pin me there. And Frazer... he was even more likely to slip.

I turned to him, ready to tell him he could wait on the bank if he wanted.

"I know what you're thinking, so don't," Frazer warned.

My head dropped in defeat.

"Shall I go first?" Rell said. He didn't sound particularly keen.

"Do you know exactly where the entrance is?" I asked John.

"Yes."

"Then I'll go first," I said, hoping my reluctance wasn't too obvious. The edge of the pool was lined with large black boulders, all slick with spray. I picked my way along them, with Frazer following, then Rell. Alice and her boys made up the rear. Shao, who was last, kept a close watch on the bank. I was worried Elijah would see our predicament and run forwards. Strung out like this, fighting for balance, he could easily pick us off with his pistol. We had nowhere to go.

When I was five metres from the waterfall, it was so loud that talking became pointless. The round surface of my bracelet lit up a dull amber and began a slow flash. John had said he would use the flashes to guide me to the entrance; when the flashes stopped, I'd be there. All I could think was that all those schematics in his memory must be very accurate.

Three metres from the waterfall and the spray was thicker than the shower in Tressaco, drenching me. The force of the spray on my head was already disturbing. I forced myself to move slowly, to make sure my feet were secure after every sideways step before attempting another.

Until I was a metre away, I wasn't even sure there was a gap between the back of the waterfall and the endwall. But there it was, barely wide enough to hold me, and congested with spray. I pressed myself against the rock, hands flat against it, fingers searching out little fissures to grip.

Slowly, slowly, I inched along. I only knew I was behind the immense torrent because of the darkness that'd closed in on me. The air itself was vibrating now – I could feel it shaking my bones. I switched on the torch I was holding, though the only thing the beam showed was an eternal white spume. I didn't even dare risk shaking my head to get the water out of my eyes. The weight and power of the cascade would tear me from the endwall in an instant if it caught any part of me. Claustrophobia tightened its grip, making breathing hard work. I tried to focus on the bracelet but my vision was just a blur. I could see a splodge of amber but had no idea if it was flashing or constant. Below my hands, the rock had turned slimy. Algae and ribbons of weed were smothering every square centimetre of the endwall, I could feel them squishing about through my soles, increasing the danger of slipping.

I was badly frightened now. This was an utterly ludicrous idea that was going to get me and my friends killed. All my own stupid fault. If I'd just had the courage to show John to Chief Sedilko, he would have understood. But no, I didn't trust anyone – too self-important and selfish.

I brought my arm up until my wrist was almost touching my nose, then squeezed my eyes closed for several long seconds. The idea was that when I opened them, I might have banished some of the water haze. It worked – after a fashion. When I opened my eyes, I saw the amber flashes on the bracelet coming very fast now, several a second.

That gave me courage. The entrance must be close. Another little shuffle along.

Long blink. The flashes were practically constant now. Further shuffling. Hands sliding across the slick endwall, unable to find any purchase at all. Then the rock started to curve away, creating a wider gap.

I checked the bracelet. The amber light was steady. I slid my hand across the cold, slippery rock in a wide sweep – out, up and down, further out, stretching...

My fingers tracked across emptiness. I froze. This was the moment of maximum danger. I had to be really careful bending down. The gap between rock and pounding water might be a few centimetres wider, but I mustn't think that was going to make this manoeuvre any easier.

I slowly traced the edge of the entrance. It seemed to be a hole that started at about ankle height with a top below my shoulders. With that established, I lifted one foot and pushed it round the edge of the hole. It was still slimy inside. I shoved my foot deeper in, carefully bending my other knee to lower myself. One hand went inside, and there was a ridge that I gripped so tightly I thought I might crush the rock.

With a leg and arm inside the hole, I slithered round the edge as if I'd become boneless. Then I was inside and wriggling away from the waterfall.

I shone the torch around. The access passageway was barely a metre and a half high. It was pitch black ahead while the waterfall roared past with lethal force behind me. I turned round, scraping elbows on the hard walls, and stuck the torch out of the entrance, pointing it back the way I'd come, then waved it up and down. Frazer would see that and know what it meant, that the torment would soon be over.

Before long, I saw his hand creep round the edge of the entrance. I grabbed it, praying the touch wouldn't make him jump in shock. Thirty seconds later he was lying beside me in the passageway, eyes wide with shock or fright – probably both. He opened his mouth, shouting. I couldn't hear a word he said. Then he was jabbing his hand, pointing down the access passageway. It was easy enough to understand – we couldn't both wait at the entrance for Rell as there wasn't enough room. I gave him a thumbs up and started to walk along the passageway, practically bent double. Behind me I saw Frazer stick his hand out and wave a torch about.

Ten metres and the passage ended in a door. It was soaking wet but there was no algae here. Because there was no light, I guessed. I played the beam round and saw a metal handle set into the wall. John had said there would be one, an emergency manual release. It took plenty of tugging – I wound up hanging my whole bodyweight off it – but it eventually hinged out. Then I had to rotate it – almost as difficult.

Abruptly I heard something, a metallic screech that blended into the awesome roar of water. When I shone the torch again, I saw the door had opened a centimetre. I tried to move the handle some more, but it wouldn't shift any further. I was sobbing, I was so exhausted and cold.

Then Frazer was worming his way up beside me. He too gripped the handle and together we started to turn it.

The door slid open and a white glare shone out through the gap. I scrambled through onto some kind of metal grid.

I'd emerged in a cavern twice the size of the Tressaco vestibule. It gave me the first real glimpse of what *Daedalus* had been like before the Mutiny. There were racks along the floor, stretching the length of the chamber. They were made from some translucent white material, like carved marble – not in here the nailed-together shelves that came out of Dad's carpentry shop. Everything the Builders had created had an elegance to it and these were clearly designed to last.

There were cybots resting in the racks – not many, maybe thirty in a chamber clearly meant to house hundreds. Some were similar to the cleaners in Tressaco; others were a lot bigger – as tall as me. Six long arms sprouted from their upper rim, looking more animal than mechanical as they hung almost to the floor. Where hands should have been were black metallic tools I didn't recognize.

"Finally," John said. "Some help."

"Are they working?" Frazer asked in fascination. All the dread I'd seen back in the access passage moments ago had vanished; this was the Frazer who'd just scored another goal, built another contraption. A chamber full of cybots was his own personal heaven.

"Some are inactive," John said. "But nearly half are in standby mode. I am activating them now."

Rell came crawling through the open hatchway, dripping water from his saturated clothes. He staggered to his feet and I clung to him. The shakes running up and down my body weren't just from the cold. All that numbing dark fear kindled by traversing the back of the waterfall was taking a long time to subside. But the way his arms hugged me helped a lot.

"You okay?" he asked softly.

I just nodded, tightening my grip.

Tamran emerged, with Alice sloshing along behind him. Then Shao was in, and I felt a wave of relief.

"We made it," I said, almost laughing at how outrageous we'd been. Defying the waterfall was the stupidest thing I'd ever done. I couldn't bear to think about how dangerous it had been. If one of us had made the tiniest mistake…

I kissed Rell, then made my way over to Alice. "Still think following me was a good idea?"

She managed a half smile. Her gaze swept round the chamber. "I didn't believe before, not really. Being with you, defying the Regulators, was just….exciting. But this – it's all real, isn't it?"

"It's real," I told her.

"Is the air running out?"

"Yes."

"So will these things fix it?" She gestured at the cybots.

"No," John said. "These are general-maintenance cybots. The type of cybots that can tackle the Swirl leak are up on the main engineering level."

"Please tell me there are no more waterfalls between here and there," I implored.

"There are no more waterfalls."

"Good!" The relief made me feel incredibly tired, a sensation stronger than the cold gripping my flesh. Just about the only thing keeping me on my feet was the way Rell held me. "We need to rest."

"We need to get dry and warm," Alice grumbled through chattering teeth.

"There are offices at the far end of this chamber," John said. "I suggest we look there to see if there's anything useful."

"Not yet," Rell said. "We need to deal with Elijah first."

"Simple enough," Frazer said. "Just shut the hatch. If he is following us through the waterfall, the light from here will be shining down the access passageway, telling him where we are. Close it, and he won't be able to see a thing. He'll have to go back then."

"No," I said. The thought of anyone trapped behind the waterfall in the pitch dark, not knowing what had happened or where to go, chilled me more than my saturated clothes ever could. I couldn't do that to another person, not even Elijah.

So much for all my bravado. Besides, if we could get Elijah to accept the truth then anything was possible. And if he saw the forward chambers and the command Ais, he'd have no choice but to believe.

"No?" Rell asked, and he sounded disappointed too.

"You know what it's like behind the waterfall. If he doesn't make it into the access passageway, he'll probably get swept away."

"He wants to Cycle us!" Alice exclaimed.

"I want to be better than him," I said. "I want our future to be better than it'll be with him and people like him in charge. We deserve that."

They grumbled. They pulled miserable faces. But, in the end, we clustered round the open hatchway and waited.

"Why put the access passageway here anyway?" Tamran asked. "It's not like they could ever use it. The waterfall would smash the cybots about too, if they ever tried to go out."

"The waterfall would be switched off before they travelled down the passageway," John said. "Standard procedure. There are access passageways to most parts of the habitat."

"You can switch off the waterfalls?" Frazer asked.

"They are not natural but are part of the habitat environmental system. In fact it is surprising the water pumps have worked so well for five hundred years without interruption. They have multiple redundancy, but even so…"

It was several more minutes before a wet, cold, exhausted, and scared Elijah came crawling out of the hatch. He blinked round at the cavern in astonishment.

Rell pulled the pistol from Elijah's holster, and the Regulator didn't even protest. He didn't question the welder I pointed at him either. I guess my attitude told him all he needed.

"You have a choice," I told him. "You go back the way you came, carry on lying to people about me, or you come with us and see what's here."

He looked at all of us in turn. There was still a universe of hate and anger in his eyes, but I could also see suspicion. The start of doubt.

"Where are you going?" he asked.

"I told you. We're going to switch on the machines that can repair the Swirl hole."

He shook his head. "The Electric Captain will never let you interfere with the machines. Not here."

"Then what have you got to lose?"

"You really are this stupid, aren't you? It's not an act."

Rell started forwards, his fists coming up. I gripped his shoulder and pulled him back. "That's what he wants," I said. "Ignore him."

"But–"

"Do as you're told," Elijah mocked.

"You need to behave," I said wearily. "You need to be more… civilized."

"Or what?"

And suddenly I'd had enough. I was risking my life and those of my friends to help people, and this was how I got treated! "John, bring the biggest cybot on line, please. Use it to restrain Elijah."

One of the general-maintenance cybots slid forward. I could see it seemed to be rolling on top of some football-sized spheres that were fixed in its base. Elijah gave it an alarmed look and took a step back. The cybot brought an arm up *fast*. A three-finger pincer closed round Elijah's wrist. He tried to jerk it away, but the pincer didn't budge.

"Guano!" he exclaimed. "Hey, stop this. Get it off me."

"If you annoy me, if you make trouble, if you say something nasty about my friends, I will shoot you with your own dart. Do you understand?"

"I'm not going to put up with…"

He trailed off as I snatched the pistol from Rell and flicked the safety catch (old Shamus had showed us how that worked on one of his school visits). "*Do you understand?*" I roared.

"Just stay calm," Elijah said. "I get it, okay? It's been a day like no other – we're all exhausted and on edge. So let's all calm down here. We'll go where you say this flight-command machine is. Hell, maybe you're right, maybe there is a leak."

I shoved the pistol back at Rell. There was no way I was going to start explaining the deception John had pulled back in Akebia's hall.

* * *

Seventeen cybots came with us to the offices, including the one that held Elijah. There wasn't much inside, just some chairs like the one Frazer had used back in Tressaco and some desks, and a couple of chest-sized machines that looked like smaller versions of the medicine machines in Ixia village hall.

"Can you turn the temperature up?" I asked John, without much hope. I was still shivering.

"There is a manual temperature control on the wall behind you."

I followed John's instructions and soon had warm air blowing out of the vents in the ceiling. I stood under it, waiting for my clothes to dry out. It took a lot longer than I was expecting. I was practically asleep standing up when I decided I was slightly comfier. At least I'd stopped shivering.

"I will keep watch," John said. "The cybots will act as sentries."

I was way too tired to ask what they were going to watch out for, so I lay down next to Rell. His arm went over me. I managed a cosy smile at that. There were a lot of things I wanted to say to him.

I fell asleep right away.

I was walking down the tunnel when something started moving behind me. I knew it was there because of the scratching sounds it made as it scrabbled along. Every time I turned round to look, the tunnel became even darker. The scratching grew louder and louder. I started to run, but my feet slipped and I went sprawling in the filthy water. The darkness closed in like a solid force as the scratching became deafening.

I woke up with a start, my arms fighting off the nightmare. Alice and Frazer were sitting together, talking quietly. They both looked at me.

"You okay?" Frazer asked.

"Bad dream," I admitted.

"Oh. I slept for hours. I feel a lot better now."

I saw Alice grinning. "Good," I said tartly. "I'm glad." When I looked round, I saw a pair of cybots standing just outside the office door. More of them were spread out across the chamber. Elijah had somehow managed to curl up round the base of the one that was attached to him. He looked ridiculous, which cheered me up.

"How long did I sleep?" I asked John.

"Seven and a half hours," John said.

That would explain why I was ravenous again.

"There is a drinks dispenser in the second office," John said. "It has no network connection so it may work."

Alice and I trooped over to investigate. Our whoops of delight woke everyone up. You couldn't really blame us. John had recommended something called a Hot Chocolate.

"Sweet Captain!" Alice exclaimed after she'd taken her first sip. "This is almost as good as boys worshipping me."

"You may be right," I agreed. The taste was astonishing. "This makes everything worthwhile."

"If you bring this to the villages, they'll crown you mayor of *Daedalus* by the end of the day."

I sipped down some more. I wanted to take larger gulps but it was too hot for that. "I will rule wisely and kindly as long as everyone does as I tell them."

"As long as I can have more of this, I'll do whatever you say."

"Why don't we grow chocolate?" I asked. "Is it a plant or a meat – what?"

"I'm surprised you are unfamiliar with chocolate," John said. "The cocoa bean grows in climates similar to the habitat. However, it does requires a long process to turn it into an edible product."

"That's us," Alice said wistfully. "We can't afford time for anything decent." She pressed the button for a refill.

That was when I looked round to see everyone else crowding into the doorway. Even Elijah and his cybot warden was there.

"What are you two crazies talking about now?" Frazer asked.

"Drink this and tell us we're crazy," Alice challenged, and held out the cup.

I was impressed the dispenser didn't run out of cups. Even Elijah had three, not that he said thank you or anything.

"So now what?" Alice asked when everyone was bloated from a breakfast of chocolate and more chocolate.

"The engineering department level is two kilometres above us," John told us. "It is divided into twenty separate sections. The nearest to the swirl will be Section Seventeen."

"Two kilometres?" Tamran said. "That's above the sky."

Elijah snorted in contempt but didn't say anything.

"How do we get up there?" I asked. I kept thinking of the last time I was in the Tressaco lifts, when John had fought his strange invisible fight with the Electric Captain to control them. No way did I want to get caught up in that kind of battle again.

"There are several routes. I don't know which are open. There are no active network nodes in here."

So once again all my anxieties came surging back. "You mean you don't know what's on the other side of the doors?"

"No."

"Which door out of here opens up the largest number of route options?" Frazer asked.

"The third."

We armed ourselves. Rell took the Regulator pistol. Frazer handed the crossbow over to Shao – Rell told us he'd been shooting ducks and swans since he could walk. I gripped the welder.

"What about me?" Elijah asked.

"What about you?" Alice asked.

"If there is something bad waiting, like you claim, I won't be able to run with this thing attached to me. Or do you not believe in what you're saying?"

I glanced at Rell, who shrugged. "Okay," I said. "John, release him – but keep watch, okay?"

"Yes, captain's daughter." He always made a point of calling me that when Elijah was close.

The cybot's metal pincer let go of Elijah. He rubbed his wrist slowly, giving me a thoughtful look. "What is that bracelet thing?"

"John? He's an independent machine from before the Mutiny. He can talk to all the other old machines."

"And has the Electric Captain confirmed that?"

"No." John said. "But when I have a network connection to whatever the Electric Captain is, I suspect we will have great many subjects to discuss. Legitimacy will be high on the list."

John deployed the cybots in a semi-circle around the door. We stood behind them. "Is everyone ready?" he asked.

"Do it," I told him.

One cybot used the manual release above the door. Another pulled it open. It was completely lightless on the other side.

"No active network nodes," John reported. "There is a switch for the back-up lighting circuit one metre to the left." A cybot rolled forward thorough the door and turned left. A moment later, the lights came on to reveal a wide corridor that seemed to stretch away forever.

Ten cybots rolled out. We followed.

(17)

We passed so many doors. Some small, like the front door at home, some big, and some so big I couldn't imagine what went through them – something that would have completely filled the corridor. I wanted to look in the rooms and compartments behind all those closed doors. So did Frazer.

"If we look in every room, it will take a month just to explore this level," Rell pointed out. "Once we've mended the Swirl hole, you can spend years investigating the forward section."

"Okay, I get it," I said. "Where are the stairs?"

"There is a main vertical access shaft one point two kilometres from here," John replied.

We must have gone another kilometre when we saw the scorch marks. They were all around a crossroads – deep gouges ripped into the pearl-white walls, their edges with a melted look underneath a spray of black soot. The floor around them had discoloured streaks that were nearly faded, made by things that had been dragged about, things leaking fluid.

As well as the scorching, there were little craters as if the walls and floor had been repeatedly struck by some kind of big heavy hammer.

"Fight," Shao announced.

The fact that he said something surprised me almost as much as what I was seeing.

"There was a battle here, five hundred years ago," Rell said reverentially.

"Loyalists and Mutineers," Tamran said. "This is where it happened."

"One place?" I said. "The Mutiny went on for over a year."

John directed me into the mouth of the right-hand corridor and I pressed the secondary lighting switch. The lights came on ahead of me, revealing seven bodies and a whole pile of wrecked cybots.

I'd never seen a human skeleton before. Why would I? The Cycled were taken away to the composting machines and returned to us in the form of guano. Oh, I'd seen pictures in one of the school's books, but an actual skeleton? No. There was something both fascinating and repellent at the same time. The strangest thing was that they were still wearing clothes. Those super-tough fabrics had lasted for all this time, even though they were badly tarnished by the putrefaction they'd enclosed. But inside their fancy jackets and trousers, the bodies had rotted away and dried out.

"How does that happen?" Alice asked quietly. "There's practically nothing left of them."

"Decomposition of all living tissue begins at death," John said. "It is a natural function of the body's own chemicals and enzymes, followed by bacterial activity to complete the process. Bones, however, can last for thousands of years, though they do become more brittle over time."

Rell bent down for a closer look. I almost blurted, *Don't touch them!* Some deep instinct wanted me to leave them in peace. I thought of my corpse being examined by someone long after I'd died. There was something sacrilegious about the whole prospect.

But Rell was frowning at the corpses, examining them as closely as Dad scrutinized the grain in wood he was about to cut. "See this? There's a huge cut in the shirt fabric, and the ribs underneath are damaged. And this one, the arm is nearly severed at the shoulder."

"What are you saying?" Alice asked.

"That something practically ripped them apart. Oh, but not this one; every rib is broken. It's like she was crushed to death."

I rubbed at my arms, even though I wasn't cold. My thoughts were back in the garage under Cobaea station, where all the machines had been smashed up. The Mutiny had unleashed so much violence. Did all people have that ability at their heart?

"Oh my dayz," Frazer said quietly, and clicked his fingers. "Yi, type two."

I gave him an uncomfortable look. "You don't know that. We don't even know if they're real."

"I know. But Narline said something had smashed up the wall she saw to try and destroy the pictures. If you can do that to a wall, you can certainly do this." He gestured at the corpses and ruined cybots.

"What are you two talking about?" Alice asked nervously.

"One of the Tressaco residents saw something," I said. "A long time ago. It was a picture of a creature that even John doesn't have a memory of."

"And... what? It's here?"

"I don't know." I thought about whatever had been in the tunnel pulling the Cycled bodies along, and the back of my knees did that vertigo tingle again.

"It's a strong possibility," said Frazer.

"Frazer!" I hissed.

"What? We don't know what was in the tunnel with the Cycled bodies."

"Yes, but – ugh!" I gave up.

"Do you ever actually listen to what you say?" Elijah asked, shaking his head.

"Aren't you even remotely curious how they died?" Frazer asked the smug Regulator.

"I know how they died. It was in the Mutiny, fighting these things." He pointed at a broken cybot. "That's what stabbed them and smashed their bones."

Frazer gave the cybots an uncertain glance.

"You need to stop building a castle of lies to justify your actions," Elijah said. "We all know how this is going to end."

"Let's go," I snapped.

Elijah chuckled, but walked with us.

John manoeuvred two cybots to open the door into the vertical access shaft. As expected, the other side was in darkness. A cybot slipped through and a moment later the lights came on.

I don't know what I was expecting. A bigger version of the stairs in Tressaco, I guess. I walked out onto a broad balcony that stretched away on both sides, with a rail at chest height.

My brain couldn't work out the perspective at first – it took me a while to understand what I was seeing. The lights formed a delicate glowing circle around the wall of the shaft but revealed very little. The balcony circled a giant column of darkness, as if space itself had broken in to fill the void. I suddenly didn't want to question how much emptiness there was above and below me. Judging by the way the air soaked up every sound, the answer was: a lot.

"Wow," Frazer said, crowding onto the balcony. "How high does this go?"

"Three kilometres," John said before I could stop him. That was twice the height of the habitat sky! My hands tightened on the railing.

"Cool," Frazer said. "Where's the stairs?"

"Turn right," John said.

We found them just a few metres away. A cybot switched their lights on. That was even more daunting. The stairs formed a precarious line curving up the wall in a full spiral, revealing just how disconcertingly wide the shaft was.

"Sweet Captain," Rell muttered.

The first cybot moved to the base of the stairs. A small mechanical attachment swung out from under its base and clicked into a slot that ran up the wall. It started to slide up.

"I was wondering," I admitted.

Three more cybots went up ahead, then Rell took my hand and we started to climb.

It took an age to get up to the next level. Our initial pace quickly slowed to a plodding monotony. Even then we had to take breaks every so often. I had no idea climbing was so exhausting. I like to think I'm reasonably fit, but this was relentless. All of us looked tired and strained by the time we reached the next balcony.

The lights were switched on, forming another delicate ring around the abyss.

"More?" Alice said in dismay.

"Two more flights of stairs," John replied.

I think all of us greeted that with a groan.

"It will get better," John said. "As we go up, gravity will reduce, and with it your weight."

"How?" Frazer asked.

"*Daedalus*'s spin is configured to produce a standard Earth gravity on the habitat floor. It decreases proportionally as you rise above that. The axis has no gravity at all; it is called freefall, where you will simply float about in the air."

"Oh my dayz! Can we go there?"

"After we fix the Swirl," I reminded him.

Up we went.

John was right. I started to notice the lower gravity about halfway to the next balcony. When my foot shoved down on a step to take me up to the next one, I'd find myself going a lot further than I expected, almost like I was doing a mini-jump. Once I got used to it, I started exerting my leg muscles a lot less – which my aching calves were most grateful for.

We started to spread out a little to avoid knocking into each other. I didn't realize Elijah had come up behind me until he spoke.

"You know he adores you," he said. "That doesn't make him a bad person."

"Who?" I asked.

"Zawn."

Some rogue instinct made me glance ahead to where Rell was skimming along. "Right," I said brusquely.

"He told me why, once. I didn't get it until now. I thought it was just because you look amazing."

I didn't rise to the compliment; Elizabeth Bennet always resisted flattery. But– "Get what?"

"This crazy forcefulness you have. All your anger, the way you always argue and defy everyone."

"I do not!"

"Yeah." He gave a mocking gesture, taking in the shaft. "Just an everyday walk, this, like cleaning the chicken coop."

"We have to be here. *Daedalus* is dying. Don't you get that yet?"

"And *there* it is. You either intoxicate people, sweep them along with you, or you scare them guano-less, which turns them against you."

My cheeks started burning but I didn't say anything.

"Those weeks the two of you were together: my brother had never been that happy before."

"I'm sorry. I know I didn't handle it well. I just–"

"Yeah, you just wanted more – from the village, from life – and you didn't think he'd be able to give you that."

"He's a Regulator. His life is fixed. It would be the same as every Regulator for the last five hundred years."

"Everybody's life is the same as always. That's how the Cycle works – the Cycle that's got us this far."

My turn to gesture at where we were. "That life wouldn't have got us here."

"I'll tell you something: if Zawn had been allowed to come on the Tressaco raid, it'd be him in here helping you right now. And I think you know that."

"So what? He wasn't allowed to come, was he?"

"All I'm saying is that when we get back you should give him a chance."

"You still don't get it, do you? There is no going back after this. And even if I did, you'd kill me and throw me down the Cycling shaft behind the village hall."

"No. I wouldn't. You changed everything. Tressaco changed everything."

"Hah. And you just want everything to go back to being the same."

"I don't think you believe that, not really. What do you expect is going to happen when Frazer walks – walks! – back into Ixia?"

"Everyone will see the truth!" I told him proudly.

"Yes. They will. That means you've won."

"What?"

"You heard. You've even got me asking questions, because I know things aren't quite right. How's that for a victory? I still don't believe you about the Electric Captain, but I was down in those tunnels yesterday, and now I'm in the forward compartments with working machines and I'm actually quite interested to see what we're going to find."

I'd never thought I'd hear him sound remorseful. I suppose I should've been graceful about it, but all I could say was, "We're going to find an engineering-section command AI."

"Or we're going to find the Electric Captain. As near as I can figure out, they're the same thing."

"No, they're not."

He grinned. "See? Straight to the arguing. You know you're right."

"Of course I am. If you were right, I'm a Mutineer under a death sentence from the Electric Captain."

"You don't get politics, do you? How long would Fininen remain mayor if Atov put you and Frazer on the Cycling platform now?"

I frowned. "What do you mean?"

"I mean you seriously need to start thinking about what's going to happen when we get back, what you need to say to people. And, speaking as his brother, I'd like you to give Zawn some proper consideration. That's all."

I gave him a sullen look and carried on upwards. I hated that I could still feel guilty about Zawn, so I did my best to shove everything Elijah had said out of my head. I needed to concentrate on fixing the leak. Nothing else was important.

By the time we reached the third level, I was almost appreciating the low gravity. I was taking the steps three or four at a time, gliding up between them. I'd learned the hard way there's a big difference between weight and mass, as illustrated by the bruises on my legs where I'd been overconfident and gone drifting (ha!) into the safety railing. Those railings had got progressively higher the further up we climbed. When we left the second level, it was like they'd grown into a cage enclosing the stairs.

Looking through the mesh on the third level, the balcony and stair lights cut curving lines through the darkness below. The first balcony was almost too faint to see.

"This is a problem," John said when we glide-walked to the closest door. There was a red light blinking above it.

"What is?" I asked.

"That's an emergency light," he said. "The environment on the other side is harmful."

"How harmful?" Frazer asked.

"Without an active network, there is no way of knowing what is on the other side."

"So what do we do?" Alice asked.

"Try the next door."

That had a red light flashing above it, too. As did the next. We walked round the entire balcony. Every door on that level was warning us not to go through.

"I may have deduced what the problem is," John said. "We are close to the Swirl. Whatever punctured the *Daedalus*'s shields will have torn its way through this section. If so, then this whole area will now be a hard vacuum."

"So how do we get to the engineering department?" I asked.

"We go around," John said. "To do that, we must go down to the level below."

It was irrational, I know, blaming him for that, but the thought of more stairs was hideous, even though I'd be going down.

But down we went, all of us grumpy and bad tempered. Descending felt like defeat. So much for being an efficient self-supporting team.

There was no red light on the door at the bottom of the stairs. A cybot slid the release rod into its hole and pulled the door open.

I was almost disappointed when the secondary lights came on. It was a corridor identical to all the others in the forward section.

"So do we go to another vertical shaft?" Frazer asked.

"Not immediately," John replied. "There is an auxiliary craft hangar on this level. I believe it would be instructive to check it."

John directed us to a door he said led to a flight-preparation facility. I was holding my breath when the cybots slid it open, worried that the air would go rushing away into space.

The room's far wall was made out of glass that curved outward. As always, there was only blackness to see beyond, but the room itself had several tall semi-circular desks with tall rectangles of glass rising out of the top, which John called work consoles. There were even spiral stairs winding down from the middle of the floor.

"No active nodes," John said. "Frazer, can you check a console for me, please?"

"The bioweapon?" Frazer guessed.

"Yes."

Frazer soon sliced open the inspection hatch at the bottom of a console. "It's here all right."

"In order to look into the hangar, we will need to switch the lights on," John said. "That will require activating the console."

"If we cut the bioweapon fibre, she'll know we're here," Rell said.

"When we reach Section Seventeen and switch on the repair cybots, she'll know where we are anyway," Frazer countered.

Everyone looked at me – gratifying, yet worrying at the same time. I've never been a decision-maker, carefully weighing up the options and outcomes and smoothly delivering a wise, convincing answer. I ran on impulse. Maybe that's what Elijah had been on about, that I had to think about the politics more.

"Do it," I told Frazer.

He grinned and switched the D-blade back on.

A couple of minutes later, the console surface was alive with symbols and text. The glass sheets were also crawling with grids of numbers that resembled complicated maths.

"I'm linked to the console," John said. "The ship's primary network is completely closed to me, but the hangar lighting circuits are controlled through a local network. Power is available."

Bright light abruptly shone through the glass wall. As one we walked over to it, none of us speaking.

The hangar was carved out of naked rock, measuring at least two kilometres long and maybe half a kilometre high. Most of the wall surface was covered in pipes and conduits and grid-like structures of metal. Blocks of machinery were stacked up like small villages on the floor. And parked in the open areas between them were the auxiliary spaceships.

My fingers tightened on Rell's hand, I was so awestruck by the glimpse into my own history, so completely different to how we lived in the villages. Frazer was wiping small tears from his cheeks, he was so overwhelmed. The spaceships entranced me. The biggest were the spheres that bizarrely wore tight coats of silver-white fabric, with rectangles cut out to reveal long black windows. Mechanical legs, which must have been copied from insects, made them look like they were crouching down ready to pounce. The bottom of the fuselage had a clump of three nozzles sticking out – the engines, I guessed. Other spikes and dishes jutted out of the fabric coat at random. Then there were the smaller, egg-shaped craft, with plain metal hulls and small bulging windows. They looked sleek and exciting. I imagined them travelling very fast.

Not all of them had survived. John had been right. Whatever hit the *Daedalus* had punched clean through the hangar. I could see a fifty-metre hole high up on the opposite wall. Just imagining the fury of the impact that could do such a thing was terrifying. The rock itself had melted. I didn't even know it was possible for rock to do that – the temperature must have been phenomenal. Grey waves of molten stone had gone running down to spread across the floor before cooling and solidifying. It had engulfed all the machines and vehicles in its inexorable path.

"And this is after twelve kilometres of solid shielding," Frazer said in awe. "What did we hit, a moon?"

"What are those ships for?" Alice asked.

"They are multi-functional," John said. "The larger ones are Armstrongs, for external maintenance and short-range exploration. The smaller are Gagarins, for inspection missions and cargo manoeuvring."

"Are the Armstrongs the ones that'll take us down to the new world?" Frazer asked.

"No. The landing craft are stored in the lower forward level. They are considerably larger than anything in here."

Now my senses had calmed slightly, I began to notice how tarnished the spaceships were. On all of them the side of the fuselage facing the puncture hole had darkened. Some of the mechanical bits had sagged – the heat from the impact must have softened them. I guessed that even the ships parked at the far ends of the hangar would need a lot of work before they'd ever fly again. And five minutes ago I didn't even know *Daedalus had* auxiliary spacecraft, let alone that they might be damaged. Looking at them just underlined what a daunting task we faced to get the *Daedalus* fully operational again.

"The breach is a good route towards Section Seventeen," John said. If the Electric Captain is now aware we're in here, she will lose track of us in that."

"But it's a vacuum," Frazer protested. "We wouldn't be able to breathe."

"You will if you wear spacesuits."

We went down the spiral stairs into the EVA room.

"It stands for extra-vehicular activity," John said. "Which basically means going outside the spaceship."

The EVA room had a long row of lockers. The doors were higher than me, and almost twice as wide. I followed John's instructions and turned the handle on the first, twisting then flipping it back. There was a hiss of gas, then the door swung open.

Frazer practically shoved me aside. "Oh, wow!" he exclaimed in delight. If anything, the spacesuit was making him even happier than the spaceships had.

It was made from what looked like shiny orange leather, with a big bubble helmet on the top. There were cylinders incorporated in the sides of the torso section, which produced bulges in the fabric. Various tubes and cables were plugged into sockets on the side of the locker. "Life support," John said; then: "Air supply."

"How do I get in it?" Frazer asked.

"Unplug its network cable. That's the blue one."

Frazer yanked the blue cable out.

"Now press the power reset button next to the black socket."

I heard the tiniest whining sounds coming from the suit. Lights built into the helmet came on, then dimmed. Blue and amber symbols skipped across the transparent visor.

"I'm linked to it," John said. "Running the start-up sequence."

"I am not getting into one of those," Elijah declared.

"Okay," I told him. "You know the way back. Goodbye."

"You can't do that. You can't leave me here."

"Scared?" Alice asked maliciously.

"No!"

"You have a choice," I said. "Either come with us or you go back. I'm not going to *argue* with you either way. You made this problem for yourself."

"Did you see the spacecraft hangar?" Frazer asked maliciously. "Do you think that puncture hole is normal, that the Builders put it there? Or maybe *Daedalus* did hit something and the air really is leaking out. And your Electric Captain hasn't fixed it."

Elijah stared at Frazer for a long moment, but that dark anger that always seemed to power him was gone.

"Isn't it a Regulator's duty to protect the citizens of his village?" Rell asked in that level, reassuring tone of his (he's going to make a great doctor). "If the habitat air is leaking out of a hole, then you should help us try to seal it."

"If there was a puncture, the Electric Captain would have done something," Elijah said stubbornly.

"If–?" Frazer began indignantly.

I held a hand up, and by some miracle Frazer shut up. "I don't mind what you do," I told Elijah. "But I think you know now that we are genuinely trying to help the *Daedalus* and our voyage. So we're going to put on these spacesuits and climb up to the engineering level to switch on the repair cybots. You're welcome to join us."

I turned my back on him, and for the first time I wasn't worried what he'd do. He clearly needed time to adjust, and I was happy to give him that. In return, I might actually start considering what I was going to say to everyone when we all got back to Ixia, and how they'd have to release everyone they'd arrested at Tressaco. I possibly, maybe, perhaps ought to have a thank-you prepared for Zawn, too.

It took the spacesuit a couple of minutes to charge up.

"It's active," John announced. "The systems are fully functional. Are you ready?"

After my little speech to Elijah, I could hardly back out, so…

We took it out of the locker. There was a slit up the back, following the spine. I started to wiggle my way in. Head up into the bubble helmet first, then legs and finally arms, having to shove my fingers firmly into the gloves.

"The suit is now ready to seal," John said. His voice was coming from somewhere inside the helmet. I didn't like how tight and confining the suit was, and the helmet which had looked so big was actually quite small, so there wouldn't be much air, which was scary.

"How long will the air last?" I asked.

"For as long as there is power, so about three weeks," John replied. "The suit simply recycles the air you breathe."

"Oh, okay. Seal it up then."

I stood there with everyone in a semi-circle around me, watching. I could feel the slit closing up by itself. Then something strange happened: every part of the suit contracted. I let out a yelp of shock.

"It is expelling the surplus air," John said. "Don't worry. If you went out into the vacuum with air inside, it would expand and inflate the suit like a balloon. You'd be unable to move."

"Okay. Er... what's a balloon?"

"A sphere of flexible material that is filled with gas. They used to be popular with children on Earth."

"Right." I think I understood what he meant. When I tried moving my arm around, it was actually quite easy. I'd been distracted, so I hadn't realized I was now breathing the air that the suit produced. "Seems okay," I said.

We took half an hour to get the rest of the suits powered up. John switched on a radio in each of them so we could talk to each other.

"I would suggest you all take a standard maintenance pack," John said.

"Why?" I asked.

"They contain tools which will be useful. Some of them would also be considered small weapons if applied with malice."

The image of the skeletons in the first level corridor flashed up in my mind. "Good idea."

I opened the smaller lockers at the end of the EVA room. The maintenance packs were like small backpacks, but with multiple pockets containing various gadgets. John told me which ones were potential weapons – a laser vacuum seam bonder and a directional cutting field, more powerful than the D-blade (of which there was also one). I hesitated for a moment before handing one to Elijah, but he'd committed to coming with us. I suppose I was starting to trust him a bit.

The airlock was a big circular chamber at the end of the EVA room. Five of the cybots went in first. The big door swung shut. Above it, the light changed from green to red.

"They made it through," Frazer said. He was pressed up against the window, looking out into the hangar. I could see the cybots rolling over the floor.

"Let's go," I said.

(18)

I was expecting the airlock to be claustrophobic, but being in it with everyone else seemed to keep that particular phobia at bay. I held hands with Rell as the air was pumped out. I realized I'd been doing that a lot. It happened so easily. His hand was always there whenever I reached out.

Green-and-purple diagrams appeared in front of my face, riding up the curve of the helmet visor. John explained them to me and the others. Suit integrity. Power levels. Medical read-outs. Communications "icons". Rangefinder. I watched, fascinated, as little violet figures showed me my own heart rate. It was quite high, edging into amber – but what do you expect? Nobody in Daedalus had done anything like this for five hundred years.

One benefit I noticed was that the air in the suit almost immediately banished my low-level headache.

The airlock's outer door swung open and we walked out into the hangar. That's when the impact of what we were doing finally arrived – the huge hangar, the abysmal impact damage. It wasn't like I'd never believed the habitat was part of a giant spaceship, but walking among the auxiliary craft made me confront my life full on. My heart-rate numbers went up, turning a darker orange, verging on red. I took a deep breath and made an effort to calm down.

The remaining cybots came rolling out of the airlock and we headed for the puncture hole. Now we were out on the hangar floor, I could see the second rent in the wall, opposite the one we'd seen from the EVA room.

"We really did get lucky," Frazer said, looking up at the hole. "Imagine if it had been this big when it broke through into the habitat. The air would have been sucked out in a day."

I knew he was right but there was no need to share that thought with us.

There was a layer of rubble skirting the slope of solidified rock. I carefully picked my way over it, then I was on the grey incline. My helmet lights shone overlapping circles on the rock. The surface was surprisingly rough, but that gave me decent traction, which was useful in the low gravity. On top of all my other worries, I could now add falling over and tearing the suit fabric. Somehow, I suspected that might be quite difficult. Wearing the suit and seeing all its functions shining on the visor was giving my confidence a boost.

Rell was walking beside me, also being careful how he moved as we climbed higher. The cybots were deploying ahead and behind. I'd been curious about that. They'd got up the vertical shaft by using the slot rails. Here, the sphere wheels underneath them had extended wide on the end of what resembled stumpy flexible legs. The spheres themselves had produced hundreds of tiny spikes, giving them a good grip on the uneven rock as they rolled onwards.

It got darker quickly when we ventured into the hole itself. Standing there on the rim, I could see a thin white vapour streaming past. I put my hand out, expecting to feel wind buffeting it, but there was nothing.

"Is this the air?" I asked.

"Yes," John replied.

"Wait, you can see it?" I frowned at my wrist where the bracelet was underneath the orange suit fabric.

"I am linked to your suit sensors, so yes. The camera and spectrometry sensors are showing me a standard nitrogen–oxygen gas with water vapour."

"But I was expecting a jet of it, a strong one."

"This part of the breach is nearly fifty metres in diameter. As Frazer said, if that width was constant it would drain the habitat's atmosphere in a day. This vent is small but continual. The atmosphere that is coming through the hole in the sky has expanded considerably by the time it reaches this part of the breach. Consequently the pressure is minimal."

I turned to Elijah, who was just coming up the last part of the slope. "This is the air leaking out," I told him. "You can actually see it here."

He didn't answer.

I faced into the hangar and stared down the chasm on the other side. It was just a bleakly disappointing black void. I was probably being naive but I'd kind of been hoping I'd see stars at the far end. I've always wanted to see them since I was little. There are pictures in the school books for the youngest kids, but I never believed gold diamond shapes were what they actually looked like.

The cybots shone their beams around as we moved into the puncture hole. All that did was make me feel small and insignificant as the bright circles slid over the rock. We walked deeper into the darkness, angling upwards the whole time. Around us the walls began to change. From unbroken crinkly rock with congealed runnels, I began to see stubs of material poking out, bits of *Daedalus*'s equipment stubborn enough to resist the heat. There were even crevices that led back into burned corridors. After a few hundred metres the puncture hole's diameter was noticeably smaller and the gaps in the walls wider, revealing more of the chambers it had burned through. The vapour was slightly thicker, so I convinced myself I could feel it gusting against the spacesuit.

I saw two of the lead cybots turn off and disappear through a fissure.

"This one," John announced.

The chamber was badly mangled from heat and the violent loss of air. Its walls were buckled and blackened, all machines and conduits ripped away. Doors were missing and the corridors outside were equally devastated. I began to understand why we hadn't been able to get out of the vertical shaft onto this level.

We followed the cybots along the usual maze of corridors. My helmet lights played along the walls, showing me doors that were all closed. Some had buckled while others just bulged. There was no secondary lighting available.

Finally we came to a door which looked intact. An orange light glowed above it.

"I will try and open this," John said.

Two of the cybots rolled over to it. There was a panel on the wall, just above the floor. Their arms reached down, tools glowed violet and the panel came off. Then more tools were inserted through the hatch. I saw slender finger-like manipulators moving so fast they were practically a blur.

"Disengaging the pressure guards," John said, "and activating the emergency doors on the other side. You will need to stand back. There will be a blast of air when this door is opened."

We all walked away hurriedly. A cybot slid a release rod into the hole above the door. Air howled out past us as the door was pushed open, exactly the way I'd thought we'd find in the breach hole. The gust only lasted a few seconds but I nearly lost my footing.

A big emergency door had come out of the corridor walls on the other side, similar to the ones below Tressaco. We waited until the cybots closed the door behind us before they went to work on the emergency door.

Air came flowing round it as it started to open. The display on my suit visor showed me the atmosphere pressure growing.

"You can open your helmets now," John said.

I checked the small keypad on my forearm and pressed the buttons he told me. The visor clicked and flipped up. Air hissed out.

"Oh my dayz," Frazer said when his visor came up. "We walked in space! Actual space!"

Alice's face wore a huge smile. "I can't believe we just did that. We can do anything. We can fix the leak." She put her arms round Tamran and Shao, who both looked dazed and enormously pleased.

The secondary lights came on. I'd seen the cybots still working on the wiring inside an inspection hatch but hadn't realized what they were doing.

"How far to Section Seventeen?" I asked John.

"Not far now. We are in the engineering department. We just need to go up half a level."

More corridors. A couple of junctions. We glide-walked along, chatting excitedly.

The secondary lights went out.

"What happened?" Rell asked.

"I don't know," John replied.

I skipped to a halt. My helmet lights were shining on Rell. "Where's the nearest light switch?" I asked.

"The corridor network nodes have come on," John announced.

"Is that because we switched the lights on?" Tamran asked.

"No. I am detecting signals directed at the cybots. Someone is trying to access their processors and gain control of them."

"Who?" Alice asked.

"The Electric Captain," Frazer said in a flat voice.

"Can she do that?" I asked.

"I have encrypted their systems," John said. "They will only take instructions from me."

"We need to go," Rell said. "Where do we get up to the next level?"

"There are some lifts in three hundred metres, with a stairwell beside them."

All of us started moving at once. The cybots closed in around us, shining their lights on the walls and floor ahead.

"So what happened to the lights?" Rell asked.

"I believe they have been switched off deliberately," John said. "With the local nodes coming on at the same time, it is not a coincidence."

Glide-walking took a lot of concentration. I wished we could move faster, but the low gravity prevented that. If I tried to run, the force of shoving my feet against the floor simply pushed me higher, and it took longer to reach the ground again. The cybots didn't seem to have any trouble increasing their speed. John sent four of them on ahead to open the stairwell door for us; they leant forward on their stump-legs and accelerated.

"The decryption routines are more powerful than I expected," John said.

"John!"

"The Electric Captain may yet manage to take control of the cybots. I will warn you if that is about to happen."

"Oh, guano. Okay."

"When we get up to the next level, how far to Section Seventeen?" Rell asked.

"It is directly above us," John said.

"Will we be able to get in?"

"Section Seventeen is under the control of a command AI. If it survived the Mutiny, it should let us in."

"If!"

"All the primary sections were designed to be self-contained in case of emergency," John said. "They have their own power and life support. If the Mutineers tried to attack an engineering AI then it would have responded by sealing itself away, physically and electronically."

"Then why hasn't it already come out and helped us?" Frazer asked.

"This can only be speculation; however, if it survived then it is completely isolated. First it would wait for a call for help from the Loyalist survivors. If none came immediately, it would wait for circumstances to change."

"I hope you're right," I grumbled. Somehow the notion that there might not be a command AI waiting to help wasn't one I wanted to consider.

Up ahead, the four cybots were clumped together around a series of doors. Their beams splashed broad white circles on the wall. We were only twenty metres away when John said: "The cybots are detecting movement."

"What?"

"One of the doors further down the corridor."

"The Section Seventeen AI," Frazer said breathlessly. "It knows we're here."

"I dunno," I cautioned.

One of the cybots rolled on down the corridor, shining its beams ahead. Then the main lights came on abruptly, flooding the corridor with a white glare.

A door was opening. Blackness swept out, seemingly composed of undulating bulbous shadows. Then I focused properly, seeing glistening ovoid bodies the size of dogs tapering back to a fat fish tail. I could make out a mouth at the crest of each body, a circular hole seething with burgundy cilia, emitting a very high-pitched squeaking. There were no eyes, at least none I could recognize. The creatures had long coiling tentacle-limbs sprouting from their midsection, maybe eight or nine of them, that lashed about in synchronized pulsations, propelling them forward in quick, jerky motions as if they were spasming. As they approached, they made a leathery slithering sound I'd heard before, back in the underground transport tunnel.

"Yi," Frazer said in a dead tone. "Type two."

"What the hell!" Alice shouted. Tamran and Shao closed in protectively next to her.

"No," Elijah exclaimed. "No, no, this isn't possible." He sounded more angry than frightened. "What are they?"

"Aliens," I said simply.

Rell calmly took the laser bonder from his pack. I struggled to pull my e-beam welder out.

John brought the cybot to a halt. "The unknown always triggers a fear impulse in humans," he said. "Do not automatically assume they are hostile. We need to establish intent. It is a measure of humankind's moral superiority that rational examination of circumstances should be–"

The leading Yi reached the stationary cybot. Long tentacle limbs lashed out, coiling round its arms and body, twisting the joints with daunting strength, and pincers on the ends of the tentacles snapped at the more delicate manipulators on its arms.

I drew an astonished breath. I'd seen a pincer like that before, mounted on the prow of Kirill's barge. And that unnervingly strong tentacle waving it round: back in the guano, the ribbon of putrefying flesh I'd assumed was some animal intestine. "Sweet Captain."

The cybot was almost invisible beneath the Yi. It toppled over. I could hear metallic screeches as metal joints were wrenched apart. One of its arms clattered to the floor. The rest of the Yi Type Twos flowed round it, slithering towards us.

"They do appear to be hostile," John said. His voice changed, becoming firm. "Humans under threat. Defence protocols activated."

Most of the remaining cybots swivelled round and headed for the Yi.

Rell and Frazer started firing their lasers. Whenever a slender ruby-red beam touched one of the dark alien bodies, a puff of steam and smoke shot out and the Yi thrashed furiously, which sent the beam scoring longer wounds across its skin. But the Yi kept coming.

I fired the electron-beam welder. The dazzling flash left a bright purple afterimage across my vision and the bang pummelled my ears, but I saw it strike a Yi. The front of its body burst apart like an overripe fruit, splatting on the floor.

"Cybot restrictions disengaged," John said.

And suddenly the cybots were zooming past us, their arms extending, tools on the tips activating – drills spun up; blades glowed scarlet and purple. They charged towards the Yi.

Now Elijah, Tamran and Shao had joined in, firing their lasers at the stampede of writhing aliens. It was creating a burst of crazy colour flares along the corridor. I took aim as best I could and fired the welder again. In my mind, all I could see was the scorch marks on the walls we'd seen in the lower corridor, which must have been made by lasers and welder beams the same as ours. How many battles exactly like this had been fought against the Yi? And humans had lost them all.

"John!" I cried. "Get us out of here!"

"Proceed to the lifts," he said.

I could see the three cybots remaining by the doors still working on a little inspection hatchway. One had a couple of its mechanical arms deep inside. But the Yi had almost reached them.

Then more lasers started to fire. The cybots John had sent charging forwards were using their tools to strike at the aliens. And now it was difficult for us to get a clear shot at the Yi. I didn't want to fire the e-beam welder for fear I'd hit one of our defenders.

The two sides collided. Cybot blades cut deep into dark alien bodies. Lasers sliced through tentacles, leaving the severed limbs twisting about on the ground like landed fish. A putrid yellow fluid came squirting out of the wounds, spreading fast across the floor. But the Yi fought back. Tentacles wrapped tightly around metal, crushing and bending. Pincer claws snapped at delicate sections. Tips hammered and gouged at vulnerable instrumentation.

They knew! They knew the cybots' vulnerabilities.

Two or three Yi would fling themselves at a cybot, wrapping their tentacles round it, and their flailing and squirming would quickly knock it off balance. Once a cybot toppled over, it stood no chance; more Yi would swarm over it, pummelling madly. They were losing dozens to the cybot attack, but that didn't seem to inhibit them. They had numbers on their side. I couldn't count how many there were now, and they just kept coming.

One of the lift doors slid open. A cybot rushed in.

"Get inside!" John ordered.

Everyone ran for the open door. I saw the cybot firing its laser along the side of the stairwell door, fusing it to the rim, making it impossible to open.

I dived into the lift beside Tamran. Inside I bounced off Alice. The cybot had the control panel off and was working fast on the exposed wires and components. Rell and Elijah were backing in, still firing their lasers at the surging mass of Yi.

"Ready," John said.

"Get in!" I bellowed.

Elijah and Rell practically fell backwards. The lift doors slid shut.

For a moment we were encased in silence. Rell hugged me and we tried to kiss – difficult in spacesuit helmets. We just wound up with our helmets clattering together.

"You okay?" he whispered.

"Yeah. You?"

"Still here."

There were some dull thudding sounds and the lift trembled. I was pleased my helmet visor was up so I couldn't see any graphics; sweet Captain alone knew what my heart rate would be.

"What was that?" Frazer asked.

"I removed the safety limiters on the cybot power cells," John said. "That is permissible under defence protocols. The cells shorted out and exploded. I believe the blast will have terminated a great many Yi."

"What were those *things*?" a frantic Elijah demanded. "What is going on?"

"They are aliens," John said calmly. "Origin and intent unknown."

"They probably helped the Mutiny," I said. "There's a bioweapon inside *Daedalus* that's crippled all the machines. It didn't come from Earth."

Elijah's face was stricken with confusion and fear. "There can't be aliens on board the *Daedalus*. How could they get on board?"

"A command AI may be able to tell us," John said. "Speculation without facts is pointless."

"How many of them are they? Where have they been hiding?"

"We don't know," I said, and amazingly I felt sorry for him. "But we'll find out, okay? We'll stop them."

"How!?" he cried. "They're monsters. How will you stop them? Oh, sweet Captain, what if they get loose in the habitat? The villages–"

"Hey!" Alice shouted. There were tears streaking her face, but she looked angry rather than afraid. "We know as much as you, okay? But Hazel will find the answers. And when she does, we'll know how to stop them. Just trust her."

Elijah gave her a nervous nod and glanced at me for reassurance. *Guano!* I had no idea how to reassure myself, let alone him.

"We're almost at one of the command AIs," I said, "so we just take this in stages. Get into Section Seventeen. Get answers. Then we decide what to do."

"Right, yes, okay. Sorry. But–"

"I know."

"We all know," Frazer said.

"The lift is at the engineering-department level," John announced.

All of us gave the door an extremely anxious look.

"Are they outside, do you think?" Tamran asked.

"Unknown," John said. "But I suggest you get ready to shoot."

Seven weapons were abruptly pointing at the door.

"Opening now," John said.

The door slid open with a courteous *ding*. Bright white beams from our helmets swept urgently across the darkness beyond.

No Yi.

There was a spray of sparks from the lift panel which the cybot had opened. It withdrew its arm.

"The lift systems cannot be accessed from the network now," John said rather smugly.

The cybot rolled out and immediately started sealing up the other lift door.

We were in a short corridor with several doors. Fifty metres ahead was a huge semi-circular door. Our helmet beams slipped across it. Something had at one time tried to get in. All sorts of metal fragments and stones lay scattered around – they'd clearly been used to hammer against it. The surface was scratched and dinted. I think a fire had been started along the base, too, as streaks of soot coated it like a painting of black flames.

"Is that Section Seventeen?" I asked as we approached the big door.

"Yes," John confirmed. "It does appear to be secured."

I let out a breath I didn't realize I'd been holding.

"Now what?" Frazer asked.

"The door control panel is on the right hand side," John said. "It has a node but it doesn't seem to be active."

When we got close, it was easy to see why. A filigree of white fibres was growing down the wall like a malignant leafless ivy. A big knot of them had formed over the panel.

Frazer leaned in close, frowning at the weird invader. "What do you think, John?"

"I am viewing this through your suit sensors. I can only suggest you cut the fibres around the panel, then use your laser on low power to burn them from the panel itself. We will be able to assess the damage then."

"Okay." Frazer pulled out a D-blade and began slicing.

The corridor lights came on.

We all glanced up.

"Uh-oh," Rell muttered.

I looked back at the open lift door, then the one next to it where the cybot was still working. I didn't need Frazer's brainpower to work out what was going to happen next.

Elijah and Tamran were both pointing their lasers at the lift. I glanced round the rest of the corridor. There must have been more than a dozen doors. The cybot wasn't going to be able to seal them all.

"How long do you think we've got?" I asked John.

"Impossible to determine."

"Frazer, you need to hurry."

"No kidding!" He finished using the blade and brought up his laser. The intense beam spread out in a fan, and he swept it up and down over the panel. Wisps of smoke rose from the fibres as they shrivelled.

A melodic *ding* came from the door of the second lift. The cybot rolled back a metre and all its arms came up, ends poised pointing at the blank metal, which made it seem amazingly antagonistic.

I held the e-beam welder with both hands, ready to shoot alongside the cybot. "Frazer?"

"Almost done."

Something hit the lift door, a metallic sound that reverberated down the corridor. Alice stood on one side of me, Rell on the other.

"*I'll* find the answers?" I asked her out of the side of my mouth. "That's the best you've got?"

"What's the alternative? We wait for Mayor Fininen to take charge? Of *this*?"

"Good point."

Another thump came from the door, then another. The banging became regular, as if the Yi were drumming. I saw dints start to distort the metal.

"What the hell are they hitting it with?" Rell wondered.

"Frazer!" I called.

"The panel's clear."

"Now what?" I asked.

"I cannot detect an active node," John said. "Hazel, remove your spacesuit glove."

"What?"

"You need to touch the panel. It will run a DNA scan."

I didn't even know the spacesuit glove came off – seemed like a bad design idea to me – but there was a seal around my wrist which started to peel back, reminding me of a lip puckering up. I tugged at the glove with my other hand.

"There!" Shao shouted.

Everyone looked at him. Even me.

"Hazel!" Rell shouted. "They're coming!"

One of the other doors, thirty metres away, was sliding open.

"Shoot into the gap," John said. "Constant fire. Do not give them the opportunity to get out."

The corridor filled with brilliant red flashes as the others fired their lasers. That set off a high-pitched whining from the Yi on the other side of the door; it wasn't loud but the sound seemed to pierce right through my skull.

I got the glove off and slammed my hand on the panel. It took all my determination to keep it there; the panel was so hot it felt like my palm was frying.

"Is it working?" Alice shouted.

"Not yet."

Somehow two of the Yi had got through the barrage of laser shots, hurtling out across the floor, their tentacles squirming so fast they created a confusing grey haze round the bodies. Rell and Tamran tried shooting them, missing. The lasers scored deep pocks in the wall.

"Hazel?" Frazer implored.

The door might have been a rock carving for all the movement it was making. I took my hand off the panel, then slapped it down again and again, ignoring the heat and pain, pounding on the rectangle. "Open!" I pleaded. "Please. Ashleigh Kruger is my ancestor. Please!"

Tamran finally managed to shoot one of the Yi, his laser cutting into the front end of the body. But three more had managed to come through the gap. The aliens spread out, darting from side to side as they approached us, constantly changing speed, presenting an incredibly difficult target.

A bass rumbling sound came from the door. It started to slide up slowly. "It's opening!" I cried.

Tamran, Rell and Shao had dropped to their knees, still trying to track the Yi bounding about the corridor, firing repeatedly. The cybot had finished with the lift door and now was rolling across the floor, chasing a Yi.

The bottom edge of the Section Seventeen door had risen nearly a metre off the floor. Bright light was shining out of the opening, along with a strong rush of air. "Let's get out of here!" I shouted. Frazer was first, diving down and sliding under the door. Alice and Shao followed.

"Rell, move!"

I fired the e-beam welder. A chunk of floor detonated in front of a Yi; smouldering fragments slammed into it, sending it reeling back. I fired again. Again. Then my finger was stabbing the button and nothing was happening.

"It's out of power," John said.

"Guano!" I started to wriggle my way under the door. Elijah was backing towards it. I could see Yi pouring into the corridor now. The cybot was firing lasers and slicing away, but they swarmed it. Rell and Tamran were still shooting as they scurried backwards. They didn't even have to bother aiming properly, there were so many Yi closing on them.

Then I was through into some massive chamber. "John, we have to close the door. The Yi will come through."

Elijah came sliding through on his back. He was firing his laser past his feet, roaring wordless defiance at the horde.

"I have a network link," John said. "Requesting door closure."

"Run!" I screamed at Rell.

Frazer was on his belly, shooting under the door. I dropped down beside him, trying to pull a laser from my backpack. I could see Rell and Tamran on the other side, crouching to duck through. The door started to slide down.

"Rell!" I reached for him. And he was under the door, scrabbling towards me. My hand closed round his arm, and I tugged hard, pulling him through. "Sweet Captain," I groaned. I was so frightened he'd left it too late.

Tamran was on the floor beside him. "That's—"

A tentacle wrapped round his ankle. He gasped in shock. "Alice!" he yelled. His hand was thrown out desperately towards her.

Alice jumped for him. "No!"

Tamran shot back under the door. I froze for a second, I think all of us did. Then I was flinging myself down flat, trying to see what was happening on the other side, trying to find something to shoot. Tamran was almost invisible at the centre of a seething cluster of tentacles. Those hideous toothless mouths were expanding, gurgling loudly. I heard him scream. Yi were slithering under the door, coming for us.

We all opened fire, shooting blindly. Then the door was squashing the Yi beneath it. I heard vile crunching sounds. Their sickly yellow blood spilt out. And the door shut.

(19)

The silence that followed struck me like a physical blow. I felt nothing. It wasn't real. It hadn't happened. It couldn't have happened.

Then all I could see was Alice. Her face was centimetres away from mine, our helmets banging together.

"Open the door," she shrieked at me. "Get it open. We have to get him back."

"Alice–"

"Open it. Open it."

"Alice, there are dozens of those things out there," Rell said. "He's gone."

"No!"

"I'm sorry."

"Hazel," she begged. "Please. Open the door."

"I can't," I whispered. And that's when the tears came. I sat down hard on the floor, and just cried and cried. Tamran was dead. Dead because he came with me. Because he'd trusted me. Dead.

Alice put her arms round me, and we sobbed helplessly together.

"The Section Seventeen command AI is online," John said. "I have been informing it of our situation."

I wiped the tears from my face. Sweet Captain, I felt so dreadful. Shao was on his knees trying to comfort Alice, though his own anguish was as profound as hers.

Rell took my hand. "I know this is hard," he said, "but we need you, Hazel."

"Did you not see?" I asked. "Their tentacles were crushing him! There were so many tentacles, the pincers–"

"Don't," he said. "I grew up with Tamran – he was like a brother – but we have to mourn later. If it'd been me they snatched, he'd be telling you the same thing right now."

"Don't say that." I pulled him tighter. "Don't you ever say that. You can't die. I need you. Do you understand? I need you."

His hand stroked my cheek. "And I need you, more than you know. But right now we have to talk to the command AI."

I hated myself for nodding, but nod I did. "Okay."

With Rell helping, I slowly got to my feet and looked around.

The compartment was big, maybe three hundred metres across. There were machines everywhere: big spherical cybots sitting on racks; machines that looked like larger versions of the medicine machines back in Ixia and Tressaco. Although they were bulkier, they somehow seemed more powerful – which I know is silly, but that's the impression they gave. They were sleeker, too, like they'd been sculpted out of white glass and ebony. I thought that was a good omen – Dad loves ebony even though it's really rare in *Daedalus*. As well as the machines, there were tall translucent columns standing all over the floor, similar to the ones behind the Electric Captain.

"Hello?" I said.

"Hello, Hazel," a deep male voice replied. It came from all around. And an old man was suddenly standing inside each of the columns. He was dressed in a blue-and-green robe, with long white hair flowing down his back and a thin beard that came halfway down his chest. His gaze (all of them) was directed at me.

"Who are you?" I asked.

"I am the command AI of Engineering Section Seventeen, but I think the name that fits best in these circumstances is Lazarus."

"Lazarus, our friend Tamran that got taken–"

"I'm sorry, Hazel. There is nothing I can do about Tamran. But I cannot adequately convey how glad I am to discover there are still humans alive on the *Daedalus*. John has downloaded his memory files to me, so I am aware of your situation. It is strange."

"What are those things out there?"

"They are Yi, classified as type two."

"I don't understand – how can there be aliens on the *Daedalus*?"

"They are Kianira's indigenous species."

"What's Kianira?"

"The name of the first world *Daedalus* flew to. It means *dawn*. Kianira was to be the new beginning for all the humans on board, fulfilling the dream of the Builders."

"So that part's true, then," I said. "There were aliens there. But our school taught us they weren't sentient."

"That is what we believed. Kianira was mostly an ocean world with a scattering of small islands. The Yi we encountered were a semi-aquatic species, growing on the shoreline and practically immobile. In their young form, they swim in order to find themselves a clear section of shore where they attach themselves to the rock like terrestrial anemones. This is where they stay and grow to full adult form. They have a root system as well as gills that ingest small sea creatures. Our scans revealed a large brain in the adults, making nearly two-thirds of their body mass. We believed there was a strong chance they would evolve to full sentience. This is why Ashleigh Kruger reluctantly gave the order to abandon Kianira. Human ethics simply wouldn't allow us to usurp an indigenous species in order that we could colonize a world for ourselves. So *Daedalus* departed for another world fifty light years away, one we knew didn't have any alien life."

"How do you know that?" Rell asked.

"Because one of the early seeder starships reached it and began terraforming it centuries ago."

"I don't know what terraforming is."

"There was a lifeless planet orbiting the star. The ship seeded it with life from Earth – bacteria first, to release oxygen into the atmosphere, then more sophisticated plants, and finally insects and animals. This is terraforming, a process which takes centuries, but by the time we arrive, it will have a biosphere identical to Earth."

"That is true, then," I said. So much of what we'd been told was a lie, I'd been ready for the "second world" to be just one more terrible false promise from the Electric Captain.

"It is," Lazarus said. "In fact, we should have arrived by now. Which is why I am so pleased that you are here."

"The Yi," Alice said in a dull voice. "How did they get here?"

"We brought them on board before we left Kianira."

"You *brought* them on board. Sweet Captain, *why?* That's crazy!"

"We were going to take them with us to the second world, to share it with them. Biological life, we have found, is extraordinarily rare in this galaxy. We regarded preserving it to be a moral duty."

"So what happened?"

"The Yi we brought on board settled in well and began to flourish. They released eggs into the water. What we didn't realize until too late was that there was more than one type. The type ones, the brain queens, started to entwine their roots. You see, they're more than just roots, they're nerves, too. Their thoughts merged, becoming one mind shared between many bodies, and so its intelligence grew each time a new brain was incorporated. All of which we were unaware of."

"Oh my dayz, the brain-queen roots!" Frazer exclaimed. "That's what's growing everywhere, along all the conduits and into the machines."

"Indeed," Lazarus said. "They started to physically infiltrate our network, their nerves fusing to our electronics. They subverted some AIs with their thought routines. They used our own technology to develop antagonistic programs which could attack even command AIs. Then they struck. They took over several command AIs and used their processing power to advance their own control. Those of us remaining were left without communications. The power grid was shut off and buildbots deactivated. That is when the new types of Yi emerged. The type twos you have just encountered appear to be general workers, while the type threes are the soldier class." Lazarus's face showed infinite weariness. "Each of those islands on Kianira was home to a single mind living inside thousands of brain queens, sending out its forces to conquer other islands. The wars they must have fought beneath the waves! We saw none of it, of course."

"Type twos are just workers?" Frazer gasped. "They're not even the soldiers? Very not cool."

"What happened when they attacked?" I asked.

"We were completely unprepared," Lazarus said. "I used my buildbot facilities to modify some tools into laser weapons for humans trapped in the nearby forward sections, who went out to fight. But even before *Daedalus* left Earth, humans had not fought wars for centuries. The people on board were not soldiers. After they went out, I detected an electronic attack against me, directed by the Yi brain queens, and shut down my network connections. After that, their nerve roots began to invade the network junctions around Section Seventeen, so I had to seal myself up and hope that I could contribute later. I know several other command AIs did the same, though some of us fell. That was five hundred years ago."

"So the Electric Captain...?"

"Is a visual construct of the Yi brain queens, produced by the subverted AIs. The brain queens have used it to keep you subjugated."

"Why?" I bellowed. I was so furious, and frightened. I'd been expecting the command AI to be reassuring, to solve everything, to begin repairing *Daedalus*. I'd built it up in my head to be our goal, that everything would be okay again when we reached it. Instead, I'd found I'd spent my life a slave to alien monsters. We all had. "Why did they do this? What do they want with us?"

"I do not know. Their psychology and reasoning is not human. However, they must have some purpose for the *Daedalus*. They would not have kept it functioning otherwise. I can only speculate they wish to travel to the second world themselves, and transfer to the surface where they will make it their own."

"What do we do?" I asked. "I don't know what to do."

"I do," Lazarus said. "Your arrival has consequences that require a swift response. I am able to determine the only valid course of action."

"What is that?" Rell asked, in a voice that was shaky with dismay.

"Obviously, the habitat atmosphere leak must be sealed. I am currently preparing a fleet of cybots with the appropriate tools and materials."

"Morphtallic?" Frazer asked. "Is that what you're going to use?"

Lazarus gave him a kindly smile. "It is, Frazer. Well done. I will prepare an educational package that you can take with you. There is so much for you to learn afterwards. So much knowledge that can benefit you and your friends."

Frazer gave the column closest to him a puzzled glance. "But you can teach me everything I need to know."

"That is not going to happen."

"Why?" I asked, dreading the answer.

"Section Seventeen is perfectly safe when sealed off. However, when it is opened it will become vulnerable again. And I must open it, both physically and electronically, which will expose me to the brain-queen attack programs. They will eventually overwhelm me as they have the other command AIs, for together they have more processing power than I."

"No! You can't just sacrifice yourself like this."

"There is no alternative. And I do it gladly – now that I know the *Daedalus* habitat was punctured, my only duty is to repair it so humans may continue to live. This will involve dispatching a team of cybots, enough to get through the swarm of type two and three Yi who will be gathering outside. If that was all that was needed, I would seal the section up again as soon as they were out. But I also have to establish a link to the cryogenic tanks containing the ship's reserves of oxygen and nitrogen in order that the habitat atmosphere can be replenished. That is why I must reconnect to the network."

I took a step closer to the nearest column and gave the figure inside an imploring look. "But we need you. None of us knows what to do. You have to tell us. To help."

"I understand," Lazarus replied with an ancient sympathetic smile. "And I am sorry. But you are far more important than me; what you have started must continue. Hazel, you have tell the rest of the humans in the *Daedalus* what has happened. You must warn them – they must understand it is no longer their ship. Then you need to contact the other command AIs that have survived. They will be able to formulate a strategy to ensure you reach the new world safely."

I couldn't believe it. I was already so bone-achingly tired after everything we'd done, and now I was being told I'd barely begun to help *Daedalus*. I just stood there, staring mutely at the unreal man within the column. Just when I thought I might start crying again, Rell's arm went round me. I can't express how comforting that was.

"You said the Yi were gathering outside?" he asked.

"Yes. You coming here has upset a status quo that has lasted for five hundred years. The brain queens will want to stop your sedition from spreading. They will try to prevent you from leaving and re-joining the villages, especially with the knowledge you have acquired. They will try very hard. And they are utterly ruthless."

"Can you get us out?"

"I believe so. When the brain queens came on board, *Daedalus* was home to a beautiful and passive civilization, devoid of aggression. Captain Kruger presided over the pinnacle of human accomplishment, a peaceful, inclusive society born from millennia of struggle and suffering. Because of that, all the brain queens know is a seemingly docile, easily intimidated species. But humans were not always so passive. I have so many war histories in my memory, including the tactics deployed in those dark ages. When I open the doors, all that I am will come out fighting. Every processor, every cybot, every weaponized tool, every attack program will immediately strike at the Yi. I expect to lose, but before I do there will be a great deal of confusion. That will give you an opportunity to slip away unnoticed."

"No," I said.

Lazarus raised an eyebrow in polite query.

"Sorry, but I have to see the puncture repaired. After everything we've been through to get here…"

"I quite understand. You can leave with the major-incident cybots. They are large enough to overcome most obstructions. After you get clear and the repair is complete, there are several potential escape routes back into the habitat. I will prepare them for you."

"Thank you, Lazarus," Rell said. "I'm sorry this will end you."

"Please do not think of me as life as you know it. I would not want you to be encumbered by sentiment. Ultimately, I am a program. Protecting you is part of my function. It is, if you like, what I live for."

"I'm not sure we deserve you," I said.

"You do," Lazarus said. "By simply getting to Section Seventeen against all the odds, you have proved that. Besides, I will not be completely finished. I can back up my core personality and store it physically in a safe place. When you ultimately succeed, you could reload me."

My lips twitched into a grin. "Like John."

"Indeed. Let us hope I don't have to wait five hundred years."

"If I'm still alive, I'll reload you," I promised solemnly. "You can make your back-up."

"I already have. I began enacting the strategy as soon as I received John's download. Everything is ready."

"But..." We'd barely been in the engineering section for ten minutes. "That was quick."

"The faster I get you out of here, the less time the brain queens have to organize, the greater our chance of success."

"Right." When I checked round, everyone was looking surprised – except Frazer, who was nodding eagerly. "Okay, then."

"When I reconnect to the network, I will launch a purge program to neutralize the brain queens' control of the nodes," Lazarus said. "It will only be temporary – the subverted AIs will initiate countermeasures. But I may be able to reach the screens in the villages for a small time period."

"That's good?" I ventured.

"Indeed. Please think of what you will say to them."

I blinked. I'd heard the words clearly; they just didn't quite make sense. "Excuse me?"

"It is an excellent opportunity to warn people about their true situation. The start of your campaign to reclaim the *Daedalus*."

"*Me?* You want *me* to talk to everyone on board?" Me who had even hunched her shoulders up during the Cycling Day ceremony because I was the centre of attention for everyone I knew? And I'd *wanted* to be the flower girl! Now I had to talk to every human living on the *Daedalus*? "Uh... wouldn't that be better coming from you?"

"I will cease to exist within the hour. You are known – real – and you will return to the habitat villages to focus the fight to reclaim it."

"Mutiny," I said. "I have to start a mutiny against the aliens controlling *Daedalus*." All I could do was stare across at Elijah, who responded with a sardonic smile.

The major-incident cybots were being readied in Section Seventeen's main assembly room, situated below the entrance chamber. We trooped down a set of spiral stairs to the room, which was over four hundred metres long and easily fifty high. Despite the slow-burning trepidation which came from knowing what I was about to face, I was captivated by the section. Lazarus was immersing us in life as it had been all the way back in Ashleigh Kruger's time. Lights, warmth, air at the correct pressure, machines humming and moving, cybots gliding about, screens and panels alive with graphs and numbers and words. A world of commonplace miracles that worked smoothly and efficiently. And it belonged to me and my friends. This was the ship that had been taken from us. I'd lived in a bamboo cabin my whole life, yet I'd always known something was missing.

"Sweet Home Alabama," I murmured as one of the major-incident cybots trundled past. It was almost the size of the cabin I'd grown up in, a combination of tanks and complicated mechanics. And it moved! For some reason it reminded me of Bronwyn, the horse we'd borrowed when Frazer and I first fled Ixia. It had the same slow, purposeful momentum that was clearly destined to last for centuries. I managed to resist the impulse to pat it. Besides, hand-sized cybots with stick limbs were crawling over it, machine spiders as busy and fast as their living counterparts, working on open apertures. More cybots were marshalling across the massive floor, examining and modifying one another the way cats preen each other.

I walked along an avenue between them, trying to imagine all of *Daedalus* restored to this glory. The lights in Tressaco seemed so insignificant in comparison now. But they were a start. Maybe it could be done.

Then I remembered Tamran and his final screams and shuddered. I'd be lucky if I survived the next hour, let alone lived to see *Daedalus* as my ancestors knew it.

Three white-and-purple cybots were waiting for us by an archway in the rock wall. They resembled the general-maintenance cybots that had accompanied us up to the engineering section, but there were slight differences. I couldn't say why, exactly, but these appeared sleeker somehow, more powerful, sort of like an improved version. They were a lot cleaner, for a start, with shorter, more agile arms. Each of them had additional equipment clamped to their body casing.

"These will be your escort after the repair," Lazarus said from one of the columns that lined the assembly room's walls.

"Won't the brain queens be able to take control of them?" Frazer asked. "John said they were close to controlling the cybots that came with us earlier."

"I have deactivated the network nodes in the machines I am deploying; they will all function independently. The brain queens cannot take control of them."

"Right."

"And I have prepared items which might help you," Lazarus added.

The white-and-purple cybots held up small backpacks for each of us, and a belt with a holster.

"On the belts are lasers with a much higher energy rating than the ones you have used so far. The small discs beside them are power cells incorporating a five-second timer trigger, which will short them out. Activate the trigger and throw them in the direction of whatever is threatening you."

"They'll explode," Frazer said in approval.

"Correct. In the backpacks are medical kits and some ultraviolet-based communication systems which the Electric Captain cannot jam. They will interface directly with your suit systems."

"Thank you," I said. The idea we were being given some decent weapons helped lift my confidence slightly. Not that weapons had done Ashleigh Kruger any good in the end.

"Frazer, I placed an educational tablet in your pack."

"Sounds cool," Frazer said.

The air was suddenly full of loud bass whining sounds as the major-incident cybots all began to move at once. They dispersed down the broad archways cut into the assembly room's walls. Then the rows of smaller cybots began to roll away.

"Are you ready, Hazel?" Lazarus asked.

"Uh, I suppose so. What do I do?"

"Face one of the columns containing my image. I will open Section Seventeen and initiate the network purge. If the purge is successful, you should make a quick statement. As soon as you've finished, you can ride out with the major-incident cybots I assigned to seal the Swirl."

Rell and Alice smiled encouragingly at me. Frazer gave me a thumbs up.

And I didn't have a clue what to say. Like every unpleasant task I knew I'd face, I'd put it at the back of my mind where it could be safely ignored.

"Some advice?" Elijah said quietly.

"What?" Yes, I was that desperate.

"Consider the impact you're going to have. Just seeing you appear on the screens rather than the Electric Captain is going to be the greatest trauma the villagers have ever had in their lives. Don't tell them everything at once – that the Mutiny never happened, that there are aliens on board. It'll be too much."

"So what do I say?" I asked.

"Preparing to open in twenty seconds," Lazarus announced.

"Get them ready for the real shock. Make them want to ask what's happening."

"How do–?"

"Five seconds," Lazarus said.

"We should stand beside you," Alice said. "That'll let everyone know that you're not alone, and that we're all okay."

So my friends were suddenly crowding close, pushing their faces forward inside their open helmets so they could be seen properly. Which was another few seconds when I wasn't thinking what to say.

"Opening," Lazarus said. "Cybots moving out. Reconnecting to *Daedalus* general network and launching purge program."

I just stood there, staring dumbly at the image of Lazarus, not knowing how long anything would take. Did I just start talking? I saw his image flicker. He didn't seem quite as substantial as before. Then a frown creased his forehead.

"They are powerful," he said in a troubled voice. "I might not last as long as I expected."

I sucked on my lower lip – and suddenly I knew what I was going to say. It was obvious: prepare them for the really bad news that was to come – just as Elijah said – and help Alisha and the others from Tressaco, as well as making everything I said believable. I grinned. And I hadn't even had to ask Frazer.

"Network purged," Lazarus said. "Accessing habitat screens. Hazel, you're on."

I opened my mouth–

"Mum, Dad, I'm okay!" Frazer yelled, waving frantically.

An exasperated Alice shushed him.

"My name is Hazel," I said, telling myself not to speak too fast, to try and sound confident, like this was so utterly ordinary. "I'm from Ixia village. Right now my friends and I are in an old engineering compartment beyond the forward endwall. We've come here because *Daedalus* has been leaking air into space ever since the Jolt. We collided with something which punctured the habitat – our atmosphere is draining away through the Swirl above Akebia. But there are pre-Mutiny repair machines here that are still working. We've managed to switch some of them on, and they're on their way to seal the hole. In a minute, new air is going to be released from reserve tanks. I think it's going to be cold, but don't worry, it's all part of making everything better." I took a breath. Out of the corner of my eye, I could see some red and green flashes in one of the big archways. "When I get back, I'll tell you everything else that we've found. But the really good news is that we don't have to Cycle any more. The machines here told us we're close to the new world." A thin jet of smoke erupted horizontally from the archway, accompanied by a loud commotion. Our trio of escort cybots began to move in protectively. "One of the seeder ships has reached the planet ahead of us, so it's already got all the plants and animals from Earth. That's why Ashleigh Kruger chose it – because it's ours, and it's going to be beautiful."

"The Yi are now inside Section Seventeen," Lazarus said. "I'm sorry, Hazel. I didn't think they would be so quick."

"So don't Cycle anyone," I implored.

A smashed-up general-maintenance cybot came flying out of the archway in mid-air. The wreckage hit the floor in a shower of sparks and went clattering along until it struck the opposite wall.

"Run!" I yelled.

The overhead lights went out, leaving us in the gloom cast by smaller lights dotted across the assembly room. Beams from our cybot escort came on, showing us the way as one of them raced on ahead. Our spacesuit beams added to the waving pool of illumination. My helmet visor snapped down and irritating purple graphics swept across my vision.

There were more scarlet and green flashes behind us. Then a brighter orange flare bloomed. The explosion almost knocked me over; I stumbled but managed to keep going.

Three major-incident cybots filled the corridor ahead of us. The rear of the last one had a bench along it. I jumped on and helped Frazer up beside me. Then we were all sitting together, arms round each other as if we'd just won a game.

"Goodbye, Hazel," Lazarus's voice said inside my helmet. "I knew Ashleigh Kruger well; she would be so proud of you."

The major-incident cybot passed through one of the huge semi-circular doors and we left Section Seventeen behind.

(20)

I could hear the ominous high squeaking sounds of the Yi somewhere ahead. Being on the rear of the cybot, facing backwards, wasn't ideal. I wanted to see where we were going, what was ahead of us.

Then the lead cybot must have encountered some Yi. Flashes of scarlet laser light filled the corridor. Yi squealed loudly – then there was silence. We trundled on past several open doors.

"Lazarus ordered all the doors to open," John explained as the cybots turned off into a smaller, curving corridor. "That way, when the Yi brain queens regain control of the network, they won't be able to track us through opening doors."

It was lightless inside the new corridor, the walls only just wider than the sides of the big machines. The small square of light that was the entrance soon vanished round a corner and the major-incident cybots seemed to pick up speed.

"It's a spiral," Frazer said. "We're going up again."

He was right – even sitting on the bench, I could feel the gravity dropping off. I heard Alice sniffling miserably in the dark, trying to hold back her grief for Tamran. Normally I would have gone to her – it's what we do, comfort each other when something bad happens – but now it was Shao with his arm round her, while her helmet rested awkwardly on his chest. For someone who barely speaks, he seemed to be doing a good job.

After ten minutes, we emerged into a normal corridor. I could hear a sharp sizzling sound up ahead and tensed up, thinking the cybots were firing lasers at another swarm of Yi, but a moment later I saw glowing gashes on the walls.

"The cybots are physically disabling the nodes," John said. "When the brain queens regain control, they'll still be unable to monitor us."

"Are they regaining control?" I asked.

"They are. I am monitoring the local nodes. Their countermeasures are expunging the Lazarus purge program."

"Have they attacked him yet?"

"Yes. But he will progressively erase himself as they break through his defence layers. No knowledge of your escape will be available to them. Instead he will leave strategic memory caches intact for the brain queens so they believe they are victorious. Some are booby-trapped with slow infiltrator packages, which will take weeks or even years to inflict damage on the subverted AIs."

"That is such a weird battle."

"I know. But ultimately it will contribute to the fall of the Yi."

I didn't have an answer for that. John hadn't said much while we were in Section Seventeen. It felt good to talk to him again. Strange how some things become familiar in such a short time.

We entered a big empty chamber with several doors, all of which had red warning lights flashing above them. A couple of medium-sized cybots closed the door behind us. Then my suit visor display showed the atmospheric pressure reducing fast.

We climbed off the back of the cybot. The biggest door with a red light above was opening. I saw streamers of mist appear in the thinning air to streak through into the darkness beyond. My display showed I was in a full vacuum again.

The major-incident cybots eased their way through into a jumble of fused and melted wreckage. Powerful lights mounted on their front came on, cutting clean across the ruins and filling the broken chamber with a confusing geometry of twisting shadows. At the far end were several fissures in the naked rock wall, glassy edges softening their jagged profile. The first major-incident cybot extended a big circular cutting tool and started to slice through the rock. Fist-sized chunks of rubble tumbled away. Several smaller cybots scurried through and began to examine the puncture hole.

It took another five minutes before the fissure had been widened enough to admit the major-incident cybots. I stood beside the opening and peered in. Even now I couldn't quite believe what I was seeing. From a whispered secret at the Cycling ceremony, through tragedy and dread via panic, to this: actually seeing the leak being repaired. It was the happiest, greatest sight I could remember, yet somehow my limbs were trembling as if I was in shock.

Right in front of me a couple of the major-incident cybots were inserting black cylinders as thick as my leg into the glazed rock, turning the inside of the hole into an oversized pincushion.

"How does that help?" I asked.

"This is stage one," John said. "The anchors. They will activate the seal soon."

Sure enough, with about thirty of the black cylinders protruding into the puncture hole, one of the major-incident cybots began to extrude a globe of mirror-bright liquid metal which I guessed to be morphtallic. It flowed over the cylinders along the bottom of the hole, engulfing them, before starting to stretch upwards. I saw wisps of vapour starting to curve over the upper surface of the morphtallic blob. They began to thicken as the gap grew smaller, moving faster than the waterfall. The silver metal began to shake as it forced itself higher, fighting the flow of air.

A low roaring sound began. Something started to push at me, gently at first but with increasing force. *This* was what I'd been expecting the first time we'd ventured into the puncture hole back in the hangar.

Then the morphtallic had filled the hole, forming a perfect plug. It changed, turning dull. At the same time, I knew it wasn't fluid anymore; in some indefinable fashion it had become as solid as the rock to which it clung.

The sound died. My helmet visor displays told me the pressure outside was high enough to breathe.

"We did it," I said numbly. "Rell, we did it!"

We hugged each other hard, helmets clattering together.

"You did it," he insisted.

"Oh yeah, this is seriously cool," Frazer said. He was running his hand over the morphtallic as if he was trying to find a weak spot. Then he frowned at the major-incident cybots who were now inserting a second batch of the black rods into the rock walls. "What are they doing?"

"Preparing a second seal," John replied. "We cannot rely on a single seal. Suppose it breaks? They have enough material to construct at least five. After that, a more permanent seal should be made – but given the circumstances, that may have to wait."

"Whatever." All I could think of was Alisha, wondering if she'd seen the screen when I'd appeared. I couldn't wait to see her again, to tell her what we'd seen. Alisha would know what to do and say next. "Do you know if Lazarus managed to open the reserve air tanks?" I asked.

"Yes," John replied. "The vent into the habitat has begun. However, I have now lost contact with the network; I conclude the nodes are back under the control of the brain queens."

"We'd better get out of here," Elijah said.

I didn't argue, even though I was quite keen to see the second seal being established. We retraced our steps to the door, which the three escort cybots opened. If John was right, the nodes that had been destroyed would mean the brain queens still didn't know where we were.

The escort cybots moved along the corridor, with us hurrying after.

"Do you know our escape routes?" I asked John as we passed a junction.

"Yes. Lazarus sent me a great many information files. Do not worry, he mapped out several alternatives in case one or more exits become blocked. All of them are good."

"So where are we going now?"

"We need to reach the environmental-maintenance department."

Which was an answer that meant nothing.

"You might want to have your weapons ready from now on," John added.

Up ahead at the next junction were several broken cybots and a couple of type-two bodies that had been sliced by lasers. My fingers tightened on the laser Lazarus had supplied. The fight was very recent; I could see wisps of smoke still coming out of a cybot. One of our escort cybots moved into the junction like an anxious kitten exploring its world for the first time.

"Clear," John announced.

Just as we set off, the sounds of a skirmish came echoing down the corridor from behind. I heard the high-pitched antagonistic screeches of the Yi, followed by the violent crump of an explosion. The escort cybots started to speed up.

A battered cybot came careering out of the junction in front of us, its casing smeared in Yi blood. I brought my laser up, ready. Sure enough, it was followed by several Yi type twos, and some cybots who were fighting them. All of us started firing. The beams scored deep smouldering slices in the Yi. Several severed tentacles dropped to the ground, where they writhed about energetically. More Yi appeared.

"Down!" Rell ordered.

I hit the ground as he threw one of the power-cell discs at the junction. The explosion kicked out a huge blaze of white light and the blast shunted me backwards, arms flapping about. I landed hard on my arse. I was really glad I was wearing the spacesuit – I think the sound would have broken my ears otherwise. Even inside the helmet it was ferocious.

When I looked up, the Yi were all dead and ruined cybots were on fire, churning out thick black smoke. Alarm sirens went off and a thick deluge of water rained down.

We picked ourselves up and raced along with the escort cybots. A couple of minutes later, we were outside a closed inspection hatch. Rather than opening it, the cybots used something like a D-blade to cut out a rectangle.

"Now the brain queens have regained full control of the network, we don't want to use door mechanisms in case they spot us," John explained.

My spacesuit helmet lights showed me an open square platform on the other side, surrounded by empty blackness. I stayed as far away from its edges as possible, which wasn't easy given it was only about two metres across. On top of that, there was a strong air current gusting down, making it feel even more unstable. The vertigo feeling electrified my muscles as everyone else started crowding on behind me. We were in another of those vertical shafts, only without balconies and spiral stairs. My helmet beams couldn't find the opposite wall – somehow I was quite glad about that. I forced myself not to look down, not to see how close my boots were to the edge, not to see if there was a bottom somewhere down there in the blackness.

A cybot began to weld the hatch back into place behind us. That didn't help my nerves.

I concentrated on the coloured displays splashed across my visor. My heart rate seemed quite high. "What now?" I asked.

"We go down a level," John replied.

Again I studiously avoided looking down. "How?"

"This is an air-circulation shaft that filters particulates out of the atmosphere. It descends into the habitat environmental section, and beyond."

"Didn't need to know that," I said firmly.

"It's okay, Hazel, we've done this before," Alice said. "Where are the stairs?"

"This is a subsidiary shaft, not a primary," John said. "There are no stairs."

"Then how the sweet Captain do we get down there?" Elijah asked curtly.

"The cybots have brought winches."

I risked half-turning my body. The cybots had removed cylinders which had been clamped to them. Their arms extended upwards and used some kind of tool to fix them to the wall above our heads. A cable came out of the free end, with several straps dangling from the end.

And I suddenly realized what was going to happen. My knees felt weak, but there was no way I could get out of it now.

"Nobody ask or say how far down the next level is," I announced. "Clear? I do not want to know."

Judging from the subdued mutterings of agreement, I wasn't the only one who was having doubts – or, if I'm being honest, scared out of my skin.

We helped each other fit the safety harnesses on. I admit the harness seemed secure – I had loops round my legs and arms, a metal buckle locked four straps together in the middle of my chest and clipped in to the winch cable. It was pretty much impossible to slip out of it, which gave me some confidence in the system.

But not enough confidence, it turns out, to step off the side of the platform and start the descent. Not to be the first one to do it, anyway.

Frazer, of course, had no such inhibitions. Or maybe it's because he understands and loves machinery and all the things it can accomplish.

He gave us a thumbs up as he followed John's instructions. Standing on the platform's edge, with the rest of us watching in horrified fascination, trying not to shine our helmet lights into his face, he leant back before allowing the winch to tighten up slightly. It lifted him, confirming the cable could take his weight; for a moment he was dangling in the air, with his boots above the platform, before Rell gently pushed him out over the edge.

"Starting to lower now," John said.

The cylindrical winch began to unwind. Frazer sank below the platform.

"Wow, this is cool! I'm spinning a bit. Hey, there are slot rails in the wall. Is that how the cybots get about in here? Oh, just saw another platform."

I forced myself to look over the edge. I could see his helmet lights shrinking below me. And *nothing* else.

"I'll go next," I said. And I could feel cold sweat suddenly run out of every pore, as if my whole body was crying. But I had no choice – that was my little brother down there. If he could do it, so could I, even though the idiot didn't know the difference between brave and reckless.

I refused to focus on the visor displays as the winch lifted me a few centimetres off the platform. Then Rell was pushing me out over the edge and there was only blackness beneath me.

"Lowering now," John said. And suddenly it was way too late to ask about those alternative routes.

There are times in your life when you are absolutely helpless. Events just sweep you along. Sometimes these are good and you laugh and smile as they occur – away dances, for instance. Just because Ixia's girls get invited to Akebia or Viride doesn't mean you have to go, but once you say yes you don't have to think – it just happens like it's happened a thousand times before. And what follows is lovely and exciting and sometimes – like with Scott – really rather nice.

Then there's the opposite. When Marana was operating on Dad in her surgery after the accident, all I could do was wait outside with Mum and Frazer. There was nothing I could do, nothing I could contribute that would make the slightest difference to the outcome. I'd never felt so utterly powerless, so out of control of my life. It showed me a kind of vulnerability

I'd never realized could exist. I came to despise that sensation – so much so, I'd promised myself I'd never get in that position again.

Yet there I was, dangling in complete darkness, in a shaft of unknown size (but suspected: *big*), completely dependent on a cable and winch made by a command AI my own arrival had killed. Hunted by aliens. My home and family abandoned.

Totally vulnerable to fate once more.

I thought I'd get all teary and self-pitying as I slid smoothly and silently down the seemingly infinite shaft. Surprisingly, I found I was angry. At Ashleigh Kruger for bringing the Yi on board. At my ancestors for not fighting back harder. But mostly at the universe for doing this to me. I don't suppose the universe cared, but I put it on notice that I was going to stop allowing these things to happen to me.

"Almost there," Frazer said.

When I looked down, I saw him a couple of metres below my feet. And the invisible distance under me didn't freak me out anymore.

His arms were stretched up, and he grabbed my ankle, pulling me onto the platform beside him.

"Thanks, Frazer," I said as we hugged.

"That was wild. Not sure I want to do it again, though. I started thinking about the stress on the cable."

"I'm going to kill every Yi on the *Daedalus*," I told him. "Then we're going to fly down to the new world. There will be no more living like this."

His helmet touched mine, and I could see his smile. "I know."

Alice was next down. She didn't say anything, but kept a firm grip on my shoulder until Shao landed on the platform. Then they wrapped their arms round each other.

After Rell and Elijah came down, John told us to unbuckle our harnesses. When the straps came free, the winches retracted. A few minutes later, the cybots came sliding down the side of the shaft using the slot rail. They cut through the inspection hatch and we were out of there.

"This is the environmental-maintenance department," John told us as we walked along a dark corridor. "We are close to the exit now."

I knew we weren't at the habitat floor level; the gravity was a lot stronger than it had been up in Section Seventeen, but not yet full. "How close?"

"We should be out within quarter of an hour."

Which wasn't quite the answer I was looking for. John was being unusually evasive.

The chamber we crept into was empty apart from a three-metre-diameter pipe which ran across the floor. It was surrounded by girders that supported a walkway that ran along the top. We went up the metal stairs to the walkway and I saw a big circular hatch on top of the pipe with a wheel in the middle.

"You want us to go inside, don't you?" I said. No wonder John hadn't given anything away about the route. He knew I hadn't liked the underground tunnels yesterday. I suspected the pipe would be worse.

"That is correct. Lazarus determined that this would provide a route into the habitat which the brain queens will not suspect," John said as one of the cybots began to turn the metal wheel. Latches around the rim of the hatch rose up, unlocking the seal.

Two cybots pulled the hatch open. We looked over the rim, shining our headlight beams in. The pipe contained a metre of water that flowed along quickly.

As I gazed at it uneasily, a cybot manoeuvred itself into the opening and lowered itself down. The water surged round it as it began to move slowly downstream.

"I'll go first," Rell said. He held his laser ready as he swung his legs over the edge, then slipped down. I saw him struggle to keep his balance in the water.

"It's not too bad," he said.

With a sigh I followed him in.

Elijah was the last down, followed by the two remaining cybots. I was already twenty metres down the pipe when I heard the hatch close with a loud *clang*.

The current was powerful, always trying to sweep my feet away. It made for slow progress. I learned that keeping my feet wide apart helped me keep stable. At first the water came up over my knees, but there were grids on the apex every fifteen metres or so with more water pouring in through them. After a few minutes, the pipe began to slope down and the flow increased. It was everything I could do to stay upright. I didn't want to think what would happen if I slipped – where the water would take me.

"How much further?" I asked.

"Fifty metres," John said.

"And what's at the end?"

"The waterfall feed chamber."

"The waterfall! That's our exit? You are joking."

"It is perfectly safe. The spacesuit will work as well underwater as it does in a vacuum."

"But it's so high!"

"The fall distance is within safe tolerance limits for humans."

"Oh, guano!"

I saw a pale patch of light ahead. The pipe began to expand as we approached, widening into an oval shape, which thankfully meant the water grew shallower.

I stood close to the lip and peered out. Our pipe was one of fifteen forming a ring around the top of a steep funnel that must have been thirty metres high. Water cascaded down its sides, rushing away into a big hole at the bottom.

There was no walkway above the pipes, no hatchway in the domed ceiling. The only way out now was down the funnel and into that hole.

(21)

"No way," Alice murmured, gripping my hand. "I can't jump down that."

"The winch will lower you to the intake opening," John said. "Once you reach the rim, you can release the cable. It is a short distance to the waterfall, and you will be carried there swiftly."

"Makes sense," Frazer admitted grudgingly.

"It's crazy," Alice protested.

"We got here safely, didn't we?" Frazer said. "And there's no Yi between us and the habitat now. Lazarus knew what he was doing. I'll go first if you like."

"No," I exclaimed. I knew that it probably wasn't very risky, that Lazarus would have done a million clever calculations to make sure we'd be okay, but that drop down the funnel looked terrifying.

"I go first," Shao announced.

Nobody argued. I don't suppose we knew how.

"What was that?" Rell asked.

"What?"

"I thought I heard something."

As one, we all turned and stared back down the pipe. Our helmet beams reached maybe ten or fifteen metres into the darkness. The only thing moving was the water.

"I can't hear anything," Elijah said.

"It was a bang, like the hatch made."

"Let's get moving," Alice said nervously.

The cybots began attaching winch cylinders on the top of the pipe. I slipped into my safety harness, locking the cable into my chest buckle.

Shao gave us a thumbs up and began to slide down the funnel slope. Water poured onto his shoulders, creating a curving torrent of spray that practically engulfed him. Seeing that, I knew I'd be glad of the helmet when it was my turn.

He was halfway down when Alice suddenly said, "To hell with waiting. I'm going."

She sat on the edge of the pipe and the winch began to unwind, lowering her after Shao. I watched her go, creating her own fast surge of spray.

"No so bad," she declared.

I looked at Frazer, who made an exaggerated shrug in his spacesuit.

I went next. The water gushing down the funnel was fiercer than I'd realized. It pummelled my shoulders as I ploughed my way down, creating a chaotic eruption of surf. I was right – without the helmet protecting my head, it would have been impossible to breathe.

I squinted through the dense spume and saw Shao reach the inlet rim. He was having trouble holding himself in place against the churning water while he tried to unlock his cable. It took him several attempts before he succeeded. Then he was gone, swept away instantly, plunging down into the chaotic white-water whirl.

Alice was almost at the rim.

"Hey!" Frazer exclaimed. "What's happening?"

I tried to see him, but the water was surging across my helmet, blotting everything out. "Frazer, what's wrong?"

"I'm going up!" he cried.

I pushed my feet against the funnel wall, forcing my torso out of the water. The cascade pounded into my stomach, but I managed to twist so I could look up. They were all there above me, Frazer, Rell and Elijah, hanging at the end of their cables. Then I screamed and flung myself aside. A cybot came hurtling down, spinning as it fell, and smashed into the side of the inlet. It was instantly sucked down into the vortex.

"Help!" Frazer shouted.

"What is it?" Rell demanded.

I stared upwards, not believing what I saw. Something was filling the end of the pipe. It wasn't a type two – this mass of dark flesh was huge. A tentacle thicker than my leg was gripping Frazer's cable, pulling him up.

"A Yi!" I screamed. "Frazer, release the cable. Now! Release!" Then I gasped. More tentacles were weaving sinuously out of the pipe, reaching for the remaining cables.

Frazer was thumping madly on his chest buckle. It opened, and he was abruptly swinging upside down, snagged by the harness straps round his shoulders and legs. His cry of pain burst into my ears.

I stopped going down.

"I can't reach it," Frazer groaned, his arms waving feebly against the streaming water. The cable was still attached to his buckle, which was now suspended above him.

Overhead another tentacle began to pull. I started to slide slowly up the funnel. The hammering I was getting from the water became worse. My hand went straight to my chest buckle, then I realized if I unlocked it now I'd end up in the same tangle as Frazer. I went for the laser instead.

Aiming was always going to be difficult, but that huge flank of slick Yi flesh was a big target. I fired. The scarlet beam shone brightly in the eternal spray. Droplets detonated into steam. The slender beam frayed, diverging before it reached the Yi.

"It's got me!" Rell said.

He was trying to aim his laser at the monster. The water around him was even thicker than the deluge I was trapped inside.

"I can't use the laser," Alice said. "The water's too strong."

I glanced down. Alice was on the intake rim, almost invisible amid the raging water. "Unlock your cable," I told her. "Get free."

"I'm not leaving you!"

My feet slipped and I crashed painfully into the funnel wall. "Alice, get out. You have to warn people."

"No."

"Do it. Please, Alice. Please."

"Hazel, I can't! I can't lose you as well. I just can't."

"Escape. For me!"

I saw her struggle with the buckle lock. Then the cable was free, lashing about in the air, and the water slammed her over the rim. I brought my arm up, knowing it was useless, trying to find some sort of target through the relentless flood. Above me, a tentacle was tugging Elijah up, but he was swinging vigorously from side to side. His feet kicked savagely against the funnel wall to propel himself a little wider each time. He'd almost reached Frazer's cable.

"Elijah, what are you doing?" I yelled.

"I'm a Regulator," he grunted. "I have to look out for everyone. It's my job."

Then I saw he was holding a glowing D-blade in his hand. His swing took him past Frazer's taut cable, and he slashed.

Frazer fell, wailing in shock as he went. He careered off the side of the funnel to splash straight into the centre of the intake.

Without his weight, the tentacle that had been pulling him jerked upwards. I felt a judder transmitted down my own winch cable. A new, thicker tentacle appeared, winding purposefully through the air towards Elijah. It was twice as broad as the others, with an open orifice at the end lined in small curving fangs. The gullet behind pulsed in waves as its cilia beckoned greedily.

"Look out!" I shouted. I fired my laser, heedless that I couldn't get a decent aim.

Elijah swung wide, and the questing mouth-tentacle missed him. He slashed again. Rell plummeted down.

I gasped as momentum began to carry Elijah back. He was heading towards my cable. The big tentacle caught him, its myriad little fangs engulfing his shoulder and biting down hard into the spacesuit fabric.

His scream of agony and fury was something I'll never forget, piercing straight to my heart sharper than any knife. "Elijah!"

The tentacle-mouth began to chew its way across him, expanding like snail flesh to devour his neck and arm.

"Give Zawn a chance," he said in a frighteningly calm voice. "Elijah?"

As the mouth started to scrabble its way over his helmet, his free arm shot out. The D-blade sliced through my cable.

I fell. My leg struck the funnel wall, sending me cartwheeling. The universe rotated around me, and beneath my feet I saw Elijah's hand slap down on the power-cell discs clipped to his belt. Then my shoulder smacked onto the intake rim and I crashed into the chaos of the maelstrom. Furious water clawed at me, squeezing my body tight. I fought for breath, panicking as darkening bubbles seethed around my helmet. Then the light drained away and the forces gripping me increased their hold, carrying me down and down.

A white light abruptly seared through the liquid night from above. I felt the shockwave through the water, punching me deeper.

We each had six of the power cells on our belts. When Elijah triggered one, it must have detonated the others in a colossal multiple explosion.

After a long moment, the buffeting began to ease off, though the pressure against my skin was still intense. I could hear my frantic breathing against a backdrop of dull rumbling. The helmet lights showed me nothing but a grey-green blur, which had to be the pipe walls rushing by at unnerving speed.

"John?" I bellowed.

"You're almost there," he said in that wondrously calm way he has.

He wasn't lying. A pale uniform light was seeping into the water around me. Moonlight! A bright patch of it rushing towards me.

"You might want to–" John began.

I never did find out what. I shot out of the waterfall outlet, flying through the air, my arms and legs waving round as I traced a long arc down to the pool below. I splashed down hard, then flailed about for a while as I orientated myself before rising to break the surface.

"Who was that?" a voice asked.

"Hazel?" Frazer's frantic voice echoed round my helmet. "Hazel, is it you?"

"Yes," I moaned.

"I knew you'd make it!" Alice exclaimed. "I just knew it."

"Are you all right?" Rell asked urgently.

"I guess." Though the hot bruises that were now throbbing mercilessly down my arms and legs and ribs were telling a different story. "How about you?"

"I'm just happy you're okay."

"Shao?"

"Here."

"Where's Elijah?" Alice asked.

For a moment I was engulfed by the darkness again. "It's just us. That *thing* caught him. But he took it with him. He used the power cells…"

"Oh, sweet Captain."

"Type three," Frazer said.

"Whatever." I no longer cared. When I looked round, I saw helmet lights bobbing about in the water. One seemed closer to the bank than the others so I started paddling my way towards it.

My arms moved sluggishly. The spacesuit had suddenly become very restrictive. It took ages before my feet touched the mud on the bottom, and then I had to crawl over the slippery boulders lining the edge of the pool.

Someone gripped me under my shoulders and helped haul me onto dry land. I told John to release the helmet seal and took it off before I flopped down onto the grass. There was something very wrong with the habitat air – it was so cold it was practically burning my cheeks. "Air from the reserve tanks," I muttered. John had said it needed to be super-cold to turn to liquid for storage. But even that didn't matter because Rell was there beside me, his lovely face all creased up with concern.

"I thought I'd lost you," he said, as if he was in the most profound pain.

"I've only just found you," I told him. "I'm not letting go that easy."

We kissed, and I didn't ever want it to end. My hands were stroking his face, just to make absolutely sure he was real.

"Habitat pressure is almost back to a standard atmosphere," John declared.

My shoulders slumped. Rell and I grinned at each other.

"That personal adaptation learning routine you have," I told John. "It needs to work on your timing."

"You did it," Alice said weakly. "Hazel, you did it! You fixed the hole in the sky. We're going to live." She burst into tears. "He'll never know, he'll never see any of this."

Shao put his arms round her as she sobbed helplessly.

Frazer was on his feet, hands on hips, staring straight upwards. He frowned. "What is this?"

I took Rell's hand and tipped my head back. The pale light strips above had become strangely difficult to see, as if some sort of haze was filling the air. Little white flecks were drifting softly down around us. I reached out and touched one. It vanished as soon as it came into contact with my gloved finger, turning into a drop of water.

"That's odd." When I glanced at Rell, I had to smirk. More of the flecks had landed on his hair, forming a sparkling fringe. "Good style," I teased.

He dabbed at his head, as bemused as me by the white stuff that swiftly turned to water.

"John, what's happening?" I asked.

"When the temperature falls below zero, water freezes into ice, its solid form. Did you not know this?"

"We've never known the habitat to be this cold," I replied.

"Oh, I get it," Frazer said. "This is the night rain."

Rell and I held hands, smiling at the sight of each other getting covered in the soft flakes of weird solid water. "It's lovely," I said.

"The village idiots will have to believe you now," Alice said from inside Shao's embrace. "You told them this would happen."

"Not quite this," I said. "But yes, it might help."

"Does it have a name?" Rell asked as he caught a flake on the tip of his tongue.

"Snow," John told us. "It's called, snow. On Earth it signals the arrival of winter."

"Winter?" I asked.

"A new season," John said. "The harshest of them all. But if you can survive through winter, spring awaits."

Hazel's story will continue in

THE CAPTAIN'S DAUGHTER,
BOOK TWO OF THE ARKSHIP TRILOGY